DAYS OF WINE AND ROSES

BLACK SWAN

DAYS OF WINE AND ROSES
A BLACK SWAN BOOK : 0 552 77236 4

First publication in Great Britain

PRINTING HISTORY
Black Swan edition published 2004

1 3 5 7 9 10 8 6 4 2

Set in 11/13pt Melior by
Kestrel Data, Exeter, Devon.

Black Swan Books are published by Transworld Publishers,
61–63 Uxbridge Road, London W5 5SA,
a division of The Random House Group Ltd,
in Australia by Random House Australia (Pty) Ltd,
20 Alfred Street, Milsons Point, Sydney, NSW 2061, Australia,
in New Zealand by Random House New Zealand Ltd,
18 Poland Road, Glenfield, Auckland 10, New Zealand
and in South Africa by Random House (Pty) Ltd,
Endulini, 5a Jubilee Road, Parktown 2193, South Africa.

The Random House Group Limited supports The Forest Stewardship
Council® (FSC®), the leading international forest-certification organisation.
Our books carrying the FSC label are printed on FSC®-certified paper.
FSC is the only forest-certification scheme supported by the leading
environmental organisations, including Greenpeace. Our
paper procurement policy can be found at
www.randomhouse.co.uk/environment

Printed and bound in Great Britain by Clays Ltd, St Ives plc

www.booksattransworld.co.uk

Contents

Foreword	Jerry Hall	7
Poetic Justice	Diana Appleyard	11
Aunt Hesther	Charlotte Bingham	23
Portfolio Woman	Elizabeth Buchan	37
Sheep's Eyes	Mavis Cheek	49
The Birth of Venus	Tracy Chevalier	61
Waking Beauty	Amanda Craig	73
Second Showing	Edwina Currie	87
Portrait of Auntie Binbag, with Ribbons	Helen Dunmore	99
'You've got a book to write. Remember?'	Barbara Erskine	111
Falling	Nicci Gerrard	125
Looking for Perfect Peony	Karen Gunning	135
Aunt Margaret's Visit	Maeve Haran	147
The Perfect Village	Wendy Holden	161

Pastoral	David Lodge	175
Second Honeymoon	Angela Lambert	189
The Wagon Mound	Val McDermid	201
The Clean Slate	Hilary Mantel	213
Forbidden	Edna O'Brien	227
Not the End of the World	Imogen Parker	241
Barley Sugar	Julie Stradner	255
Mrs Hamilton's Garden	Mary Swann	265
The Reiki Master	Sandi Toksvig	277
Is Anyone There?	Barbara Toner	287
Angel	Joanna Trollope	299
The Yellow Door	Lynne Truss	313
The Hawthorn Madonna	Salley Vickers	327

Foreword

As a supporter of Breast Cancer Care, I am honoured to write the foreword for this book. It is fantastic that these prominent contemporary female writers have contributed their entertaining and memorable stories to help raise money for Breast Cancer Care, the UK's leading provider of breast cancer information and support. All of the stories have appeared in *Woman & Home* magazine who have made a significant contribution to the charity by raising money and awareness. At least £1 from the sale of each book will go towards ensuring Breast Cancer Care can continue to provide free and confidential support and information to those affected by breast cancer across the UK. This book is being published as part of the 11th Breast Cancer Awareness Month in the UK and as a celebration of the charity's work getting people talking about breast cancer and increasing breast awareness.

So many of us will have been affected by breast cancer in some way, with over 40,000 women diagnosed with the disease each year in the UK. I was touched personally by breast cancer when my twin sister Terry was diagnosed in 1998. Her diagnosis left her feeling frightened and isolated. I recall her panicking and unable to remember ordinary things or talk about anything else. When I found out I immediately went home to support her and her family.

Terry's children were 13 and 16 at the time and found it hard to accept their mother was ill. They were used to her being strong and running the household. Her husband also found dealing with her diagnosis difficult, choosing denial as his way of coping.

Terry's experience of breast cancer made me realize how important it is for women and their families to have access to the type of information and emotional support that Breast Cancer Care offers. Through services such as their helpline, the charity has been listening to people affected by breast cancer for over 30 years so they know what they're talking about.

The helpline is a confidential telephone service offering an all important listening ear, as well as access to up-to-date medical information which helps women make informed choices about their treatment. Calls are answered by specialist nurses and trained volunteers who have had a personal experience of breast cancer. Through the charity's centres in Glasgow, Cardiff, Sheffield and London, the helpline can also help put people in touch with a specially trained volunteer who lives near them and has been through a similar experience with breast cancer.

Like Terry's husband, many partners can find it difficult to express their feelings or acknowledge that they are finding it hard to cope. Breast Cancer Care's helpline is there for them too and, if they wish, they can also be put in touch with a volunteer who is also the partner of someone with breast cancer.

In addition to the helpline and peer support service, the charity runs telephone support groups for younger women and those living with secondary breast cancer.

Breast Cancer Care also offers a prosthesis fitting service, a hair loss advisory service, courses on complimentary therapies and how to live healthily with breast cancer and they produce booklets such as 'Talking with your children about breast cancer' which would have been useful for my sister at the time.

For those who don't feel comfortable talking over the phone or have a hectic schedule, they can email Breast Cancer Care's Web Nurse who is available through the website and can give answers to technical questions on breast cancer and treatments. The charity's website also hosts a unique chat room whereby people living with breast cancer can exchange information and share experiences at all times of the day or night.

Through all of its free services Breast Cancer Care reaches over 750,000 people each year in the UK. By listening to the concerns of those with breast cancer and providing opportunities to talk to an expert or someone who's been there too, the charity provides the chance to combat the isolation and distress that is so often associated with having breast cancer. Through their specialist services and expertise Breast Cancer Care links people together who can support one another.

Terry's experience of breast cancer made her realize just how important it is to have emotional support. Now in remission, she currently supports women in her home town who are going through treatment for their breast cancer.

The incidence of breast cancer is rising but happily people are living longer with the disease due to earlier diagnosis and improved treatment. As a result demand for practical and emotional support like that provided by Breast Cancer Care is increasing all the time. Your donation will help the charity continue to meet this need.

If you or someone you know is going through breast cancer or has a breast health concern please do call the Breast Cancer Care helpline free on 0808 800 6000 (textphone 0808 800 6001) or visit www.breastcancercare.org.uk where you can also find the contact details for your nearest Breast Cancer Care centre.

Thank you again to the authors who have contributed to this anthology. Enjoy this book.

Jerry Hall

Diana Appleyard is an author and journalist. She lives in Oxfordshire with her two daughters: Beth, 16, and Charlotte, 10, and is married to Sky News reporter Ross Appleyard. A regular contributor to *Woman & Home*, Diana has also written four novels: *Homing Instinct*, *A Class Apart*, *Out of Love* and her latest, *Every Good Woman Deserves a Lover*.

Poetic Justice

It seemed so harmless, so innocuous, just to flick onto the website to see if anyone interesting had logged on, or maybe left some riveting details such as 'Am now a wolf scientist in Siberia', or 'Am living in Hackney with five children and a huge mortgage', which would make her feel substantially better about her own vast overdraft.

His name burnt its way into her soul. Jed Cunningham. No – not Jed, surely not Jed, it was so unlikely that he would bother to post his name on the Friends United website. He always hated to look back, and his mantra was that you lived for the day. He was seizing the day long before the film *Dead Poets Society* was made, and the last thing he would ever be interested in doing was attending a school reunion, because even when he had been at school he had never seemed a part of it. He was an old head on young shoulders, who stood apart and watched the world mockingly, making his teachers uneasy. They accused him of disrespect for their authority, but the reality was that they feared him, feared his searing intelligence and his inability to fit into the common herd. He saw through them, and they found that disconcerting in one so

13

young. Their job was to mould minds, and his was already formed.

Putting her own name up there had triggered off a response from old friends – well, no, not all old friends, some of them were girls she'd like to have seen roasted on a spit. But now, being an adult, you could hardly feel proud of being overcome with loathing just to see a former foe's name flash up in your inbox. Hardly mature, to snigger twenty years on about her chubby knees and the fact that she was known by the boys at school as the Chinese wrestler.

He was the last person she would have thought would log on. I mean, he was Jed, Jed who always stood outside the herd, the coolest of the cool with the fashions everyone else followed, from scarves draped casually round his neck to the tie at half-mast, school trousers worn low on his hips. Who resolutely refused to be in with the in crowd, and gathered about him an eclectic group of friends from the deeply weird scientist nerd to the incredibly popular and handsome head boy, a dead ringer for Pierce Brosnan.

It was bizarre, how just a name could create such a welter of emotion. Her fingers resting on the keys of her computer, her eyes closing, she could see him so vividly – tall, thick black hair with a tuft at the front, blue blue eyes in pale skin, broad shouldered but so skinny, his mouth curved into a sardonic smile. Even at seventeen, he was a cynic, worldly-wise, with a taste for unusual authors, Camus, J.P. Donleavy, Waugh. He said he was going to be a poet, and travel, and he'd never do anything that was ever expected of him. Oh, how she loved him. He was the first, ever, who met her intellectually, who made her laugh and unleashed in her something she'd never expected before, a kind of wildness and irreverence. He wrote her the most wonderful letters, unexpected, witty, dangerous. It was, in a way, an adult love affair among children – she wanted to marry him. He caught and held something in her which was so precious, so very individual. They complemented each other. They were two sides of the same coin. Eyes still closed, she saw them walking in the park behind the school – he'd be teasing her, laughing at something she'd said, an illicit cigarette waving in his hand. Every other boy at school smoked their cigarettes cupped into their hands in case a teacher appeared. Jed didn't – he smoked like an Irish poet, which in a way, he was.

Then, in her mind's eye, she saw him grabbing the scarf which mirrored his and pulling her to him, his eyes abruptly ceasing their laughter until they were wicked and dark blue and his mouth was on hers. Stop. Her heart beat wildly. Stop. You were too young then, and now you are too old. They had never made love, never. When you're seventeen, and still living with your parents, where do you go? There was the car – he had a beaten-up car his father had given him – but that was too wrong, too cheap for them. They knew other friends did, indeed boasted about it, but they didn't, she wasn't quite sure why. She would have if he'd asked her, but he didn't, and in a way their love was the more passionate for it, vibrating like a harp with no release, it burned on and on.

They lived their two years together in a bubble, a bubble full of secret codes and messages and looks that no one else could understand. They lived in a mad, crazy parallel universe, and in a way it was like being a child again, being with Jed, children who longed for something they dare not reach. Maybe making love would have ruined it, spoilt somehow the odd innocence of their love.

How did it end? She remembered tears, and anger, something being thrown. And him driving off saying she would never see or speak to him again. He was as true as his word – he disappeared from her life, leaving no ripple to say he had ever been. Apart from in her heart. God, they'd had a row, hadn't they, about future expectations and he said she was so bourgeois in that she wouldn't come with him – where, oh where was it? Now she remembered, now she knew, that was why she'd thought of the Irish poet. He wanted, at eighteen, to go and live in Ireland and work, labour at anything, to earn money and buy a tiny cottage and write and drink and not have to be anyone that his life expected of him. And she'd told him he was mad, and stupid, that it was an impossible dream, something they'd talked about but it wasn't real. She had the weight of family expectations of going to university and getting a career and being a grown-up and being a success. Surely that was what all that education was for. And he'd laughed at her, but bitterly, saying that was not the point, not the point at all, surely the act of reading Salinger or Donleavy made you realize there was so much more and that success was in your head, not in the eyes of others. She'd never thought he really meant it, it was just their secret dream. But he had meant it, and she had broken their dream. So he left, and she stood in the drive of her parents' house, aware that the best in her had gone and life would never be the same again.

She heard he had gone to Ireland too, how his parents were furious with him because the day after he left the letter arrived detailing his dazzling success at A levels, success which would have taken him to the top universities and on to the road of success, the well-travelled road of safety and security and a chance for your parents to relax because now you would be safe. Banker, lawyer, doctor, candlestick-maker – a career, a step on the path towards middle-class nirvana.

But he'd gone in the swirling dust from his bald tyres and taken the wildness out of her. Now here I am, she thought. Here I am. I sit in front of my keyboard tapping out a series of articles, each almost identical to the last, and I do it for money, and I hope for fame, and I'm not sure what that fame would bring. Would it make me myself again? Would it bring me long blond hair and tanned skin and a man who loved me rather than was used to me? Would it take away my middle-aged spread tentatively held at bay by twice-weekly aerobic sessions and the reliance on the latest miracle skin cream and the certainty that the best in my life has gone? And what would he think of me? How very disappointed would he be in me?

Her hand hesitated, and then clicked on his name. The computer whirred. It was too old and slow and everything had to be faithfully copied onto the hard disc and then back again with a machine-like groaning noise, like a very old clerk thumbing through files with arthritic fingers. Gradually, the screen revealed itself. It said, 'Where are you?'

She stared at the screen. Oh yes, she thought. Of course. How very, very typical. No 'I am an accountant living in Walthamstow and I have three children and a corgi'. No, 'I'm the managing director of a thrusting new software company – hey, check us out at www. etc etc'. Just three simple words. 'Where are you?'

I don't have to respond, she told herself. Beyond this locked door of my office I have two children and a husband and two dogs and a cat. I have a normal life. I need to book my car in for a service. The small lawnmower has packed up again. The curtains are still at the dry-cleaner's and I need to buy some Chemco for the Aga because it's covered in sticky gunge. My daughter has a party on Saturday and I'm not sure how to get to the house and there are some jumpers stuck on the delicates cycle in the washing machine. I'm wearing socks with open-toed sandals, which is a heinous crime, my jeans are too tight and I have a roll of flesh hanging over the top of my waistband. My T-shirt is too tight too because it belongs to my teenage daughter and I have no make-up on and bags under my eyes. I am not alluring or desirable or wild. My wildness spiralled out of me when you left and it's never come back. Wild isn't part of my life any more. I can't even do hangovers because they hurt too much and I'm scared of letting go because I'm not sure I know the person who might come out. I am reserved. I reserve my emotions to the point where I'm not sure I have emotions now which are not banal or unsurprising. I would disappoint you.

Reply. Should I reply, she thought? It's such an innocuous little button. I could just click, and then tap out something funny, or curt, or unrevealing. Maybe I could tantalize him with some mysterious signs of success. Or maybe I should just tell him that I do not exist any more. The person I have become would not exist in his eyes.

'I am listening,' she wrote. Then clicked Send.

The rest of the day hummed by in all those endless, exhausting tasks which make up a day, tasks which don't end but just repeat themselves over and over again, from emptying the dishwasher to walking the dog to putting the milk bottles out on the step and loading and unloading the washing machine and defluffing the tumble-dryer and poking out the gunge

18

from the plughole in the sink. Amid all these life-enhancing duties she worked, and wrote, and sent off an article, seeing its satisfying bottom disappear into the 'sent messages' file, another job done.

But she did not look in her inbox, although it told her she had three new messages. They'd be junk mail, exhorting her to click on to the Lolita teenagers engaging in unspeakable Internet activities, or enlarge her penis, which was a bit of a no-hoper, or clear all her debt NOW. They wouldn't be from a poet trying to find her.

At the end of the day, dog-weary, dying for a coffee and a book but knowing she had five minutes before she had to pick her youngest daughter up from school and say, 'How was your day?' and hear 'Boring' before listening to the same Harry Potter tape for the tenth time because all the other tapes were in her bedroom and they kept forgetting to bring a new one into the car, she screwed her courage to the sticking post and logged on to hotmail. Inbox, 4 messages, it said. Four, eh? A one-in-four chance of there being something of interest among all the junk and porn.

The message said very clearly, Jed Cunningham. She took several deep breaths before clicking on his name. Even clicking on his name felt like an act of betrayal. She could have ticked the box and then deleted it and no one would ever have known.

'Who are you?' it said. 'Can you still spell biscuit and do you still make a habit of leaving your coat behind a wall?'

She laughed. 'It's love, not biscuit, and I am not the stranger who chucked her school coat behind the wall. Surely you've put all that behind you?'

'I am grown old, and dull, and sad,' he said. 'My hair is grey and I have a large dog called Roger.'

'Mine is called Bramble. How sad is that?'

'OK, you win in the sad stakes. Bramble, please. At least Roger is funny. Do you live in the country, or the town?'

This is like twenty questions, she thought. 'Animal, fish or mineral,' she tapped back. 'I am a country mouse.'

'Good.'

'Good, just good? What about an exchange of information? That is what the email system is for.'

'OK, country too. A remote place, by the sea.'

'You sound a bit mad.'

'Quite probably. I live alone, you see.'

Alone. 'Why?'

'I drove my wife to the point of insanity.'

'Why?'

'Because she was not you.'

She stopped. Her fingers, which had been whizzing over the keys, ceased – she was going to be late, her daughter would be the last one standing on the steps of the school, forlorn, trailing her bookbag, her school shoes dusty, her blazer hanging from one finger. Too much, she thought. Too much, for a Monday. A Monday of work and school runs and many chores. He was out there somewhere, sitting in front of his computer, in a remote place by the sea, alone, thinking about her.

Her fingers hovered over the keys. Very, very deliberately, she slid her mouse on to the Reply button, then kept it moving. Kept it moving up to the little square which she ticked, and then she kept it moving, all the way up to Delete.

It went, that last message, into infinite cyberspace.

Stretching, she rolled her neck on her shoulders, feeling the click. Then she stood up, opened the door to her office, walked to the kitchen, pushing away the Labrador which lay heavily against the door. It rose sullenly and stiffly, stretching out one back leg. She picked up her car keys from the wooden dresser, then walked into the hall. In the mirror, she paused to look at herself. Blond hair, caught up into a bun, tendrils escaping. She smiled, and watched the skin under her eyes bag and wrinkle, the dimples appearing in her cheeks. Not an old face, she thought, not really. A nice face. An unexceptional face. The face of a mother about to collect her daughter from school, the face of a mother who lives a very acceptable life. Not a life to tinker about with, or test. Not a life to risk in a remote place by the sea. She smiled to herself. It's a transfer, she thought, a simple transfer. You give all that passion, all that expectation and the excitement of the unknown to your children. You don't go out and seek it yourself. To do more would be a sin, and only a poet could be happy with a life of sin. And I'm not a poet, she thought. Not any more.

Charlotte Bingham comes from a literary family. Her father the crime novelist, John Bingham, having sold a short story to H. G. Wells when he was 17. She herself published her first book at twenty, and went on to write for television with her husband the author/playwright, Terence Brady. Together they contributed to such series as *Upstairs Downstairs* and wrote comedy and drama series such as *No Honestly*, *Nanny*, and *Forever Green*. Her latest novel *The House of Flowers* is her twenty-eighth published book. She lives in an early eighteenth century rectory in Somerset together with Terence, two dogs and assorted horses. They have a son, Matthew Brady, the literary agent, and a daughter, Candida Ogilvy who, when not producing films, has found time to give them two grandchildren, Barnaby and Matilda.

Aunt Hesther

Lucy Hayward lived with her mother in a semi-detached house near enough to the river Thames to make life bearable on a hot day, but not so near to footpaths and such like as to be what her mother always called 'murky'. The house would have been plenty roomy enough if Jane Hayward had not had a penchant for rescuing animals of all kinds, and if she had not also fancied herself as a sculptor.

'The trouble with sculpting is it's a bit messy . . .' Jane sometimes said this, not in an apologetic way, but in a slightly puzzled manner, as if she had only just discovered this fact. She also usually said it when she saw Lucy with the vacuum cleaner of a Saturday morning.

Their mother and daughter role-reversal had happened gradually over the years, following the early death of Lucy's father. What with Lucy going out to work to pay the mortgage and Jane staying home to sculpt, inevitably Lucy became the parent and her mother the helpless teenager, always in faded jeans and T-shirt looking vague before, typically, cadging money from her daughter to go round the corner to the pub.

Happily, at her office, Lucy was considered to be everything that she should be, and this despite the fact that she always lunched alone with a book from the library, and never went on communal holidays with other singles from her department. Not that she was stuffy or anything, it was just that she had different interests from her colleagues, although her mother thought otherwise.

'You're just like your Aunt Hesther, your father's sister, really you are,' Jane often grumbled after she'd had two gin and tonics of a Sunday. 'She was always stand-offish. Toffee-nosed, we used to call her.'

Lucy hated being compared to someone she had never met, but nevertheless accepted her mother's version of herself and her father's family: that the Haywards were stand-offish, snobbish and, generally speaking, without much appeal. Her mother's family, the Fauns, on the other hand, were talented, artistic, good-looking and had always been popular, at all levels. Lucy had accepted this version of both sides of her family until, quite suddenly, Aunt Hesther died.

'I see she never married,' Lucy said, staring at the short obituary about Hesther Hayward in the newspaper.

'No, she didn't.' Her mother turned away quickly and started to pick up the usual bits and pieces that she collected from the kitchen before going to her studio at the back of the house. 'No, she never did marry, poor soul. Oh, by the way, I have found a home for the tarantula now he's got over his nervous breakdown,' she went on, cheering up as she always did when she had effected a cure for one of her hastily adopted creatures. 'Yes, a very nice man, lives round the corner from the pub, and has been looking for one, for a tarantula, for a long time. He says it's not unknown for them to lose all their fur off their legs, if stressed. He's quite impressed, you know, that we got him back to full fur on his legs.'

At that moment there was the sound of a duck quacking from the downstairs cloakroom.

'Oh dear, Duckie needs his bathwater changed, after that – you know where to find me.'

Minutes later Jane disappeared out of the front door, leaving Lucy to cook Sunday lunch. As she did so, Lucy thought over the little matter of her aunt's demise.

She knew that her mother had never been popular with her father's family. Even so, they would have to write condolences to the family. The only trouble being that Lucy had no idea to whom to write.

She picked up the newspaper again, and turning to the obituaries she noted the time of Aunt Hesther's funeral. She stared at the place in question. It was in the south of England, a long train journey from where they lived. Yet it was necessary. After all, she was a Hayward – going to the funeral to represent her father was only decent. Obviously she would have to take the day off, but that could not be helped. She imagined that Mr Mulcahy, her immediate supervisor, would not mind since she had never taken a single day's sick leave.

'Going to a funeral, did you say?' Mulcahy was a small man. It was not just that he was short in height, every aspect of him was small, including his face. As a consequence of this, his horn-rimmed spectacles seemed to take up his whole face. He now focused them on Lucy. 'Is it a very near relative, a parent or some such, perhaps?'

It was no exaggeration to say that Lucy had probably

only told half a dozen white lies in her whole life. She had certainly never told what could be described as a black lie before, but she did now.

'My mother, actually.'

'Your mother.' This at least caused Mr Mulcahy to pause, before going on to ask, 'Old, was she?'

'Quite old.'

Mr Mulcahy sighed. Even he had enough imagination to see that refusing an assistant manager permission to attend a parent's funeral was tantamount to committing a felony.

The man who refused to allow a colleague to go to her mother's funeral.

'Very well.' For one second Lucy thought that Mr Mulcahy was going to add, 'Don't make a habit of it.' Instead of which he did not add anything, merely turning away and clearing his throat instead.

On the train Lucy felt as if she had been let off school. It was ridiculous, and not quite proper, to feel so liberated by having been given a day off to go to a funeral, of all things, but not that surprising.

She had worked her way up, diligently, from the bottom to her present position of assistant manager by dint of not missing a day at the office, and by way of always staying late and arriving early. If anyone had been the epitome of a goody-goody, it was Lucy. Always anxious to please Mr Mulcahy, always crossing her fingers that she would somehow manage to get a rise, that her mother would not spend too much, either at the pub, or, which was even more expensive, at her second favourite place after the pub – at the vet's.

The trouble was that bills for twenty-five pounds to examine a lame duck or a tarantula made Lucy feel impatient, principally because her mother was not so successful a sculptor as to warrant that kind of

28

expenditure. More than that, and far more than the vet, the casting of her sculptures also cost Lucy a lot of money.

How often had Lucy found herself staring at her mother's latest piece and wishing that it would indeed be cast, although not at the foundry, but into the river at the bottom of the road. It seemed that the Fauns had all been unsuccessful artists of one kind or another, and Jane was yet another. When Lucy was small she had thought it exciting and different to have a mother who was artistic, but once her father died and money was tight, it became a great deal less so.

Yet nothing could or would induce Lucy to tell her mother that she was about as talented a sculptor as Mr Mulcahy was at public relations. To do so would be to take her reason for getting up in the morning away from her. To do so would be to take away the one thing that she knew Jane really enjoyed.

Because Jane did not sell anything did not mean she did not have a right to go on being a happy failure. It was just a fact, and, knowing this, Lucy, sighing – and all the time knowing that whenever Jane finished a new piece, bang went any chance of a foreign holiday – paid up and shut up.

Arriving at the station, Lucy waved at a taxi cab. It was countrified of aspect, more like a doctor's car, and the driver was of a cheerful countenance, despite the fact that he was already flushed, for the day was hot. So hot that Lucy could only be thankful that she had invested in her new lightweight dark suit and the vaguely low-cut black blouse.

'I always think funerals are worse in hot weather, I don't know why,' the driver said, glancing at his passenger in his driving mirror after he had taken the address. 'It seems all wrong, a nice day and a funeral.'

29

It appeared that all the mourners were expected to meet at the church. Lucy knew that she would know no one, and when she took her place in a pew and looked round she realized how right she had been in assuming this. She did indeed know no one. Thankfully there was a slip in the service programme, inviting all the mourners back to Aunt Hesther's house for refreshments.

After the service, Lucy managed to follow the rest of the mourners back to the house. Here again it was – as the taxi driver had remarked of warm weather – somehow strange to be having a wake in a house that overlooked the beach. To be talking in appropriately low voices as the sea bounded up the beach, and small children wandered about with buckets and spades looking for shells.

What was more, the stuffy Aunt Hesther, to whom Lucy had so often been compared, lived in a house completely unlike her reputation. Here was no home filled with portraits of ancestors or mahogany furniture handed down for generations.

Far from it, here was a house that was, or had been in its time, positively swinging – so much so that it was difficult for Lucy's mouth not to drop open quite visibly as she glanced from cocktail cabinets in the Chinese Chippendale tradition to pieces of sculpture of a most potent kind.

Whether a copy of Rodin's *The Kiss* or a Keith Winter original, it was quite clear where the interests of the childless Hesther had lain, and it had certainly not been in crochet and jam-making.

And yet she had never married. This was the strange thing, for everywhere there seemed to be quite clear evidence that, at one time or another, a man had occupied Gooden House, set so securely overlooking the beach and within easy reach of shops and restaurants on the south coast.

'Who are you, may I ask, if it is not – how can I say – impolite, but my father never introduced me to any of Miss Hayward's relations.'

'I am Hesther Hayward's niece, Lucy Hayward.'

The young man extended a slim, tanned hand. 'Lorenzo di – '

He was Italian, but aside from rolling off his plentiful surnames in a stream of expertly pronounced Italian, his English was perfect, indicating that he had been educated in England. Either that, or his Linguaphone lessons in English had been a great deal better than those Lucy had, a few winters earlier, tried to follow in Italian.

'How well did you know your aunt?'

Lucy looked up at him.

'Hardly at all,' she admitted, after a small silence. 'My mother thinks all the Haywards are stuffy.' Lucy smiled, glancing round the room at the intensely romantic paintings and sculptures. 'But it doesn't look to me as if she was stuffy at all.'

Lorenzo's eyes did not follow hers but remained on Lucy's pale, intense face. 'You know we are practically related? Your aunt was my father's great, great love.'

Of a sudden it all made such sense, most particularly Lorenzo's easy familiarity, as if they were indeed in some way related.

'Gracious. How scandalous.'

'It was, quite! My father was married off at a too-young age to my mother. Naturally, he and my mother quickly became tired of each other, as happens with such marriages, but, being Italian, there was no question of divorce.

'On a visit to London he met your aunt. They began

31

an affair, very intense, very passionate. Naturally Hesther Hayward would not dream of breaking up his marriage any more than he would have dreamt of divorcing his wife. So they settled on a good old British compromise.

She retired from her situation, and he bought her this house. Just what she wanted, on the beach, not too far from the shops, very settled. Every year thereafter my father came to visit, until his death last year. Are you shocked? I do hope so.'

'No.'

'Well, you might be when you hear that we have been left everything, including, most unfortunately, the cocktail cabinet with the revolving dancers, and the little opening umbrellas for the cocktails.' He looked down at Lucy, mock serious.

'I don't understand. How do you mean – we have been left everything?'

'The house, Miss Hayward, the furniture, the paintings, everything. Miss Hesther Hayward has made us joint beneficiaries. But, you know what we say in Italy, if you want to get to know someone too quickly – inherit with them! So we shall get to know each other very quickly, I think. I hope.'

In fact, Lorenzo, who ran a small family hotel near Portofino, had to leave for Italy later that day, and, in leaving, he entrusted Lucy with seeing to the wrapping up of Aunt Hesther's estate.

As soon as she heard of Lucy's good fortune, Jane Hayward took umbrage.

'Well, of course, I always knew that she was not living on air,' she kept saying, 'but I never knew that she was – well, some rich man's girlfriend. She always seemed so stuffy, so Hayward.'

Lucy was staring into the immaculately maintained cupboard housing her aunt's clothing. Row upon row of the most beautiful cashmere twinsets, row upon row of sequined jackets and crêpe evening trousers. Italian silk separates, hand-painted silk palazzo pyjamas with famous designer names sewn into the back. Hesther Hayward's clothing took up two whole rooms. It was impressive.

'It just seems too unlikely,' Jane was still saying, 'Hesther Hayward, stuffy old Hesther Hayward being someone's girlfriend. And are you really very wise to have given in your notice to Mr Mulcahy?'

'Very,' said Lucy firmly, remembering Mulcahy's peeved expression with huge satisfaction.

It took a long time to clear up the house, during which Lucy discovered that her mother had taken the whole matter of Lucy's inheritance very badly indeed. She told everyone and anyone who would listen, that Lucy's inheritance was going to destroy her life, that she was going *mad* as a result, that she was leaving all her responsibilities – which naturally meant Jane – and taking off for foreign parts without a thought for anyone else – which also meant her.

But Lucy was determined to make a new life for herself and she was equally determined that her mother should do the same, most particularly because Lorenzo had kept writing increasingly flirtatious faxes to Lucy. And when he was not writing faxes, he was telephoning her.

'I think you're quite, quite mad. Going to live in Italy.' Jane looked up, her eyes avoiding the airline luggage piled up behind her daughter.

'I know you do, Ma.'

'It is not going to be easy, me coping here on my

own. Cooking.' She managed to make the last word sound like a swear word.

'You'll come out to Italy—'

'Can't afford it.'

'I'll send you the ticket—'

'Can't leave the pets—'

'Bye, Ma.'

Lucy was already enjoying the sights and sounds of Italy before she even boarded the plane. No more grey days of Mr Mulcahy, no more worrying about her mother's endless extravagances.

She knew that Lorenzo would be sending a car from the hotel to fetch her. What she did not know was that he would be driving it.

There are some moments when a whole lifetime comes together, and the moment when Lucy set foot on Italian soil and felt the warmth of the climate, saw the blue skies and sensed the peace and fun of the life that was hurrying towards her, was one of those moments.

'For one minute I thought you would not be on the plane, and I would have to take *everything* home again.' Lorenzo laughed.

Everything did indeed seem to be *everything* – flowers, chocolates, champagne, boxes of clothes, all piled up on the back seat of Lorenzo's brilliant red sports car.

'I will take you to lunch, and you will open everything, one by one, finishing with the smallest box, in which I have placed a specially designed secret,' he told her, at the same time signalling for the hotel taxi behind him to take Lucy's luggage. 'And then all we have to do is set the date of our wedding day.'

'Lorenzo. I can't marry you.' Lucy looked momentarily stunned.

'Of course you can marry me. I am a free man. Unlike Hesther and my father, we can marry. I would never keep you for my mistress in England.' He looked down at her, mock sad. 'The sea is far too cold.'

'But – we've only really faxed each other. What do we know of each other, Lorenzo?'

'Everything. Remember? We have inherited together! I know everything about you, and you about me.'

They were moving into the main stream of traffic, and Lucy had the feeling that she was gasping for air. Worse than that, she felt panic struck; and all of a sudden she knew she wanted to jump out of the car and, of all things – run home to her mother.

And then she remembered. She could hear her mother's voice saying over and over and over to her, down the years, 'You're just like Hesther Hayward. Just like your Aunt Hesther.'

Lucy turned and stared for a few seconds at the young handsome man beside her, and then ahead of her at the pretty street, the restaurants, the blue sky, the other happy couples in other open sports cars, and she sank back.

Her mother was right. She was just like her Aunt Hesther. Now all she had to do was to prove it.

Elizabeth Buchan worked in publishing before her first novel was published in 1995. Her novels include *Consider the Lily*, the best selling *Revenge of the Middle-Aged Woman*, and her latest, *That Certain Age*.

Portfolio Woman

At 6.30 a.m. there was a muffled cry from Chloe's bedroom. It was either the cat or Jake, her younger brother by ten years. Chloe did not like her sleep patterns broken. That her sleep patterns spilt over into the afternoon was not up for debate. Or at least it was, but the debate had to be won by her. 'We agree on personal liberty,' she argued. 'That is what distinguishes us as a civilized society. I am harming no one, and this is what I choose to do.'

Jake, who at fourteen was shaping up into an intellectual tyrant, replied: 'But I choose to wake you up so that you can drag your carcass out of bed and add to the greater good by doing something useful.'

Outside my bedroom the light shifted and sharpened. I pictured it sliding over the drenched lawn and picking out the lichen on the grey stone wall. Thereafter, stronger and livelier, it danced over the field and away. This early in my day, I found my responses to light and sound extra sharp, extra vivid. They beat on my inner ear and inner eye and nudged me into wakefulness for what lay ahead.

I stretched out a leg and imagined it as the oiled, obedient limb of the marathon runner. There I was, way ahead of the competition, pounding up the road to the finish, after twenty-six miles still pumping, still upright, the cheers from the crowd sounding sweet in my ears. Naturally, I would deal with fame with ease and grace.

Will turned over and air slid protesting from between his lips. 'What time is it?'

I told him, waited two seconds for the groan which came and twitched back the duvet.

'God save us,' he muttered, 'from a wife.'

I got dressed in a charmingly ancient pair of corduroy trousers and what was left of a jumper the washing machine regarded a culinary treat, and was grilling bacon in the kitchen by the time Will shambled in, tie draped around his neck like a doctor's stethoscope. He was shivering and pale, probably the result of too much wine the previous evening. It had been one of those occasions when, Chloe and Jack occupied elsewhere, the peace folded around us in the dim interior of the kitchen. We talked about nothing much and, every so often, refilled our glasses. The claret had been a little too young. As Will in his capacity as founder and chief executive of Border Wines had explained to me more than once, all those unresolved acids and sugars and minerals, pigments and tannins required more time before the wine flowered into its personal best. Time and the requisite amount of oxygen. Then the elements of grape, primary fermentation and oak meld, mature and produce from behind their backs the all-important bouquet. Heady with ripeness and richness. 'You know,' I told my husband, 'I reckon women and wine have more in common than is generally supposed.'

'Do they now,' my supportive husband had commented.

40

'Close the window, Poppy,' Will now said. 'Please.'

I had left it open deliberately. Oxygen, I suppose. I wanted to smell the faint suggestive smells of damp earth and cold stone which made my nose wrinkle with anticipation. But I sneaked a look at Will. Actually, he did not look well. He sank onto a chair at the table and supported his head with a shaky hand.

'Headache?' I inquired sympathetically.

'Worse,' he said. 'Sick and aching.'

Automatically, I placed a hand on his forehead. How many times had I done that with my children, feeling the eggshell skin beneath my fingers and the reedy, vulnerable pulses race away from me? And how my heart had either quickened with relief or shrunk with fear. You never knew what might happen and it seemed to me that the pearly, fragile bodies of my children were ever a temptation with which fate would play games.

Will's forehead was hot and burning and the skin beneath his eyes was like a transparent crescent moon.

'Bed.'

'I can't,' he said in heroic mode. 'There's the tasting. They can't manage without me. The whole thing will collapse, and it was such a problem to set up.'

I love my husband. His sense of drama was magnificent and he never displayed the irritating feminine habit of self-deprecation.

'You can't taste with a temperature. Bed.'

Will gave in. That was the other thing. He knew when to retreat. I never did.

I was back in the kitchen sorting out the phone calls, having settled Will on propped-up pillows and served a light tempting breakfast on a tray, when Jake wandered in. He tore off a piece of bread from the loaf

41

and dipped a corner into a pot of honey. 'Cut it,' I ordered.

'We are more in tune with our basic selves if we eat with our fingers.' Honey streaked Jake's chin.

'Have I ever indicated I wished to be in tune with your basic self?'

'Right . . .' Chloe appeared in the doorway, flushed and rumpled. 'I'm moving out. I've had enough. There's no peace and no bloody privacy in this family.'

She turned to me. 'Mum, as a woman, defend me. Don't give in to this terrorist.'

Jake laughed and Chloe went a dangerous white. 'Your father is ill,' I informed them. 'So postpone World War Three.'

'Ham or cheese sandwiches, Chloe?' Jake eyed the kitchen knife and, reluctantly, picked it up.

'What do you mean, sandwiches?' Chloe extracted orange juice from the fridge and closed it with a bang.

'You said you were leaving . . .'

I looked from one to the other. Clearly, the wisdom of Solomon and the virtuous wife who is above the price of rubies had their work cut out this morning. 'Chloe, if you want to get your own back, wake up Jake tomorrow.'

'Mornings . . .' Lucia cut across this familial scene by banging on the window and letting herself in the back door. '1st good weather,' she called through.

'1st good weather,' I muttered, remembering that I had not stocked up the cleaning box as I had promised. Wearing a pink plastic barrette in her hair and black plastic high heels, Lucia tip-tapped into the kitchen, finger pointed at me.

'1st no polishes.' Her face was worked into tragic lines, desperate and worn. It was not the lack of polish or dusters or whatever household item I had failed to provide this time, but Lucia's longing to be back home in Bosnia that had engraved them on her flesh. I touched her gently on the arm. 'Have a coffee and a biscuit before you start.'

Chloe and Jake drifted out of the kitchen. I sat down with Lucia and asked if she had had any news from her brother and his family. They were Albanians in a Serb area and Lucia was terrified for their fate. A moustache of milky coffee sprouted around her mouth. 'I will kill them . . .' She meant the Serbs. 'Even if best friend.'

'You would kill your best friend?'

She turned her face to mine and the expression made me recoil a little.

'You no understand how we feel.'

Something of the blood and despair and old, old hatreds swirled around my kitchen. Whoever had invented tribes and tribalism and then linked them up with religions had much to answer for. And that applied wherever in the world.

While Lucia launched herself at the bedrooms, I mixed a strawberry-flavoured food supplement into a cup and laid up a tray with fresh napkin and water, and carried it into the part of the house where Fabia, Will's mother, lived. Or rather roosted like a great bony bird.

She was sitting up in bed waiting for what was her main nutrition of the day. One could not call it a meal. I explained that I had been talking to Lucia about the situation in her country.

'You treat that woman too well,' she said. 'It never does. They will take advantage of you.'

I reflected on the gleaming paintwork, polished floors, dust-free carpets and piles of exquisitely ironed laundry. 'I think the boot is on the other foot. How are you this morning?'

43

There was a heavy sigh and a frail veined hand went up to pat the white curls.

'Bad,' she said. 'You need to be strong to be old . . .'

I recognized the signs. Fabia wanted to be talked to. Or rather, to talk at me. She wanted me to pull up a chair and listen to stories of her other life. The one where she had been young and strong and quite a 'gel', as she put it. Listening to her, which I did, I felt a twinge of envy for the certainties that slipped from her. They were a second skin which she wore with assurance. It was so much easier to live within a set of rules and beliefs which had been, for much of her long life, non-negotiable, and easier still if you had been comparatively well off and well connected. I had heard the anecdotes from her girlhood of big-game hunting in Kenya and cocktail parties many times, but they were full of life and colour and quirky detail and I continued to enjoy them.

'About my funeral . . .' A master tactician, and having sufficiently diverted this captive audience Fabia slipped this out. I must have given a visible start. 'Don't look like that, Poppy. I count on you to help me get through the next part.'

She meant the death. A chill went through me. Fabia had never been quite so direct about the subject before.

'I don't want tiptoeing and hush and weeping.'

The last made me bite my lip. There were not many people left who would weep or tiptoe for Fabia.

'Open the top right-hand drawer, Poppy, and get out the file.'

I did not need to be told what was in the file. I opened it and scanned the handwriting which looped over the paper inside. I cleared my throat. 'You want "Nearer My God To Thee" for the opening hymn.'

Fabia poked at the strawberry liquid. 'I've been

thinking about that. I might prefer "Lead Kindly Light". Such a nice image, don't you think?'

I assured her that it was.

'Will you carry out my wishes, Poppy?'

'Of course.'

'I thought I'd ask you rather than Will because women are better at that sort of thing.'

Were they? While men did the really important things and ran the country, birth and death were women's business.

'Meanwhile, Fabia, you are very much alive. Could you try another spoonful?' I guided the spoon to her lips. 'Will is ill. Touch of flu probably.'

At lunchtime, I took Will a little lightly concocted vegetable soup on a tray. Having demolished a second helping, he announced that it would do him good to have a nap and I was foraging in the kitchen for my own lunch when the phone went. It was Allan, Will's number two. He wanted to know how Will had rated the claret. I told Allan that Will was asleep, but if he wanted my opinion, it would mature into something fairly special.

'So you think we should buy it in?'

I considered. There were several factors, but each appeared positive. The market was buoyant and growing. In our area – why, I don't know – clarets went down better than Burgundies, despite the threat from the New World, and it came from a house we wished to do further business with. 'Yes. Buy,' I said.

Next up was the arrival of Josie, the home-care help, who came in three times a week to bath Fabia. Looking thunderstruck but radiant, she burst into the kitchen. 'Guess what, Poppy, I'm having a baby!'

This was wonderful news for Josie, well over thirty,

who had been trying for years to become pregnant. 'Oh, but that is fantastic.' I felt the tears spring to my eyes with pleasure for her and also, shamefully, my heart plummet at the thought that I would have to replace her and soon.

'The doctor says,' she trilled happily, 'that I must take extra care and not overdo it.' I knew without saying it that Fabia equalled 'overdoing it'.

We agreed we would talk timetables very soon. I got into the car and drove – too fast – into town where I was due to chair a meeting on the council's proposed traffic-calming scheme for the centre. It was, as expected, a stormy session where passions were unleashed. Somehow, I managed to pilot the meeting through the agenda but, to my despair, we agreed only on one thing: to consult the consultants. No one could bring themselves to insist on one course of action over another. Myself included. I thought of Fabia and her certainties.

I left the meeting feeling jumpy and unsettled, and found myself in Boots cosmetics department where I spent a happy ten minutes browsing bright-red lipsticks, bought one and bore it home.

Will was awake. As I stood in front of the mirror filling in my lips with bright red, I briefed him on his mother and her funeral, Allan and the claret and, of course, the lack of progress on the traffic proposals. 'I'm sorry,' I added, 'but I haven't had time to shop for supper. Can you bear scrambled eggs? Chloe will be going out with her boyfriend and Jake is spending the night with Sam.'

Will adjusted his pillows to his satisfaction and sank back on them. He looked better and rested. 'I've been listening to the radio,' he said. 'There was a programme about how, in future, we must live portfolio lives. How we should have many skills, not just one. And not just one job either. It is the mark of the intelligent man.' He smiled up at me, totally without irony.

'Might be something you could consider, Poppy? Women have to move with the times as well as men, you know.'

I smoothed and tucked the sheets around him. 'Oh, do they?'

'I can't kiss you with that lipstick on.'

I glanced in the mirror. I liked the me with the bright-red, woman-of-the-world-who-might-be-dressed-in-Armani mouth.

'Later then.'

'There's a rude word for you.'

I laughed.

Later, at midnight, having fed Will scrambled eggs and cooked a completely non-fattening snack to line the stomach for Chloe before she went out clubbing, having settled Fabia for the night and checked out her dosage of pills, and after having eaten cheese on toast in the solitary kitchen while going over the household accounts, I went up to bed.

The bedroom was dark, but Will was awake. From years of night feeds and wakenings, I knew my way around without light. I slid into bed and immediately Will's hand snaked its way over my thigh. 'You know what they say about fever?'

'No, what?'

'That it heightens desire.'

My husband's body moved over me, a rehearsal and a performance of something that we had done together so many times. He was fragile from fever, but impatient and ardent. I was tired but willing, enjoying our mutual pleasure and need, and content in the quiet that followed. Images and questions slid through my mind, like water let loose. Death and funerals, a new baby, my children, traffic, cleaning, history, how it repeats and recycles . . . And had we really racked up a telephone bill of over £200? There was, of course, the wine. Each of these drifting, tangled filaments were cross-referenced, each brought the whisper and stir of memory. Each had its place.

'What did you say?' muttered Will, his breath fanning out over my bare shoulder.

'I was agreeing with you.'

I cherished Will's damp flesh with my mouth. 'A portfolio life is the mark of the intelligent and civilized man . . . and woman.'

Mavis Cheek left school without any qualifications. For twelve years, she worked at the contemporary art publishers Editions Alecto, starting as a receptionist and then becoming manager of their gallery. Mavis left to go to college, graduating in Arts, and then began writing. Her first novel, *Pause Between Acts*, was published in 1988 and won the *She*/John Menzies First Novel Prize. Since then, she has written nine other novels, including *Mrs Fytton's Country Life* and, most recently, *The Sex Life of My Aunt*.

Sheep's Eyes

Sally Parker's next-door neighbours may have been surprised that she accepted their invitation, but their surprise was nothing to her own. One minute she was standing in the back garden thinking 'sun-lounger', the next she was nodding. Worse, she was also nodding to Peter Beales's solemn undertaking to supply her with an adequate anorak should it be necessary.

'Can't trust June,' he said.

For a moment she thought he had broken out and was telling her something wicked and interesting about a floozy, but no, it was only the usual British thing about the weather.

'Just a little picnic for some pals,' said Jennifer, 'because Granny's having the children.'

Pals, thought Sally, was pushing it. Neighbours, yes. For while Sally had flown the world, the Beales had produced two noisy children and never the twain were likely to meet. They were the sort of couple who put a pond and trickling hosepipe in their back garden and ever after referred to it as a 'water feature'.

The friendliest gesture Sally ever made towards them was to stuff earplugs in on Sunday mornings when she finally took the ground job and not complain about the bloodcurdling screams that were, apparently, family fun. Which made her think that passing on marriage and motherhood, despite everyone else telling her what she was missing, was no bad thing. Besides, she was still trying to settle down to life on the ground. *Single* life on the ground. And the truth was that she enjoyed the peace of it all. But certain people kept issuing her with warnings.

Certain people like Val. Sally's old boss and a couple of years her senior. 'Since I stopped flying I haven't smiled into a man's eyes – except my dad's and he's senile – for three years,' she said. 'You think the high life is going to last and then – well, I tell you, Sal, my girl, *never* turn anything down.'

Sally smiled and nodded and said that she wouldn't. But she was unconvinced. For Sally, who had worked for airlines since she left school, dating men went with the job – from London to Karachi, New York to Moscow – never a shortage. In the last year it all began to wear a bit thin. After seventeen years chasing around exotic hot spots and 'nite' spots, Sally found that her home, and her small garden, and the neat row of houses quietly placed by the river, were seductions enough. Besides, if you were used to the flashing gold teeth of a handsome silk-seller from Karachi, or the wicked smile of a jazz man in New Orleans, Peter Beales's anorak held few charms. Maybe, she argued, she needed a little time to adjust. Val just rolled her eyes. 'While you're getting adjusted, dear,' she said, 'others will pounce.'

It was a touch too chilling. A touch too close to the ancestral jungle of the predator. Sally imagined all these women holed up in trees, skulking at the mouths of caves and hiding in undergrowth with their talons sharpened and their teeth bared, ready to fight to the last for the one potent male. Fortunately, the image of

Peter Beales as a husband went some way to dealing with such fantastical imagining.

She did try. But she was still unused to the un-attached male opening conversations with the wetness of the weather instead of the delightful silliness of how beautiful her eyes were (the Karachi silk-seller) or that he could read her soul (the New Orleans jazz man). Romance, she felt, was wanting.

'You'll be lucky,' said Val. 'Just make do.'

Which was unedifyingly like her mother's view of the world. But at least she was trying. Peter Beales's anorak or not, she would go.

The day dawned clear-skied. Nevertheless, she duti-fully put her wellingtons into the Bealeses' hatchback and they set off to meet the rest of the party some-where 'in the wilds of Oxfordshire', as Jennifer Beales put it. It all looked remarkably tame to Sally. She had, after all, driven a jeep into the Gobi desert. But she kept quiet about that.

'This is Sally,' said Jennifer to everyone. 'Our next-door neighbour. She's only just come back to England for good.' The subtext was that they must All Be Very Kind To Her . . .

She did not disgrace herself during the lengthy stomping over hill and dale as the colourful, slightly absurd (and she included herself in this) party made their way along the Ridgeway. She managed to look deeply interested in one father's remarkable child and someone's husband's detailed plans for early retire-ment and she even counselled one bright-faced mother puffing up a hill beside her about girls and languages and a career in the air.

'Obviously it's not all being a glorified waitress,' she said firmly. 'It's more like being everyone's multilingual mother, and a few other things besides.'

She did not say what these might be. The puffing mother looked anxious enough already.

There was, of course, a single male in the party. And much like children who have been brought along by their parents to be introduced because 'they'll get on so well together', she and the single male avoided each other like the plague. But at the highest point of Hickpen Hill, Jennifer announced that it was lunch-time. Sally and the single man, called Bill, were given a flask of coffee to share and a Tupperware box of assorted crustless triangles. What the Bealeses' children took to school every day, Sally guessed. She and Bill smiled awkwardly. Jennifer said, 'Bill's an actor.' And with the somewhat desperate suggestion that they admire the view, which was mostly of sheep, she left them to it.

'I always do what my sister-in-law tells me,' he said, turning to look over the fence and holding out his hand to a curious sheep. The sheep came closer. She assumed he was being ironic and laughed.

'I'll bet!' she said, roguishly.

He looked back over his shoulder, puzzled and frowning.

Oh, she thought. He *means* it – he really means it.

'Nice.'

She tried to think what could possibly be nice. 'Um . . . nice to have someone so capable, to tell you what to do?'

'Yes,' he said.

He returned his gaze to the dim-looking ram and threw it a bit of sandwich. It bounced off its nose. To no effect.

'She's certainly knocked my brother into shape.'

'Yes,' said Sally, feeling stupid in the face of such admiration.

He turned back again and smiled. 'She's trying it on me now.'

Sally shut her mouth. Personally, she couldn't think of anything worse.

'Making a good job of it too,' he said.

'Lovely,' she replied.

She studied him as he tried to entice the sheep with another bit of sandwich. He was short and squat and kind-faced, but not at all attractive. Well, not in a flashing-gold-teeth sense. Also, he was wearing a beige anorak. Actually, she thought, it's worse than that – it's a car coat. Still, an actor had possibilities. He would be perfectly acceptable if he was wearing something else. A shirt and jeans or a sweater and cords – or anything really. She heard Val's voice. 'Never turn down an opportunity . . .' Plough on, girl, she thought. She leaned against the fence and held out a piece of sandwich herself. Another daft-looking sheep approached. Followed by all the others, knocking into each other and looking – well – cretinous.

'Nice things, sheep,' said Bill. 'Don't you think? Attractive animals.'

Could he be serious? He was. Oh well, she decided, it shows that he has a nice nature. She looked at the bobbing heads, a couple of dozen with one thought between them. But she put the brightest of smiles on her face. Now or never.

'Oh yes,' she said. 'My favourites.'

One of them made a baa-ing noise at her as if it knew. She stared back at it and just about managed to stop herself, with the aid of a little cheese-filled crustless triangle shoved strategically into her treacherous mouth, from adding, 'Rosemary, garlic and mint sauce, yum yum.'

Later, at home, stretching her aching limbs in the

warm bath water and sipping a glass of sherry, she decided that she had acquitted herself very well. (Perhaps there was something in this star sign stuff – she was, after all, a two-sided Gemini.) Bill and she managed the rest of the afternoon's walking very amicably, with conversations ranging from teaching drama (which is what, it transpired, he did) to his moment of truth after being in *Crossroads* and thinking he had made it, and getting dropped six months later when his character was made to run off with the owner's amnesiac aunt.

'My job was a bit like acting,' she said.

'Really?' he replied.

'Mmm. I had to get on that plane and wow them no matter what . . . I rather liked it actually.'

'I'm not that keen on flying,' he said.

'Well, I'm not now,' she said brightly. Her face was beginning to ache with the effort.

Val came early to the party.

'Before the hordes arrive,' she said, and whipped out a chilled bottle of champagne.

'Hardly hordes,' laughed Sally. 'Only the neighbours and that walking crowd – and you.'

She opened the bottle and they sat there in the garden in the waning sunlight enjoying that special moment before a party really begins. 'I just announced it up there on the top of a hill. God knows why. Bravado maybe. I was surrounded by a load of sheep and something made me want to assert my human qualities. Partying used to be one of them.' She sighed.

'Do you miss flying?'

'Oh, don't *you* start,' said Sally.

Val stared at her.

'Sorry,' she said. 'It reminds me of having face ache, that's all.'

Val stared at her even harder. Best change the subject. Steam might appear at any moment from those ears. Sally was extremely wound up.

'So then, who else is coming?'

Sally drained her glass. Amazing the courage a glass of bubbles on an almost empty stomach can give you, she thought, and boy, if she was going to carry this thing through, did she need it.

Out loud, she said as casually as possible, 'Oh, and Bill's coming.' She giggled. 'My beau in beige.'

'Lucky you,' said Val. 'Give me half a chance. I wouldn't care if he wore sky blue with pink spots on. Or taupe.' She sighed, also into her glass. Sally refilled it. 'Cheer up,' she said brightly. 'Taupe is beige.'

After two glasses of good champagne she felt considerably better. Or was it resigned?

Jennifer, Peter and Bill arrived first. 'Don't mind if we're early, do you?' said Jennifer in the voice of one who is utterly confident. She leaned towards Sally and hissed much too loudly, 'But Bill couldn't wait any longer.' He did not look like a man who could be impatient for anything – well, not in that shade of turtleneck anyway. Stop it, she counselled, stop it . . .

'Bill,' she said, smiling with every tooth in her head, and she held out her hand. He looked relieved as he shook it.

'Tush,' she heard Jennifer say behind her. 'Peter – the present.'

Peter Beales, in a fetching royal-blue hand-knit, stepped forward and handed Sally a bottle of sparkling white wine with a pink bow on top. He – or someone – obviously thought they should make up for Bill's complete lack of colour. Actors, she decided kindly, needed to be self-effacing for their profession. Sally put the bottle down next to the half-full bottle of Veuve Clicquot. The Widow. The Black Widow. The champagne appeared (or was Sally imagining it?) to turn up its dainty, grieving nose. 'Thank you so much,' she said.

'Bill?' said Jennifer, as if she was marshalling troops. Bill stepped so smartly forward that Sally nearly saluted. Then, with his two hands, he carefully proffered a heavy and oddly disjointed parcel. He presented it to Sally as if he were laying a wreath. It was wrapped in very jolly paper with smiling clowns all over it and had yet another bow. An enticing egg-yolk yellow.

'How lovely,' she said, bright as ever. There was something about Bill that made you want (if not yearn) to be *bright*. 'You really shouldn't have.'

The label said it would remind her of their walk. 'Aah,' she cooed in a voice she did not know she owned. She unwrapped the gift slowly, letting the paper drift to the floor, where Peter Beales immediately bent down and picked it up and began smoothing it and folding it. She watched him, mesmerized for a moment, and then turned back to what she now held, unwrapped, in her hands. And then she gasped. It was a pottery sheep. But no ordinary pottery sheep; a pottery sheep of most peculiar dimensions and perspective, with a very small head and two little dots for very close-together eyes making a remarkably silly face – anthromorphically not unlike some anxious politician, with a body that ballooned out into a huge and weirdly disproportionate size. Some foolish craft notion of 'modern'. Very foolish.

She remembered the cave paintings of animals in the Levant, the Hin~i carvings of oxen and bison, the modern marble and alabaster sheep in a crib in southern Italy. Beautiful, beautiful shapes, unburdened by any need for realism, but perfect in their essential rightness. This, in her hand, was very bad art. Of the very worst kind. In art terms, actually, she thought, it's the equivalent of taupe.

'I hope you like it,' he said.

She opened her mouth to be bright. For a moment there was silence. Then Val, sitting there so demurely, her glass quite empty again, said genuinely, 'Oh, how lovely, and so unusual.' Val was never any good at artistic things.

Bill looked at her gratefully.

Sally looked at her even more gratefully. Suddenly she saw again those silly sheep in the Oxfordshire field, hustling for something they neither understood nor wanted. She handed the pottery sheep to her friend. 'Val loves things like this,' she said. 'Don't you?'

Val looked startled, but game.

'She collects them.'

Val nodded vigorously. She did now.

'And this' – Sally gave Bill's sleeve a pat and winked at him – 'is, curiously enough, her favourite colour.'

The she turned to the bottle of sparkling wine, removed the pink bow, which she also dropped on the floor, giving Peter Beales an 'I dare you' look, and opened it with a satisfactory pop for her guests.

'Lovely,' they all said.

'Lovely,' she replied.

And then she picked up the remaining Veuve Clicquot and took it back out into the garden and called over her shoulder that anyone who wished to join her would be most welcome. They followed. All except Val and Bill, who were left exclaiming and delighting over the curious sheep. As they sat at her

59

little round table (brought back from Ishafan), Sally put her finger to her lips and said, 'Shush. If you listen hard you can just hear the sound of your water feature.'

They all concentrated for ages before Jennifer Beales suddenly said, 'But I don't think it's turned on.'

It was a strain, but she pulled through, and Val, at least, went off happy. Thank God for the Veuve Clicquot, thought Sally afterwards, as she yawned herself into bed. Because, just for once (and this time she did laugh out loud), a couple of glasses of that and she wasn't anybody's.

Tracy Chevalier was born in America but lives in London with her husband and son. She is the author of four novels: *The Virgin Blue*, *Girl with a Pearl Earring*, *Falling Angels* and her latest, *The Lady and the Unicorn*. A film version of *Girl with a Pearl Earring*, the story of a peasant girl (played by Scarlett Johansson) who is forced to work as a servant in the household of painter Vermeer (played by Colin Firth), and becomes the subject of one of his most famous paintings, was released in January 2004. 'I wasn't prepared for how much I would like it,' says Tracy. 'I wanted to go straight back into the screening room and see it again. When I first saw Colin, I thought, Oh, lovely! He was perfect for the part.'

The Birth of Venus

Some things shouldn't change. Even during earth-
quakes and other upheavels, it's important to hold on
to the familiar objects and regular routines that keep a
life on track. That was what Sylvia told herself as she
sat in the waiting room, flicking through a magazine
until Sharon was ready for her. That is why I keep
coming here, she thought. I'm keeping my feet on the
ground. I'm remaining level-headed.

She reached for another magazine. These were
not rumpled two-year-old copies with articles on
celebrities who'd since dropped out of sight or
divorced or gone to prison, but gleaming, up-to-date
issues with the latest fashions and celeb gossip. That
was one of the things she liked about Sharon's salon –
besides being right around the corner from Sylvia's
flat, it always had a new and hopeful feel about it.
Sharon herself was always well turned out – her dyed
hair never showing roots, her painted toenails never
chipped – and she kept her salon that way too. She
had just had it repainted, and replaced the furniture
and carpet as well. Perhaps this time I too will become
hopeful and new, Sylvia thought each time she went
in.

Sylvia had been coming to Sharon's every two weeks for a leg and eyebrow wax for the past ten years. She knew it was that long because her first appointment had been the week before she and Richard married. Richard had suggested it. 'Darling, it will be easier for you, don't you think, not having to worry about shaving while we're in Barbados?' They were going there on their honeymoon. Sylvia had dropped hints about Cuba or Indonesia, but Richard had chosen Barbados. Richard had been right – after that visit to Sharon, Sylvia didn't have to worry about shaving on their honeymoon. And when, on their return, Richard teased her about leg stubble, she went back to Sharon, and had been going ever since, every two weeks so that the hair never got too long. She'd added the eyebrow wax when Richard jokingly said once that she looked like that Mexican woman artist famous for her one long eyebrow.

Sylvia frowned at an article about back exercises. She had forgotten the Mexican artist's name. Now, of course, Richard wasn't around to ask.

She glanced at the clock. Sharon was running late. Sylvia studied the wall. There was something different about the room. Certainly it looked better with its primrose-yellow walls and new rattan furniture. It wasn't that. Something was missing, though Sylvia couldn't work out what it was.

'Hello, dear.' Sharon bustled in from the back rooms, cheery as ever. 'Sorry to keep you – I was just getting a new client settled in on the tanning bed. How are you keeping?'

'Fine, thanks,' Sylvia answered. Sylvia always answered that. Even after Richard left her she'd said she was fine. When she did finally admit to Sharon that they'd split up, she waited till she was lying on the table with Sharon ripping the wax strips from her legs before she told her through gritted teeth; then any tears that sprung to her eyes could be attributed to the pain of the waxing.

'Oh dear, I'm so sorry,' Sharon had said. She was a kind, motherly woman and probably was genuinely sorry, as much as someone can be who knows almost nothing about you. Though Sylvia saw Sharon more regularly than she did many of her friends, they didn't even know each other's surnames. During the fifteen minutes it took for the waxing every two weeks, they chatted about their holidays, the weather, the new local shops, Sylvia's new kitchen, Sharon's garden furniture. Telling Sharon she and Richard had separated (she wouldn't dream of admitting that Richard had left her) was the most personal she'd dared to get, and they'd quickly retreated from the topic, like the neighbour's cat jumping back from water Richard sprayed at it to chase it from the garden.

Now Sylvia followed Sharon into the waxing room and automatically hopped up onto the table. After ten years she knew the drill, and Sharon had stopped asking her if she wanted anything new or different – a bikini wax, eyelash tinting, a facial. They had settled into an easy routine.

'The new paint in the waiting room looks nice,' Sylvia commented as Sharon began daubing wax onto a calf. 'Thank you, dear,' Sharon said, plastering a cloth strip onto the waxed leg. 'It does look better, doesn't it? Refreshed.' She yanked the strip off quickly. Quick and firm was best – it hurt less that way.

That could have been Richard's motto. He told Sylvia he had met another woman at the gym and was moving in with her, and indeed had packed and left, all within an hour. He'd been patient with Sylvia after he'd told her, making her a cup of tea and handing her a tissue when she cried. But even as he waited for her to calm down he was quietly folding shirts and rolling socks into balls and putting dental floss in his washbag. When the door shut behind him, Sylvia still hadn't taken in what he'd said. It was so quick that it didn't really start to hurt until a few months later. Recently when he rang – as he did occasionally, to discuss the divorce proceedings or ask her to close a bank account or tell her he was taking her name off the car insurance – Sylvia found that she couldn't speak to him because of the rage blocking her throat. She'd begun to let the answering machine take her calls, and didn't ring him back.

'I like the new furniture as well,' Sylvia said, watching Sharon's capable hands dab at a few stray hairs with the waxed cloth. 'And the carpet.'

'Got it in the sales. There. Now, just turn over onto your tummy, will you, dear, so I can do the back.'

'Is something else different in the waiting room?' Sylvia asked, her voice muffled by the towel she'd sunk her face into. 'Something you took away, perhaps?'

'Funny you should ask that, dear.' Sharon ripped another strip and Sylvia winced. The backs of her calves were her most sensitive spot. 'A client asked that just this morning. The workmen dropped one of the pictures when they were doing up the room. Broke the glass and ripped the poster so that I had to throw it away. I was going to hang up something else but I haven't had the time to get around to it.'

'Which picture was it?' Sylvia tried to remember but couldn't.

'It was of a naked lady, standing in a big shell.'

'Ah, yes. The Botticelli.' It was the shell that reminded Sylvia. The woman was beautiful, with a

66

serene expression that often made Sylvia wonder what she was thinking about. Sylvia herself could never manage to look so serene, and Richard had sometimes admonished her for it. 'Don't wrinkle your brow so, darling, it makes you look anxious. Surely you don't have anything to worry about, do you? You're with me, after all. Try to be level-headed, hmm?'

Nothing to worry about, then, except to keep her brow free of wrinkles and her legs smooth. Richard also preferred her to remain a size 10. That was one of his arguments against having children. 'But we're so happy as we are, don't you think, darling?' he would say when she brought up the subject. 'So happy and carefree. And you wouldn't want to get bigger, would you? Women always do when they have children, don't they? And the stretch marks? Oh dear me, no.'

So Sylvia had no worries, but she still was not as serene as the woman in the Botticelli painting. 'Where was that picture from?' she asked now.

'Dunno. My niece gave it to me, and she doesn't remember where she got it. She must have been popular, that lady, as so many clients have asked after her now she's gone. Isn't that always the way? All right, dear, that's done. Ready for your eyebrows?'

Now that she could no longer see the painting at the salon, Sylvia often found herself thinking of it. Once she even dreamt the salon was on fire and she had to break in to save the picture, but she couldn't get it off the wall because it had been superglued in place. She tried to recall more details about the painting. Sylvia was sure there were several people in it, but she couldn't remember where they were or what they were doing. It was funny that she had seen it so many times and yet could recall so little about it.

She did remember that the woman standing in the

shell had red hair so long it covered her nether regions. Sylvia herself had short brown hair cut into a bob that she diligently blow-dried every morning. Richard preferred short hair, and had encouraged her not long after they met to cut hers. 'Long hair is so messy, don't you think? So hard to look after. Short is so easy and convenient, hmm?' Sylvia had never had to blow-dry her long hair – instead she'd let it dry naturally. She didn't say so to Richard, however. It was true that short hair was very neat.

The next time she went to Sharon's the empty space on the wall had been filled with a poster of a tropical beach, where a couple walked along, holding hands. Sharon had got it from the travel agent next door. 'So soothing, isn't it?' she said. 'Don't you just want to be there now and feel that sand between your toes?'

Sylvia nodded obediently. She was thinking of the holidays she and Richard had gone on to the West Indies – back to Barbados ('The best place to celebrate our anniversary, don't you think, darling?') and to a resort on St Lucia for several years running, for as Richard said, it was wonderful to know what to expect each time. ('I'd swear that waiter remembered our drinks order from last year!') They had never gone to Indonesia or Cuba. 'Why would you want to go there?' Richard had said when she brought it up. 'Didn't you know that there are electricity cuts all the time? There's no guaranteeing you'd be able to blow-dry your lovely hair, hmm? We couldn't have that now, could we?'

The next Saturday Sylvia went to the local library to look through car magazines. Richard had let her keep the flat but had taken the car, and Sylvia wanted to find something smaller and less flashy. ('It won't do to cut corners on a car, will it, darling? We want something big and safe, with enough room so that your clothes don't get wrinkled, hmm?')

She went up to the front desk to ask where car magazines were kept. The librarian, a young, harassed-looking woman with wispy blond hair that fell into her eyes, pointed out the magazines, then turned away to put a stack of books on a cart. Sylvia found herself hesitating. The librarian looked around. 'Is there something else?'

'Well, yes.' Sylvia hadn't realized that there was something else until that moment. 'Do you have an art history section?'

The librarian waved a hand towards a shelf of books. 'There. But it's rather small, I'm afraid. What were you looking for?'

'A painting. A Botticelli painting.' Someone was waiting behind Sylvia, making her feel even more flustered. She tucked her hair behind her ears. 'I rather liked it, you see, and now – well, it's gone. It's gone and I would like to – well, to find it again, I suppose. Find out where it is.' She cursed herself for sounding so incoherent at the wrong moment.

'Hang on, I'll just see if we have anything.' The woman typed something into her computer terminal. 'No, nothing on Botticelli here. There's one book at the central branch, but it's out at the moment. You'll have to go there and put in a request.' She looked pointedly over Sylvia's shoulder at the next customer.

Sylvia was mortified to find her eyes filling with tears, and blinked rapidly. 'Thanks anyway,' she muttered. 'Sorry to have bothered you.'

She turned away and walked straight into the person behind her – a short, bosomy woman with long grey hair and thick glasses, the kind of woman Richard would joke read tarot cards and went to Glastonbury on holiday.

'Oh, so sorry,' Sylvia muttered. 'I hope I didn't—'

'That sounds interesting,' the woman said, talking over Sylvia's nevous chatter. 'Perhaps I can help. A Botticelli, eh? What does it look like?'

Sylvia hesitated. 'There's a woman in it.'

'Of course there is. What's she doing?'

'She's, er, naked, and she's standing in a big shell. She's got long hair,' Sylvia added, as if mentioning the hair would make the Botticelli woman more respectable.

The Glastonbury woman smiled. 'That'll be *The Birth of Venus*. The shell gives it away. Is she doing this?' She put one hand on her large bosom, another over her crotch, tilted her head to one side, and shifted her weight onto one leg, bringing her knees together so that the other foot pointed out.

Sylvia wanted to laugh at how daft she looked, and in public too. Still, the pose was undoubtedly familiar. 'Yes,' she said. 'That's it.'

'She's a beauty, that one,' the Glastonbury woman said. 'Venus arising from the sea, all fresh and new. She's in the Botticelli room at the Uffizi. It's almost ridiculous to see so many Botticellis in one room. I laughed the entire time I was there. The guards thought I was mad. Have you been to Florence?'

Sylvia shook her head. Italy was one of the many places that were off-limits to Richard. 'But we don't speak Italian. How would we get by? And all that pasta – you'd lose your figure. No, no, Sweden or Norway would be more suitable – they all speak English there and it's cooler, more like England. Don't you think, darling?'

'You should go sometime,' the woman said.

'Wonderful place. And there's nothing like seeing a favourite painting in the flesh, don't you think?'

'I suppose,' Sylvia murmured. 'I suppose I do think.'

Back at home Sylvia sat down at her computer and typed 'Botticelli' and 'Venus' into a search engine. After two clicks of a button, the painting appeared on the screen just as she remembered it from the salon. Sylvia peered at the image. Now that she saw it again, everything about the painting was as familiar as a friend's face. How could she have forgotten that the woman was floating on the sea in her shell, or that there were two angels hovering on one side, blowing so hard they'd managed to strip off the woman's cloak with the gusts they'd created? Or that another woman had caught the cloak and was trying unsuccessfully to cover up the shell woman? Or that the shell woman didn't seem much bothered by being so exposed? She wasn't trying very hard to cover up her ample body, either. She was a size 14 at least – maybe even a 16. Sylvia had been looking at this painting for ten years but had never seen that it was actually funny. Despite herself she smiled. She had not smiled in months. Not months – years. Sylvia was glad she was sitting down – she felt a little dizzy, as if she were sitting on a little boat in a rocking sea.

'Actually, I rather like pasta,' she said suddenly. She'd had pasta two or three times a week since Richard left – it was a quick and easy meal for one. In fact, Sylvia's clothes had grown rather tight from all the pasta. She would soon need to buy a size 12.

When Sylvia went to have her legs waxed a few weeks later, Sharon took one look at her and said, 'My, you look relaxed, dear. Been some place nice?'

Sylvia smiled. 'Italy.'

'Lovely. You're looking very healthy.' Healthy was

the word Sharon used when she was implying that a client had gained a bit of weight. Sylvia had never heard the word applied to herself.

'I'm feeling very healthy indeed,' she said. She held out a poster tube to Sharon. 'And I've brought you back something – something that belongs here.'

Amanda Craig is an award-winning journalist and author and lives in London with her husband and two children. Her latest novel *Love in Idleness* is a romantic comedy based on *A Midsummer Night's Dream*.

Waking Beauty

Staying in a French hotel is trying at the best of times. There are the bolsters; the carpet on the ceiling; the snooty staff who underline just why Dunkirk was a great moment in British history. But staying there with teenagers is much, much worse. Back home in England I passed for a good-enough mother, I like to think. My children weren't outstandingly clever, or beautiful (though of course I thought them so), but they were nice kids, a little exuberant, perhaps, but full of imagination and good will. At least, that's what I believed until we stayed in the Hotel d'Usse, and saw the way the Duras girl behaved.

'Sit up! Use your napkin. No, you may not have ketchup with your meal,' I hissed. 'Haven't you learnt to cut meat up without sending half of it over the table? Stop making that horrible noise with the straw. Stop it, or you'll be grounded tonight. I'm warning you . . .'

'What's bugging you, Mum?' asked Lottie.

'Are you getting PMT?' asked James.

'No I am not. Your table manners are atrocious,' I said, angrily. 'Dreadful. It's time you learnt how to behave.'

The problem was not just that they were teenagers, and so as impossible to control as a pair of ferrets. They were used, like most modern British children, to eating the kind of food that needed very little skill with utensils. The contrast with the family eating at the table next to ours was painful. Their daughter was, as far as I could tell, the same age as my Lottie, but seemed infinitely more sophisticated. The roasted chicken that was causing my kids to send their knives screeching across the china, was cut with immaculate precision at the next table. She drank watered-down wine, not Coke. She didn't speak with her mouth full, but spoke to her parents almost like an adult. By the time my own two, bored and resentful, had shot off to play together in the hotel garden, I was left to drown my mortification in coffee.

To my surprise, the couple approached me and said, in excellent English, 'Would it disturb you, Madame, if our daughter practises her English with yours?'

No, I said, it would not.

The father gave a beaming smile.

'Very good. Alors, Isabelle, parlez anglais!'

Obediently, his daughter trotted off to mine, who were by now whooping and pretending to be rock stars. Although they were fourteen and fifteen, Lottie and James were still childish enough to forget their adolescent dignity at times. Before she went, the girl curtsied to me.

'Your daughter is very polite,' I said, halfway between astonishment and amusement.

'I am of the old factory,' said the father. 'I let her have anything she wants, but she has to obey me.'

I thought this sounded marvellous, providing that you could afford it. However, it was evident that the Duras family were wealthy. Madame wore a gold necklace so thick that it looked more like a shackle than an ornament, and they drove the sort of car that I could only afford if I took out a second mortgage. They were staying at the Hotel d'Usse for a week, whereas I had booked into its creamy walls and velvet lawns for a single night, because nowhere else was available.

It turned out that the Duras family, too, were visiting castles. One, Azay les Rideaux, they had already seen, but the other, the Château d'Usse, they were visiting the following morning, like ourselves.

'Perhaps we can all go together,' said Monsieur Duras.

His wife said in a lecturing tone, 'It is the castle that inspired Perrault to write *La Belle au Bois Dormant*, that is to say—'

'*Sleeping Beauty*,' I interrupted, smiling to conceal my irritation.

We chatted for a while after that. The father was the more talkative, not just because his English was better, I suspected. This was a traditional marriage of the kind that I had never enjoyed, even if I could have chosen it. The wife was supposed to look after the house, the husband and the children and keep her mouth shut. They were Swiss. By the end of the evening I had heard as much as I ever wished to about M. Duras's business, his self-discipline and, in particular, his suspicion of foreigners, especially the wretched refugees who tried to escape across the Channel to Britain. Mme Duras joined in.

'Once, yes, once, I was in a shop with my daughter and these foreigners came in and they stole some lipsticks. If they are so poor, what do they need with make-up?' she demanded, her plump face mottling with fury. 'My Isabelle was so upset for a week after. Why did they steal, Mama? she keep asking. What can

I say? They are bad. We do not want them in Switzerland.'

Despite this, the Duras child and my own were getting on remarkably well. I watched them partly out of concern, and partly because of something else. As I have said, my own children were pretty normal. But Isabelle was another matter.

Her long, thick hair was a rich blond, which really did look like spun gold, although her lashes and brows were dark. Her eyes were a deep navy blue and her lips so red Lottie couldn't believe she wasn't wearing lipstick. Even at fourteen, usually the worst stage of a young woman's life, she was perfectly proportioned, diving into the hotel pool with the grace of a swallow.

My son said later, with a kind of awe, 'She's prettier than Claudia Schiffer,' but my daughter burst into tears that night and said that she was worried about having a fat stomach. I comforted her, but I knew what she meant.

'You must be kind to her because she's a Lonely Only,' I said sternly. 'She doesn't have anyone else to hang out with.'

They did not need encouragement. Lottie and Isabelle struck up one of those sudden intense holiday friendships. All three children played incessantly the next day, and now mine, to my relief, were not the only noisy teenagers in the hotel. In the afternoon, we all visited the Château d'Ussé, its turrets rising dreamily above its vast trees as if conjured from river-mist. The pigeons cooed in the tall boughs as we examined the stables where even the flies had fallen asleep on the enchanted horses. I had feared my children would consider themselves too old for this, but they wanted to climb the nearest tower and see the much-advertised scenes from *Sleeping Beauty*. Isabelle came with us, while her parents toured the rest of the castle. Up we went, grateful for the breeze, and soon were peering through glass windows at a room with dusty life-sized dummies in medieval costume. There were the king and queen, with their cradle, and a handful of courtiers or fairies. There, in front, was—

'Maleficent,' said my daughter, a child of Disney, 'but they call her Carabosse.'

'Gosh, Mum, she looks awfully like you,' said James.

We all looked, and it was true, there was something familiar about her.

'Mum doesn't have big black horns, though,' said Lottie.

'But you aren't bad, are you?' said my son. He gave me one of his rare smiles, the sort that reminded me of when he had been little, and that reassured me he was still brushing his teeth.

I hesitated. It's easy to be good when you're happy and secure. I had recently become neither.

'Well,' I said, 'just think what good Maleficent actually did to Sleeping Beauty.'

Isabelle opened her blue eyes very wide.

'Madame?'

'Mum,' said Lottie, rolling her eyes. 'You wouldn't like it if I went to sleep for a hundred years, would you?'

'I might prefer it to watching you with dozens of awful boyfriends,' I said.

'My father says I must never have boyfriends,' said Isabelle. 'Only a husband. He must be Swiss.'

'Oh? I think he'll find he can't stop you,' I said, drily.

Lottie sighed. 'Isabelle's parents are really really heavy, like Victorian? They won't let her get her ears pierced or wear nail polish, even.'

79

'Aren't you lucky, then?' I said. 'To have a single parent.'

By this time, the Duras family had caught up with us.

Lottie and Isabelle went to examine the second tableau, featuring a candyfloss prince waking a blonde princess in her four-poster. My children made retching noises.

'You do not like?' asked Isabelle.

'Honestly,' said Lottie, 'as if one should just lie there, waiting.'

'A princess should find her own prince,' said James, who living with a feminist mother and sister had naturally imbibed our points of view.

Isabelle looked shocked.

'But she cannot help it.'

'A spell is only a state of mind,' said James, with that adolescent pomposity I found hilarious and touching.

'It is good that they practise their English,' said Monsieur Duras, mopping his brow. I complimented him, rather stiltedly, on how well Isabelle spoke it already, and he explained that in Switzerland, they learnt English at nine, German at eleven and a third language at thirteen.

'That sounds like a lot of work,' I said.

'But of course! Our daughter works almost as hard as we do,' said his wife. 'On Monday, she have piano after school, on Tuesday gymnastics, on Wednesday tennis . . .' Her voice droned on, outlining all the extra-curricular activities that I had neither the time nor the money to give my own. I smiled and nodded, and all the while resented them for their smug, un-seeing lives, and resented, too, being made to feel like this. James was right, I was Carabosse, envious at their good fortune, and their beautiful, polite child.

All the same, nothing would have come of it if my daughter and theirs hadn't swapped addresses on departure. They promised each other, fervently, that they would be pen-pals.

We returned to England, and to our good-enough home. The children went back to school, I went back to work, and the memory of our week in France receded, although my daughter still complained about having a fat stomach, at least until acne became a greater preoccupation. I think we'd have forgotten all about Isabelle, but then a letter arrived. It was written in curly foreign handwriting, and had a stamp with a gentian on it.

Dear Lottie, I am hoping to find you well. I am well. I am writing this in my bedroom. My bedroom is pink, and my bathroom is pink also. I like pink! My family live in a house by Lake Geneva and it is very nice. I hope you and your brother will visit one day. I have a goldfish and a rabbit.

With love from your friend,
Isabelle.

Lottie read this out. 'That's so boring.'

It was boring, and what made it worse was that she enclosed a photo of herself with a house like a mini-castle in the background. Lottie refused to write back. Typical, I thought, mortified once again at my children's lack of manners. Poor Isabelle. She must indeed be lonely, to have tried to make a new friend of a casual holiday acquaintance. Then, I suddenly thought: why shouldn't I write instead? It would amuse me to plant some new ideas in that beautiful, conventional head, like weeds in a municipal rose-bed.

Dear Isabelle, Why do you like pink? [I typed.] Is it because you really like it, or because girls are dressed in pink and expected to like it? Boys are dressed in blue because they are supposed to have come from heaven, but girls are only allowed to like the colour of flesh. My own favourite colour is . . . purple!

I didn't forge my daughter's signature, as she so often forged mine, only signed with my initials. Soon another letter arrived.

Dear Lottie, Your letter was so interesting. Nobody is telling me about pink, or is making me think! Perhaps liking pink is wrong. But there are many pink flowers in nature, so is it bad? Can a colour be bad, itself, or just the way it is used by people?

Your friend,
Isabelle.

I was pleasantly surprised by this. I wrote back, still pretending to be Lottie, and received another reply. She was not stupid, and soon we were debating whether beauty and goodness were the same thing, and whether women should work when they had children. I explained to her how important it was for girls to have a career because of my 'mother's' divorce. I was then shocked to learn that in her canton in Switzerland, nobody was divorced. Women did not have the vote, and you could be fined for planting the wrong flowers in your window-box. She went to church every Sunday, never wore jeans and was expected to stay at home until she got married. Yet Isabelle could cook and sew and iron and do all the things that my own could or would not, and that, too, made me worry that in emphasizing the importance of academic work I had failed to teach my children how to be civilized. Soon, we were exchanging letters every fortnight or so. Lottie didn't notice, but James did because he liked collecting foreign stamps.

'Why are you writing to Isabelle, Mum?' he asked.

'Oh, you never know,' I said, deliberately vague. 'You might want to go and stay with her to improve your French some time.'

'Isabelle's boring,' said Lottie. 'She's just like that Sleeping Beauty. She's going to lie there like a doll and wait for her prince to come.'

'I could write,' said my son. 'I'm going to do French A level, remember.'

I was surprised. He shrugged.

'It might be better than some official pen-pal.'

'OK. As long as it doesn't become a snore,' I said. 'The secret of a good letter is liveliness.'

He looked doubtful.

'I don't know if my French is good enough.'

He wrote, however, and Isabelle wrote back – to me. She explained that it was more educational for both of them this way, for she could practise her English and James his French. I wondered whether her parents, with their strict ideas, knew she was now corresponding with a boy, and a foreigner. We were scarcely the kind of people her conventional family would approve of. By now, Lottie had decided that pierced ears weren't enough, and had gone on to have studs in her eyebrow, belly button and tongue. James insisted on wearing clothes so baggy that his trousers appeared to be held up by will power, and was deeply into garage music. His room was a chaos of old socks and decaying cups of tea positioned round his new, second-hand computer. However, he passed his GCSEs with flying colours and was predicted to get an A in French A level, so I wasn't complaining.

Sometimes at night I would hear the rattle of computer keys in my son's bedroom.

'What are you up to?' I asked, suspicious.

'Oh, just swapping emails with Isabelle.'

'You're still in touch?'

'Yeah.'

I didn't say anything. Privately, I was more relieved than not, because my son didn't seem to be too interested in English girls.

The summer after his A levels, James said, 'Mum, Isabelle wants to visit us. Can she?'

I paused.

'It might be interesting,' said James, casually.

I made all kinds of objections. I pointed out that our house was too small, messy and not posh enough for what Isabelle was used to. I was overruled. For the first time in five years, I spoke to Madame Duras as we made arrangements for her nineteen-year-old daughter to visit mine. She had never left home alone. All my hostility flooded back, as did my mortification that I would soon be judged by this child of perfection. For the next fortnight, I exhausted myself after work and at weekends getting my house a little cleaner and tidier. To my relief, James helped, repainting the kitchen, hacking back the jungle of shrubs in the garden, mowing the lawn and even getting a haircut. It was astonishing how nice he looked when clean. He had somehow been transformed into a young man. Thank God, I thought, though I still regarded her visit with dread.

At last, Isabelle arrived, smiling shyly. She was just as beautiful as before, though her hair was a darker gold and reached to her waist. My daughter was instantly overcome by self-hatred. I was also overcome. It was James who said, 'Hello, Isabelle. Did you have a good journey?'

She said, 'Hello, James. Thank you for your letters. They were very interesting. They . . .'

Then she, too, stopped.

'Oh, Lord,' said my daughter, disgustedly, looking from one blushing face to the other.

I couldn't exactly blame them. We could all see what had happened, and after a bit Lottie and I left them to it. There's nothing like love for making you feel ugly and unwanted, we agreed, hugging each other mournfully. Above our heads, wood pigeons cooed sleepily, just as they had done in the grounds of the Château d'Usse. I don't think Isabelle noticed the cracked tiles in the bathroom or the patchy grass or indeed our table manners, however. For Isabelle, far from despising us, seemed to love us all. She said that knowing my family had saved her.

'From what?' Lottie asked.

'From never being alive,' Isabelle said, passionately. 'From never being young. From never having any real friends.'

My daughter forgave her then, and took her to where she could have her ears pierced. (Isabelle refused to have a tongue stud.) They swapped clothes, they shopped, they went out clubbing and sightseeing together, but it was James who was the real focus of her interest. As she was of his. We were all under her spell: for just as my family improved her understanding of the world, so she improved us. We'd never behaved so nicely to each other, not even in a French hotel. Once we got over the shock of saying 'please' and ironing our clothes, it was surprising how much pleasanter life felt. We stopped being good-enough, and became quite good at simply being good.

I don't know at what point during that fortnight she moved out of Lottie's bedroom and into James's, for the mother of a teenager learns not to enquire too deeply into these matters. Not that it stopped there.

Her parents were mortified. Goodness knows what they had intended should happen to their daughter once she was grown up. Perhaps they hoped that she, too, would have slept on and on in the Swiss castle, and never woken up.

'But they reckoned without you, dear Carabosse,' said my daughter-in-law.

Edwina Currie is a former Conservative minister and is now an author and broadcaster. She currently has ten books to her name, including *Chasing Men* and, most famously, *Diaries 1987–1992*. She was married for the second time in 2001 to John Jones, a retired police officer, and has two daughters, aged 26 and 29.

Second Showing

The wind whistled down the High Street, scattering litter and leaves over home-bound commuters. A piece of wet newspaper wrapped itself round Diane Povey's ankles; she kicked it away and pulled her collar closer around her ears.

Darn. It was not the pleasantest evening to be kept hanging about, barely under cover, waiting for her daughter. 'Come to the first showing, Mum!' Ellen had said on the phone. 'I know you want to see that movie. It's had great reviews. Michael Caine is supposed to be marvellous.' The invitation had been pressed on her, since Ellen's latest boyfriend, Joe, was out of town: 'Bit miserable spending Valentine's night on my own, Mum. Do me a favour, come with me then we can have a meal after and a natter.'

Diane found a tissue and blew her nose. At the cinema entrance a small queue was forming, mostly couples, some hand in hand. The tickets nestled in her pocket next to her mobile; that was her side of the bargain, then Ellen would buy the dinner. They had a lot to catch up on, though it was an odd evening to be doing it.

It hadn't occurred to the girl, of course, that Diane

herself might have been feeling a bit low on this date. She took it for granted that her mother was free, and was not wrong. It was more than six years since the death of Ellen's father. Six long years since any man had taken her out, to a film or show or a candlelit supper, on this cold winter's night.

Kids! How cruel they could be, how wrapped up in their own affairs. How unwilling to recognize that parents were human too, with emotions, and needs. They had not brought up their children to be selfish, and Diane was sure that had she uttered a word her daughter would have been contrite, but the thought should have been there in the first place. It was the way of the modern world, moving so fast, with barely a moment's consideration for anyone else. Especially for the generation that had gone before, as if being over thirty meant that a person no longer counted.

Diane studied the film posters and caught a glimpse of herself in the glass. Chestnut-brown hair, a bit unkempt in the wind, but heavy and shiny, the colour still gloriously her own. Her face a little more lined than it had been at thirty, or even forty, but that was inevitable; when she smiled, her eyes lit up with amusement. Of moderate height and still relatively slim, the result of walking everywhere, for choice; when Douglas had been so ill she had taken to long energetic trudges in order to empty her brain, anywhere, the streets of the small town where they lived, or setting off along footpaths with a map and old hiking boots till she could return to the sickroom hours later, refreshed and ruddy-faced. She had regaled him with what she encountered, the pheasants in the lane, a ragged scarecrow up a hill, or the shop windows dressed for Christmas. He had squeezed her fingers and shared her delight, until one morning he had held her hand no more.

The cinema doors opened letting out a blast of stuffy air and the queue began to move. It was quite dark now, with street lamps bathing the whole area in a garish yellow glow. Not the most flattering light, Diane reflected. She worked for a film company that made television documentaries, a job that had seemed glamorous when she was younger and which kept her going reasonably well after her widowhood. The money was handy, the people mostly hard-working and creative and it helped keep her busy. Ellen had preferred the City, an investment bank where she earned many multiples of her mother's income, but most importantly it was a job the girl adored, though it tended to encroach on her personal life.

In Diane's pocket the mobile bleeped. It was Ellen, a text message.

'Mum sorry . . . got to stay late. You go in, I'll get there later. Love you lots. Ellen.'

With a shiver of disappointment Diane turned to the poster again. There wasn't much time to decide, but she did have the tickets and she did want to see the movie. The alternative was to cross the road to one of the small cafés or restaurants and waste a couple of hours alone . . . but then she might miss her daughter and the whole evening would be spoiled. She hesitated.

'Good evening. Would you by any chance be Mrs Povey?'

Diane nodded uncertainly. The man was tall, well dressed in a navy blue overcoat. A black fedora hat half hid a broad brow, a square lean face and a moustache. What hair was visible was silvered, but he was not elderly. In his gloved hands was a bunch of red roses in cellophane. He tipped his hat brim in a curiously old-fashioned gesture.

'I thought so – you have the same hair as Ellen. Horrid night, isn't it? I'm Joe's father – Matthew Lewis. Is she not here yet?'

Diane was puzzled. Joe? That was Ellen's boyfriend, the one who was away. They had been going out for several months; Ellen's conversations had been full of him. On the brief occasions when she had introduced him to her mother, Diane had been quietly impressed. But young people these days thought of nothing but their careers, so the relationship might come to nought; it did not do to set up false hopes.

'No, she's going to be late. I've just had a text message,' Diane answered. 'I thought Joe was out of town?'

'He was, but he got back yesterday and badgered me to come along. He called it a double double – the idea, I think, was that we would be a foursome. The two youngsters and us as chaperones, I guess.' He paused, removed his hat and ran a gloved hand over his hair. 'Well, that's no great problem. He's on his way. He asked me to pick up these roses. I had mentioned I was keen to see this film, so here I am.'

Diane showed the two tickets. 'Me, too,' she explained with a rueful laugh. 'I thought I was being helpful getting here early. Kids! However much you teach them, they just aren't as reliable as we were brought up to be, are they, Mr Lewis?'

He grinned. 'Perhaps we were the same with our elders. I can remember being astonished that my mother was terribly upset when I forgot her birthday – I hadn't a clue it would matter so much. I'm Matthew. You're – Diane, isn't it?'

Diane was suddenly guarded. He was respectful and

well-mannered, and clean and smart, but surrounded as they were by bustling commuters and shoppers she felt hideously self-conscious. 'Yes, that's right,' she answered formally and held out her hand. He shook it and tipped his brim again. Her eyes strayed upwards and he chuckled.

'This blasted hat? It puts everyone off. It's simply that after years in the army I feel half-dressed if I go bare-headed. Anyway, it keeps my head warm.'

'No, I think it's rather – dashing.' To her horror Diane could feel herself blush. 'It must make you easy to find in a crowd.' A gust of rain blew in her face. 'Better than an umbrella, anyway '

He glanced skywards. 'Look, it's about to tipple down. Why don't we wait inside?'

He held out his arm. What an unusual man he was, with these little gentlemanly gestures and his trim moustache, as if he had been reared in a different century. Her first instinct was to demur, indeed to go home without further ado, but that could be interpreted as going off in a huff. His suggestion made sense. When Joe arrived he would buy his ticket anyway; she would refuse any offers of reimbursement, to retain her dignity and independence. It would, however, be rude to hesitate any longer. This argument she would allow the chap in the hat to win, just for now. She accepted his arm and they entered.

It would be another ten minutes till the main feature. The cinema was a local independent with two tiny theatres and one larger one, where the Graham Greene adaptation was being shown. Several customers were crammed into a narrow bar; the atmosphere was convivial and cheerful. Diane loosened her coat as he ordered two glasses of red wine. The roses lay on the counter, their petals and glossy leaves studded with raindrops.

It was necessary to be polite, or at least not too frosty. That would only make matters worse. Diane's defences were so habitual that it required some effort to recall how to make conversation with a relative stranger. But she was also curious. 'So why didn't Joe suggest that Mrs Lewis should come?' she asked as she sipped the wine. It was a merlot, quite drinkable. He had taken off his hat and folded the leather gloves inside.

'Because there isn't a Mrs Lewis,' came the reply. The voice seemed studiously neutral but he kept his eyes on his glass. 'She left three years ago. In Abu Dhabi where I was serving as an adviser. Fell in love with the businessman next door, and that was that. I quit the army at the next opportunity and came back.'

'God, how awful.' Diane could not stop herself. 'You must have been very bitter.'

'Probably.' He lifted his head and she could see brown eyes full of sorrow. 'If I had been aware she was unhappy . . . but I wasn't. My own fault, I guess. I took hasty decisions then about leaving which I do regret now – I loved the army and could have done another turn. Now I advise security firms but it's not the same.'

'Do you get lonely?' Diane could have bitten her tongue out, but then she saw that he treated this as a kindly inquiry, not as a play for him. She held her breath as he answered, then realized she need not have worried.

'Sometimes, naturally. But to be truthful, it takes so much effort to find somewhere to live, to settle in to a new job, and to re-establish oneself – as a human being – that I haven't cared too much about all that. Civvie street alone has been a huge culture shock. The divorce was awful. I wouldn't want to go through that again. So I don't dwell on it.'

The barman leaned across. 'The picture is about to start. If you don't take your seats now, you'll miss the beginning.'

'Oh!' Diane jumped. 'But where's Joe? We can't go in without him.'

'Oh, yes we can.' Joe's father downed the rest of his glass. 'If he hasn't the decency to turn up on time . . . come on. When Joe eventually arrives, full of excuses, he can get his own ticket and find us. No doubt he will.' He helped her to her feet.

'But what about – ' she pointed at the bouquet, now looking so forlorn.

'It was supposed to be for your daughter from my son. But what the hell. Allow me,' he said, and with a sweeping gesture placed them in her arms.

It was strange, this sensation of a man's firm hand on hers as they found their seats. Unfamiliar, to hear his quiet breathing, to be acutely aware of a living flesh-and-blood body next to her own. He made no attempt to touch her, though in one exciting part of the film she almost clutched him, springing back as she realized what she had nearly done. On her lap the roses nestled as if they had been intended for her, which sadly they weren't. Never mind; her pulse was going faster than for ages.

It had been out of the question, dates with other men. Douglas had been so precious, the months spent nursing him so desperate and burned into her memory, that she had wanted no one else. She had enough money to manage on, enough activity to keep herself occupied, enough friends both at work and after not to get bored. The sex thing had not mattered that much to her when she was married, so its lack had not disturbed her too greatly. Indeed, solitude had its positive side: she could read a good book without being disturbed whenever she wanted to. Her health was excellent, a great blessing. In many ways she had a lot to be thankful for.

Last year Ellen had begun a sentence, 'Mum, you know that if you ever wanted to get married again—' But Diane had stopped her. 'It won't happen. I'm not a dried-up old spinster; I've had a wonderful life, and will make the most of whatever years are left to me. Your father would have expected no less. But other men? No, thank you.' More recently, as the girl enthused about Joe, Diane had intercepted similar hints, but without rancour. Her daughter was concerned about her welfare, that was all, and needed reassurance that there was no problem to fret over.

But . . . loneliness crept in, some nights, and shivered under the bedclothes with her. Hours of blackness when she was too conscious of being alone, with no warm body beside her. It had been her habit to listen to the tempo of Douglas's breathing, particularly once his illness was diagnosed; those nights when he slept well gave them both the strength to carry on. Without him, the silence could be overpowering, suffocating. Those were the nights she dozed only fitfully, and woke to find the pillow damp with her tears.

And now here was this man, sitting at her side, filling up his seat with a solidity and manliness which made her catch her breath; his coat folded on his lap, his hands with that extraordinary hat. The dark hid his features, except that he glanced at her and smiled; then his attention turned back to the screen, as if unwilling to embarrass her. He was a stranger, this man, this – Matthew, and yet not really; she had heard a great deal about Joe, and had begun mentally to prepare herself to welcome him as a son-in-law. Perhaps she should have been nosier about his family, but it was not her way.

The movie was drawing to its end. The outcome was sad; were her eyes pricking because of the tragedy on the screen, or because her own reflections had made her grieve? As the lights went up and the credits rolled she was dabbing her eyes and started guiltily. Matthew was standing over her.

'Oh, it was a lovely movie,' she explained, trying not to sniff as she fastened her coat. 'Don't take any notice of me. I'm an old softie. Wasn't Michael Caine great? Such a brilliant actor.'

She wondered if she was babbling on, but he supported her gracefully: 'You're absolutely right. He's seventy and still a master at his craft. Maybe there's hope for us all?'

Outside it was still damp and cold but the wind had dropped. They stood together uncertainly as she held the roses close. Matthew set the hat on his head but kept his gloves in his hand. He glanced up and down the street. 'I shall have words with my son, when I see him,' he remarked grimly.

'No, don't be too hard on him,' Diane protested. 'I'm sure he didn't mean to let us down. Anyway, I am so glad you insisted that we go in. The film was great and I have thoroughly enjoyed myself.' She did not add, 'in your company'. That would have been too forward. And too close to the truth.

'Me too,' he answered promptly. 'I haven't been to a movie in ages. Maybe I should do this more often. Am I right in thinking you're in the business?'

'Sort of,' Diane laughed. 'But not at this level. Otherwise I'd be getting free tickets and probably go too often. But I can see how it's done, how a particular effect is produced, and that's interesting.'

Matthew was gazing straight at her. 'I should like to hear more, but if you don't mind, somewhere warmer than on the street. There's an Italian place round the corner – Joe phoned and was lucky enough to get a table. Are you hungry? How about something to eat?'

'Oh, I can't . . .' She trailed off.

'Nonsense. Of course you can. And I owe you something – can't let a woman take me to the pictures, now can I? Come along. Take my arm.'

She took a deep breath. It would do no harm, not this once. Two old fools with nothing much better to do, at least for the next couple of hours. It wasn't as if anyone was watching. And the roses were hers. She slipped an arm through his.

'Oh, well. Why not? As long as I can pay my share . . .'

In a tiny café on the far side of the street two young people pushed away their plates and clinked glasses.

'Yesss!!!' said the girl, punching the air in delight.

'Hush,' said the young man, 'keep your head down. We don't want them to see us.'

The girl ducked behind her menu and peered through the plate-glass window. On the table sat her mobile phone, next to Joe's. 'I don't think they can. They seem quite wrapped up in each other. I was bothered about deceiving them, Joe, but it's working a treat. Don't they make a fine pair?'

'No finer than us, my darling, my Ellen,' the boy replied. 'Bloody good idea of yours. Especially the flowers – that was inspired. Now, what about us? We will just be in time for the second showing. Have you got the tickets? Then let's go . . .'

Helen Dunmore was the first winner of the Orange Prize for Fiction. Her latest book is *Mourning Ruby*.

Portrait of Auntie Binbag, with Ribbons

Mags, Kaff, Didi, Stu and Binnie. My mother, her two sisters and her two brothers. My mother was Mags. She's Margaret now. She stopped answering to Mags when she went to college to study book-keeping.

Margaret, Catherine, David, Stuart and Binnie. My auntie Binnie, the eldest of the five. She didn't look the eldest, with her large, soft face and her round-toed babyish shoes. She didn't look any age at all. Mum and my aunts and uncles talked about her as if she was still a child.

Binnie's so stubborn. She gets an idea in her head, and there's no doing anything with her. She lives in a dream half the time. You could talk about Auntie Binnie in a way you wouldn't dare talk about any other grown-up. She was just Auntie Binnie. Or Auntie Binbag, sometimes, on account of her clothes. *She gets dressed with her eyes tight shut. Yes, and then she feels around in the wardrobe until she finds something.* We mimicked Auntie Binbag, our arms thrust out stiffly in front of us and our eyes screwed shut. We understood that it was all right to do this in front of Mum, even though Auntie Binnie was Mum's sister.

Mum would say, 'Stop it, Sarah, Jessie. That's enough,' but not in a way that meant anything.

What made us cruel was that we loved Auntie Binnie as much as we were embarrassed by her. When we were little we'd sat on her knee and patted her large, gentle face. We'd admired the scarves that trailed from her, and the ornaments she bought us from charity shops. Auntie Binnie didn't bother about presents being for birthdays or Christmas. In fact, she was likely to forget your birthday altogether. Once she gave me a glittering china fairy with pointy toes, sitting on a bunch of china flowers. I had never seen anything so beautiful.

Auntie Binnie didn't have a proper job, or a husband, or children. My mother had all three, which was why she never had the time to go looking for treasures such as my fairy with her golden hair and bright cherry lips. It was also why Mum was more important than Auntie Binnie. When Auntie Binnie gave me the fairy, Mum explained that Auntie Binnie didn't have much money, and that was why we had to say an extra-special thank-you when she gave us a present, even if we didn't like it.

But I loved my fairy. I threw myself at Auntie Binnie and thanked her a million zillion times. It was my most beautiful possession in the whole world. It was only months later that I began to see a certain foolish-ness in the fairy's bright face. It must have been about the same time that I stopped begging Auntie Binnie to leave me her scarf collection when she died. Mum never wore scarves, or things that trailed. Everything about Mum had a clean, clear edge to it.

Auntie Binnie lived with an old lady called Mrs Bathgate. She was Mrs Bathgate's companion. She did the shopping and fetched the prescriptions and answered the phone and did the housework. If Mrs Bathgate rang her bell in the night, Auntie Binnie got up and went to her, and made hot drinks and moved pillows about. If it was a very bad night, Auntie Binnie would have forty winks on the sofa next afternoon, while Mrs Bathgate was reading aloud. Even though Auntie Binnie was the companion, it was always Mrs Bathgate who did the reading aloud, and Auntie Binnie who did the listening.

Mum said it was quite ridiculous in this day and age, like something out of a novel by Charlotte Brontë. Mrs Bathgate was a mean old devil and knew when she was on to a good thing. What did she pay Binnie? Peanuts. But Binnie was so obstinate that she wouldn't even tell Mum how much she got paid.

Auntie Binnie would trail off in one of her dangly dresses to collect yet another prescription for Mrs Bathgate. And then people would say to Mum, 'Oh, I saw your sister Binnie today, in Boots.'

They would sound as if they pitied Auntie Binnie for fetching Mrs Bathgate's prescriptions, and maybe as if they pitied Mum, too, for having a sister like Binnie, who didn't know that you don't wear a magenta satin skirt with the hem hanging down in the middle of winter.

Magenta was one of Auntie Binnie's favourite colours. Her bedroom, at the top of the house where Mrs Bathgate lived, was very small and crammed with bright cushions and ornaments and scarves. Crimson was another of Auntie Binnie's colours. Scarlet, petunia, lilac, mauve, flame. When I learned at school that the phoenix's nest was made of flames, I thought of Auntie Binnie's bedroom.

Next to the little bedroom there was another room which Auntie Binnie used for her painting. Mrs

Bathgate didn't know about the painting, because she couldn't climb stairs and her stairlift only went up to the first floor. The stairlift whizzed Mrs Bathgate up or down the stairs, whenever she wanted. Auntie Binnie longed to try it out herself, she told Mum, but she'd never dared. Mrs Bathgate had a terrible tongue. 'Why do you let that woman bully you?' shouted Mum.

In her painting room Auntie Binnie painted one picture after another, whenever she had an hour free from Mrs Bathgate. There were no fairies in her paintings, no people, flowers or landscape. Just crowds of different colours, sometimes fighting one another, sometimes agreeing. Auntie Binnie spent hours and hours painting. She didn't bother to keep her paintings when they were finished, and no one ever asked if they could have one. I didn't like them much, but I admired the way she kept right on filling up the paper with colour until there wasn't any white left.

When each painting was done, she put it behind her wardrobe for a while, and when enough were stacked there she carried them downstairs and put them beside the wheelie bin. The binmen always took them. Auntie Binnie did all this with a gentle smile on her face, as if she enjoyed the act of putting her paintings out with the rubbish.

I was eleven when Mrs Bathgate died. 'Of course she won't have left Binnie a halfpenny,' said Mum. Auntie Binnie went to the funeral in magenta and apricot, and Mum accompanied her, dressed in black. It was a beautiful sunny day. 'Do you know,' said Mum, 'Binnie was smiling all through the service. She was sat in a shaft of light coming through the chapel window and she smiled as if she was on the beach. "Isn't it a lovely day?" she said to Mrs Bathgate's son-in-law. He didn't know what to say. Not that they were a close family. I can count on the fingers of one hand the times they came to see Mrs Bathgate, in all those years.'

Mum took off her high black shoes and rubbed her feet. 'I don't know what we're going to do about Binnie,' she added with a sigh, as if I was a grown-up too. 'Twelve years she's been with Mrs Bathgate.' The way Mum spoke, it sounded as if Mrs Bathgate had been looking after Auntie Binnie, not the other way round.

But Mum was wrong about the money. Mrs Bathgate left Auntie Binnie a thousand pounds, and wrote in her will that Auntie Binnie could stay in her house until it was sold. 'Mean old devil. Mean as mustard, the lot of those Bathgates, always have been and always will be,' said Mum. 'A thousand pounds!' It sounded like a lot of money to me. I wondered what Auntie Binnie would buy with it. Dozens and dozens of scarves and ornaments. Maybe even some new clothes instead of old ones that smelled of other people. Or things for her painting. Auntie Binnie had confided in me once that she would love to paint on canvas, if only she had the money.

'I suppose she'll have to come here,' said Mum. 'We can put you girls in together, and Binnie can have Sarah's room.'

'Mu-um!'

'Or maybe you'd rather share with Binnie.'

But Auntie Binnie didn't come and live with us. The Bathgate house was on the market, and Auntie Binnie showed everyone round personally and told them everything about it. She even demonstrated the stairlift, but still nobody bought the Bathgate house. A month went by, two months.

'Would you believe what Binnie's done now!' Mum

exploded. She couldn't explode too loudly, though, because she had the car keys between her teeth. 'Just let me get these bags down.' Mum dumped the shopping, dropped into a chair and stared at us dramatically.

'She's only spent that thousand pounds already.'

'What on?'

'Would you believe it – art classes.'

'But Auntie Binnie can paint already.'

'Can she,' said Mum grimly. 'Well, she's enrolled as a full-time student at the Folk Centre.'

'An art student? Is Auntie Binnie going to be an art student?'

'Apparently,' said Mum. 'And don't eat those biscuits out of the packet, please.'

Auntie Binnie hadn't spent all the thousand pounds, however. She gave Sarah and me a twenty-pound note each, and bought Mum a huge camellia in a pot. It was called Himalayan Fire.

'Oh, Binnie, you shouldn't go spending your money on us,' said Mum.

'It flowers in January, after everything else,' Binnie said. 'The man told me.'

'It must have cost a fortune,' said Mum later. 'I hope he didn't diddle Binnie.'

Auntie Binnie was at the Folk Centre every single day. When she wasn't having classes she was working in the studios. You could work in the studios all evening and at weekends if you wanted, and Auntie Binnie did want. We hardly ever saw her. I had to wait nearly three weeks before I could ask her what being an art student was like.

'It's a traditional skill-based course in one way,' Binnie said, in the voice she used when she was repeating what the lady in Boots had told her about

Mrs Bathgate's prescriptions. 'Although each of us is on her own journey.'

'But what do you do?'

'Lots of things,' said Auntie Binnie. 'We're having an exhibition at the end of term.'

'Can I come?'

But Auntie Binnie looked doubtful. Didn't she want us there? Her own family?

'You can if you want, Jessie,' she said at last. 'But don't—'

'Don't what?'

'It's not the sort of thing your mum's going to like.'

Naked ladies! I thought gleefully. Auntie Binnie's been drawing naked ladies. Or even bare men.

'I won't tell Mum,' I promised.

It was a couple of days later that Mum said, 'Jessie, did Auntie Binnie ask you about the photographs?'

'No. What?'

'She came round when Sarah was in and asked if she could go through all the old albums. She took away lots of old photos of herself when she was little,' Mum said.

'She didn't ask me. I wasn't even here,' I said, automatically defending myself.

'But Binnie's never been interested in photos. She didn't even want a copy of that studio portrait we had done of you and Sarah. She's got no sense of family like that.'

'You could ask her what she wanted them for,' I suggested.

'Don't be silly, Jessie.'

The day for the bare men and naked ladies was drawing near. Auntie Binnie didn't say anything more to me about the exhibition, but I saw a poster outside the Folk Centre. Saturday, 7th December. The exhibition would be open all day, and tickets cost £2.

I'd never been inside the Folk Centre. None of us had. I paid my £2 to a lady with funny hair and then I went inside. I was early and there weren't many people there. The big echoey rooms were full of paintings and drawings and things made out of clay and wood and newspaper and metal. I looked at all the name labels but none of them was by Auntie Binnie. There were lots of drawings of a bare man who looked as if he didn't know he hadn't got any clothes on. Some of the drawings made his legs look strange, but some of them were good. None of them was by Auntie Binnie.

A lady was kneeling down on the floor. She was arranging lots of little clay figures on a table so they faced the door as if they expected something wonderful to come through it. Her hair was short and black, like fur. The lady was big and square and strong, but the clay figures were delicate: different from my fairy, but a bit the same as well. I wondered if the lady had made them. I moved closer. A label said *Out of the Blue* and underneath it said *Fabiola Quiggin*.

I must have accidentally read the label aloud, because the lady looked up.

'Did you make all those?' I asked.

'That's right.'

'Are you an art student?'

'In a way. I do some teaching as well.'

'My Auntie Binnie's an art student. She's got some of her paintings in this exhibition, only I haven't found them yet.'

'Your Aunt Binnie?' Fabiola Quiggin frowned. 'What's her second name?'

'Cochrane.'

Fabiola Quiggin sat back on her heels and gave me a

long look. 'Binnie's a family name, right? You're part of her family?'

'I'm her niece.'

'Are you Sarah, or Jessie?'

'Jessie.'

Fabiola Quiggin nodded.

'How did you know our names?' I asked.

'Your aunt is a friend of mine.' But she kept on giving me the long look, as if being Auntie Binnie's friend didn't necessarily make her my friend at all.

'Oh. Are her – is her painting in this room?'

'Her work's through there. In the centre of the next room. You'll find her name on the label.'

I felt that she was still watching me as I walked away. That long look settling itself on my shoulder blades.

But there were no paintings in the middle of the next room. Fabiola Quiggin had got it wrong. There was only a big thing made of twisted wire. It hung from the ceiling. I moved closer. There was a label on the floor under it. *Family Cage*, it read, and underneath there was the name: *Benedicta Cochrane*.

The wire cage swung a little. Inside there were no colours at all. Against the wire bars there were photographs of a little girl, staring out. Lots and lots of photographs, so that as you walked around the cage you saw the same little girl every time. In some of the photos she was smiling, and in others she looked sad. The wire bars made stripes across her face. From the bottom of the cage there hung plumes of colour, almost down to the floor. I stared at the colours. They were so familiar, they were—

I reached out to touch them. They were silk and satin. They were magenta, lilac, flame, crimson, rose and scarlet. They were Auntie Binnie's scarves, cut to ribbons and hanging from the base of the cage and from its bars like fountains of colour. The Family Cage, by Benedicta Cochrane.

Fabiola Quiggin was watching me from the doorway.

'What do you think?' she asked.

'I don't know.'

'I think it's beautiful. I think your aunt is a very talented woman.'

I reached out and touched a long ribbon of magenta silk. I remembered the scarf it came from, and how I used to stroke it when it was around Auntie Binnie's neck and I was sitting on her knee. I had stopped asking Auntie Binnie if she would leave me all her scarves in her will when she died.

And so here they were. I wondered if Auntie Binnie would find my fairy and put that into an exhibition as well.

'You've got a bit of a look of her,' said Fabiola Quiggin. She came across to the cage and pointed at one of the photos. 'Especially in this one. She must have been about your age when this was taken.'

I stood still, and waited until Fabiola Quiggin moved away. The girl in the photo looked out of the cage at me. Her hair was cut short and it was fairer than mine. She had freckles on her nose. I had freckles too, in summer. But surely I couldn't really look like Auntie Binnie?

The girl in the photo looked straight at me. She didn't have a big, bold smile, like Sarah's in the studio portrait. But she was smiling as if she wanted to be my friend.

'Hello, Auntie Bi—' I whispered. Then I stopped, and started again.

'Hello, Benedicta Cochrane.'

Barbara Erskine began her career writing short stories before turning to novels, the most famous of which is *Lady of Hay*, which has sold over two million copies worldwide. Barbara, her husband and two sons divide their time between the Welsh borders and their manor house near the coast of north Essex. Her latest book, *Hiding from the Light*, is out now.

'You've got a book to write. Remember?'

'It's a lonely house.' Brian Foster glanced at his passenger. 'We only ever used it for holidays.'

Caro nodded. 'I know. I've read the particulars.'

Brian had arranged to collect her from the station following her telephoned enquiry about the ad in the *Sunday Times*.

Isolated cottage
Breathtaking views

'As I told you,' he went on, 'it's just too far to come often enough to justify keeping it.' He shrugged, squinting through the windscreen at the single-track road ahead. 'Are you planning to go back south tonight?' He glanced at her again. She was a striking woman. Tall. In her early fifties at a guess. She was staring straight ahead, seemingly uninterested in Brian or his attempts at conversation.

He swung the car onto an even narrower road. 'I wish the weather was brighter,' he said with a sigh. 'But I suppose it's better to see it at one of its less glamorous moments.' Two other prospective buyers had already seen it at its less glamorous moments

113

and both had hightailed it back to civilization.

She put a hand out to the dashboard to steady herself as the old Land Rover lurched through a pothole. He grimaced. 'We – I – keep this car up here and fly to Inverness from London.'

'How long have you had the cottage?' She didn't look across at him as she spoke.

'Five years.'

'And there is vacant possession?'

'That's right. I'm staying up here long enough to sell it; then I'm off.' He tried to keep his voice light. She needn't know about the heartbreak, the anger, the misery the cottage had caused. 'You should be able to see it about now,' he added. He pointed. 'White blob on the shore of the loch down there.'

She sat forward and stared across the rain-soaked moor.

'What's that other building near it?'

'That's the broch.' He slowed the car as he approached a water-filled gully that crossed the road in full spate.

'Our local piece of heritage.'

'It's a ruin?'

'For a couple of thousand years. It's Iron Age, they think.'

He did not speak again until they drew up outside the cottage. It was a charming place, Patricia had seen to that. White-washed with a neat fence to keep out the deer. Pointless that had been. They could jump fences twenty feet high as far as he could see and had made short work of her pretty garden. Now there was heather and bog myrtle and foxgloves in the flower beds, just as there was outside the fence. Nature's way of telling you that you were here on her terms, not yours.

114

They climbed out and stood for a moment, Brian staring out across the rain-pitted waters of the loch, Caro at the cottage. He heard her sigh softly and his heart sank as he pushed open the front door and ushered her inside. The room was dark, smelling rich with peat smoke, simply furnished with a small sofa, a round table with four chairs, an empty bookcase. At the far end a sink and cooker and a small dresser formed the kitchen. He went over to the table and reached for some matches: 'As you see, no electricity, just calor gas and oil lamps. That does – did – us fine. All mod cons.' He forced himself to smile. 'Spring water and even plumbing. The bedrooms are here.' He strode towards a small lobby. Two rooms led off it, one with a double bed, the other with bunks. Both were cramped and dark and looked out onto the wet hillside behind the cottage.

'I'll take it.'

He stared at her. 'You can't be serious.'

'You do want to sell it?'

'Yes. Yes, of course.' He tried to restrain the wave of relief that swept over him.

'I'll take the furniture too. I think you said that was included if I wanted it?'

'It is. Oh, indeed it is.'

'And the Land Rover?' For the first time she gave him a real smile. 'I can't believe you want much for that.'

He shook his head ruefully. 'Indeed not. In fact, I'll throw it in for nothing.'

'Good. Thank you. I can pay you in cash. When can I move in?'

He blinked. 'When you like, I suppose. As you see, we – I've – moved all our personal belongings out. I don't want any of the crockery or kitchen stuff.'

115

Pretty kitchen stuff, so eagerly bought, so much hated now. 'As far as I'm concerned you can have it today. Don't you want to see anything else?' He was almost disappointed. Now that he knew she liked it, he wanted to show her round properly, he wanted her to admire the details, he wanted above all for her to know how much he had loved this place. Once.

She shook her head. 'I'll see it all soon enough.' For a moment her voice softened. 'It's just what I wanted.'

Her needs were minimal. All her worldly belongings, the items she had allowed herself to keep after fifty-two years of living and loving and suffering, filled a couple of large suitcases and a few cardboard boxes. The day she moved in nature decided to be kind. The sky was a soft downy blue, the water of the loch as iridescent as a dragonfly's back; autumn sunlight warmed the stone walls and shone obliquely across the deep window sills into the rooms. She wasn't a martyr. She had bought some warm woollen throws for the sofa and beds, some decent food and wine as well as the basic supplies, and she had brought an ancient typewriter. It wasn't until she had signed on the dotted line that she had thought about her laptop. It was there in one of the boxes – fully charged, but for how long? The answer would be to invest one day in her own generator, if she stayed, but for the time being she would make do and appreciate the primitive life she so craved.

Abandoning her boxes she wandered down towards the loch. Out of sight, around the corner, the long narrow arm of water opened into the sea, but up here it was calm and transparent, moving gently to the touch of the lightest wind. There might not have been another person in the world.

Except there was. As she turned back towards the house she saw the figure out of the corner of her eye just for a second on the far side of the inlet. She frowned, squinting against the shimmering reflections. No, there was no one there. No one at all. She had imagined it.

For the first thirty-five years of her life Caro had been a normal person. She had gone to school, proceeded to university, come out with a respectable degree. She had been drawn to journalism, worked on regional papers, then a national before marrying a photographer and producing two talented children for whom she had given up steady work and gone freelance. David Spalding had been the kindest, nicest, best thing that had happened to her until his God had taken him away. He had become a parson – something she had tolerated with a certain amount of horrified humour. But that had not been enough for God. David had developed cancer and seven years ago he had died. She had tried to accept it; tried to live with it; tried to come to terms with such cruel and unnecessary waste, but she couldn't. Her life had fallen apart. The children had drawn away, involved in their own careers and friends, trying to be supportive but afraid of her anger and bitterness. There was nothing left. Until she had the dream. 'Pull yourself together, Caro,' David had said. He looked much as he had before the illness started to take its toll. Tall, good-looking; his eyes gentle but firm as he stood at the end of her bed. 'You are frightening everyone away and ruining their lives and your own. Be alone for a bit. Get to know yourself again. Get away from here.' He waved his arm around the room – their room. 'You've got a book to write. Remember?' He smiled, that lovely quizzical smile, and reached out to her. She sat up, wanting to touch him, to hold him close, to smell the lovely warmth of his skin, but he had gone and she fell back on her pillow and cried.

It was the turning point. She gave the kids most of the contents of the flat, sold it and gave them each a third of the money, keeping the rest for herself. Her plan had been to travel and write that book – the book she had been going to write when she first met David. Then she had seen the ad in the paper and she had heard David's voice in her head as clearly as she had always heard it in the past. 'Go for it, Caro. You need to give yourself some space. Then start writing.'

Space! She looked round and laughed out loud. What had she done!

Two days later she saw the figure again. Just an outline really, on the shore near the broch, standing watching her as she pottered around. She narrowed her eyes against the glare off the water. It was the same man. She recognized his tall lean frame.

It took an hour to walk round the inlet. It was a cool misty day and she took deep lungfuls of the pure air as she walked. The broch consisted of two castle-like concentric circles of dark stone, with steps and passages within the thickness of the double walls. It was completely ruinous on one side, fairly intact on the other. In the centre a perfect circle of grass and weeds had grown lush, sheltered from the wind. She stood and stared, listening to the silence, the lap of water on the stones on the beach, the cry of curlew and sandpiper, the hiss of wind across the dried heather stems outside the walls. Suddenly she shivered. She turned round slowly, staring up at the blind, shadowed walls. Someone was watching her; she could feel it.

'Hello?' she called, her voice echoing off the stone. 'Is there anyone there?' There was no answer.

She did not stay long. As she picked her way back round the loch, scattering wagtails and gulls before her, a figure appeared on top of the ruined wall and watched her leave. She didn't turn back and never saw him.

'You'll be wanting to charge up your phone and your laptop while you're here?' Mrs Maclellan welcomed her into the post office with a smile. 'Mrs Foster always did that. I make a small charge for the electricity which I'm sure you won't mind.'

Caro's mouth dropped open. So that was how it was done! She had thought very little about her predecessors and was, she realized, completely incurious about them. Rich. Spoiled. A bit petulant. That was how she visualized Patricia Foster. Of no interest at all.

Slowly she fell into a routine. Once or twice a week she drove to the village; sometimes she explored further afield, and at last she had time for herself. Time to think. To remember. And to write. She bought back-up batteries for the laptop and smiled at the thought of Mrs Mac retiring on the proceeds of her battery-charging service. And she continued to wave from time to time to her unknown neighbour across the loch. Because he was still there.

The first time she saw him close up was a shock. She had been sitting on the shore with her notebook, outlining her thoughts for a series of articles – the idea for the book had still not come – when she glanced up and saw him only a hundred yards away. Dressed in some sort of rough highland garb, his hair long and unkempt, he was watching her. He was younger than she had expected; quite good-looking. She raised her hand in greeting, but he ignored it, staring right through her. She shrugged and turned back to her notes. When she looked up again he had gone. The next time, though, he looked straight at her and he smiled. She felt a shock of pleasure. The smile was warm; friendly. 'Hello!' It was the first time she had spoken to anyone for several days. He didn't reply. She wasn't sure if he had even heard her but just for a moment his gaze lingered appreciatively before he turned away.

'Who is the young man I see out by the broch?' she asked next time she was in the village.

Mrs Mac glanced up from Caro's purchases, frowning. 'There's no one lives up there. No one at all,' she said sharply. 'You keep away from there. It's a dangerous old place.'

Two days later when Caro saw him in the distance he raised his hand in greeting before turning away. She stared into the watery sunlight, trying to see which way he went. His presence was beginning to irritate and intrigue in equal measures and it was almost without conscious decision that she set off after him, intent on finding out where he came from.

The broch was shadowy, very still within the high dark stone walls. She stood in the centre looking up.

'Hello?' she called.

A pair of jackdaws flew up, crying in agitation as they circled before settling back into the silent shadows.

'Hello? Are you there?'

And suddenly there he was, standing at one of the dark recesses in the broken wall. He raised his hand and beckoned.

She made her way across the grass to the archway in the grey stone. Under it a flight of broken steps led up inside the wall. She stood at the bottom looking up into the darkness, then, cautiously, she began to climb.

'Where are you? I can't see.'

Groping her way slowly she rounded a bend in the stair and there he was, standing above her, framed by gaping stone. Seeing her appear he smiled, that warm gentle smile, and beckoned again.

She took another step towards him, eager to be in sunshine again, but as she reached the top he stepped back out of sight. Where he had been standing there was no wall. Nothing to support her at all. With a scream she found herself clawing at the stone as she began to fall.

The bespectacled face swam into focus for a moment, disappeared and then returned in more solid form. It smiled. 'So, we are awake at last. How are we feeling?' The hand on the pulse at her wrist was warm and solid. Reassuring.

Every bone and muscle in her body throbbed. 'What happened? Where am I?'

'You fell at the broch. You're in hospital, lass, thanks to Mrs Maclellan.'

Caro realized suddenly that the postmistress was sitting on the far side of her bed.

'How did you find me?' Slowly she was beginning to remember.

'Mrs Maclellan took a lift out with the post van to see you.' He paused, wondering how to describe the woman's hunches; her second sight. 'She remembered what you had said about the laddie up at the broch and wanted to warn you about him. Luckily for you, they saw you fall, from the road.'

Caro closed her eyes. She felt sick and disorientated. 'What did you want to warn me about?'

The two beside her glanced at one another. The doctor shrugged. 'It's our belief that you saw a lad called Jamie Macpherson. He lived near the broch some while ago and fell in love, so the story goes, with a young woman he met up there. One day the boy disappeared. They found him where we found you, at the foot of the wall. He had a lassie's silk scarf in his hand.' He paused, scrutinizing her face cautiously. 'Mrs Foster knew the story. She was quite obsessed about it. She would stay up here when her husband went back to London, making notes to write a book about it.'

Caro lay back against the pillow, her eyes closed.

'Poor lady. It seems she followed him to the broch one day and climbed the stair just as you did.'

Caro frowned. 'I don't understand. You said he was dead?'

He nodded. 'They should pull that old place down. It's too dangerous. The steps are broken. She fell. Just as you did. Only in her case, no one came.'

'She was killed?' Caro's eyes flew open.

He nodded gravely.

'Oh, how awful. Poor woman. How sad. No wonder her husband wanted to leave.'

'Aye.'

'Did you follow Jamie out there?' Mrs Maclellan sat forward on her chair.

Caro shrugged. 'I followed someone. Young. Good-looking. Wearing a highland plaid.'

'That's him.' The woman nodded.

'And he's a ghost?'

'Aye.' She was matter-of-fact.

Caro shivered.

'I suppose you'll leave us now, once you've recovered.' Mrs Maclellan shook her head sadly.

Caro shrugged, trying to make sense of the jumble of words spinning in her head. 'I don't want to leave. I love it here.' She smiled weakly. 'I'm a writer, too, like Mrs Foster.' Was that a voice she could hear in her head? 'Go for it, Caro. This is the book!' She looked up at them. 'Perhaps I should write the story for her? And for him?' She hesitated. 'I wonder, would that help them find peace, do you think?'

'Aye, I think that would be the right thing to do.'

Mrs Maclellan smiled at her. Was she the only one, she wondered, who could see the handsome clergyman standing next to the bed, nodding in approval.

Nicci Gerrard lives in Suffolk with her husband Sean French and their four children. She and Sean have written seven best-selling novels under the name of Nicci French, the most recent being *Land of the Living* and *Secret Smile*. *Things We Knew Were True* is the first novel written by Nicci under her own name. This story was inspired by her own recent riding accident; she's recovering from a fall that left her temporarily bedridden with broken vertebrae.

Falling

The Saturday after Sid left – taking with him his toothbrush and razor; the clothes that had gradually accumulated over the months; the hand-held drill he'd brought round at Christmas to put up some shelves and never taken away again; the cookery book he always used because of its recipes for smoked haddock pie and bacon and chicory soup and cheat's chocolate souffle and banana bread; the books on birds of prey and on English churches; the scuffed brown leather jacket and the pink tie and Bart Simpson socks and down-at-heel slippers; the CDs that stood in a crooked pile on the mantelpiece; the alarm clock that shrieked at 7.10 in the morning and which he would always ignore; the whiskey only he ever drank; the wok and the wooden pestle and mortar that smelt of cumin and coriander; the whole tide of possessions that for nearly a year had been seeping into all the corners of the house and that now flooded out again, leaving rooms bare and unfamiliar – well, on that Saturday Connie decided to go riding with her two teenage daughters. She didn't particularly want to go, she was secretly a bit scared of horses, but she knew that if you behave in a certain way, then feelings will eventually follow.

Behave like a woman who canters along an avenue of trees on a spring morning, and that's who you will be. You can lure yourself back into happiness, con yourself with misdirection. She had learnt this before and she repeated it to herself now, not believing it but knowing it to be true.

She reached up to pat the damp neck of her horse, bulky and coarse brown. His sour, grassy breath blew into her hair; his nostrils were velvet and his great teeth yellow. She could see the whites of his eyes and a tremor of nervousness passed through her. She had to use a mounting block to clamber into the saddle, where she sat trying to remember the rules: go into the forward position when cantering; don't fight the horse all the time but give and take. She didn't really know what that meant, 'give and take'; it had been ages since she'd been riding. She glanced at Zoe, who was sitting gracefully on her fidgeting horse, her silky blond hair tucked into the hat; the pure curve of her pale cheek. She looked round at Dorothy, who looked back, smiling at her anxiously, wanting her mother to be happy, or at least to be composed and orderly again, not the woman who, four days ago, had sat at the kitchen table, separating eggs in the palms of her hands, and had suddenly pushed aside the bowl and laid her head on the rough grain of the wood and howled steadily, tears coursing down her cheeks, running into her mouth. Later she'd looked into the mirror and seen a face she scarcely recognized, creased and defeated in the harsh bathroom light.

'All right?' mouthed Dorothy, before climbing easily into the saddle.

'All right,' she nodded back, smiling. Trying to smile: the ground was an awfully long way down, almost enough to give her vertigo. The trick was not to think.

Like a child's drawing of spring, the sky was a hot, flat blue, the leaves clean green. Connie felt the sun on her bare forearms, and on her face when she tipped it back. They clattered along the road towards the bridleway in order of competence: the riding instructor first, then Zoe and Dorothy, and Connie last. She looked at her daughters between the ears of her horse. In one year's time, Zoe would leave home. Then Dorothy. She looked at the way they sat very straight and yet let themselves be swayed by the motion of their mounts. Like saplings, she thought.

When they reached the bridleway, they trotted along the baked earth. Connie felt the ripple of power under her; her horse tossed his head several times, tugging her forward. Specks of foam shook from the metal in his mouth. And then, at a shouted command from the instructor, they broke into a canter; a sudden surge of freedom underneath her, as if the animal was taking off, the oxygen-gulp of fear and euphoria in her constrained urban soul, the sudden breeze in her face, blowing a strand of hair across her eyes so that she was momentarily blinded, a waft of fragrance, the echoing thud of hooves, the banks rushing past her on either side and ahead a narrowing corridor of trees down which they thundered. The earth seemed to shake. And then, the startled face of Dorothy as Connie overtook her, although she was pulling back on the reins with all her strength now, feeling her arms ache. Give and take, she remembered; adopt the forward position. She tried to lean into the horse's great neck, her body jolting heavily out of rhythm, her foot slipping clumsily in the stirrup. Then past Zoe; Connie saw her mouth open into a perfect 'o' like the mouth of a china doll. Then the instructor, shouting commands that she could no longer hear.

On the branch ahead, the unfurling leaves were so new they were almost sticky. She felt them against her face, the moist slap of them giving a last nudge to her precarious grip on the horse. The sky was electric above her as she floated effortlessly towards it, the fleck of birds, the scribble of white clouds, the curve of the shining horizon as she was lifted clear of her flailing, rejected body, her messy life, her sense of panic and loss. She saw that there were bluebells growing on the banks. She saw that the light shone down through the leaves, casting a rippling, aqueous light onto the path that streamed beneath her. There was moss on the bark of the silver birch. A bird dipped past with a rusty breast.

In the roaring silence, she remembered her husband dying, all that time ago, and the funny little grimace of surprise as he was finally loosened from her. She remembered, as if it was years in the past, Sid walking out of the house for the last time, turning in the doorway for a moment, half lifting a hand and then letting it drop. She imagined as if it had already happened how Zoe would leave home soon, waving goodbye from the window of a train that was pulling out of the station. She heard her whip strike the path beneath her; bounce twice and skid off, as her life stretched out before her.

She would lie upstairs for several weeks, during which time late spring tipped into early summer and the blossom fell from the trees and lay round the garden in drifts. Her room would fill up with flowers, a powerful odour of perfume and decay, and with chocolates. The phone would ring.

At first, Zoe and Dorothy would be extraordinarily solicitous. They would be with her in the mornings before they went to school, and in the afternoons would come straight home and upstairs. They would cook: rubbery scrambled eggs, pasta with sauces out of cartons from the 24-hour shop up the road, a sloppy tuna-fish bake which Connie spilled down her neck, fruit salads with the grapes cut in half and meticulously depipped. They left sandwiches wrapped in cling film by her bed for when they were out; thermos flasks of bitter coffee. They spent hours reading and talking to her, giving her crossword clues that she could never do. They arranged a rota of friends who appeared with tins of home-made biscuits, strawberries in green cardboard baskets with metal handles, casseroles to reheat in the oven, poetry anthologies, bath salts, nail varnish for her toes, glossy magazines, gossip from the office and the gym and the pub. They would bring her music they fancied appropriate for a middle-aged woman in great pain; Bach's violin sonatas filled the room. The girls vacuumed the carpet, plumped up her pillows self-consciously, helped her inch her way to the lavatory and back, looking away as she excruciatingly lowered herself onto the seat. Daily, they would tell her they loved her. Sometimes they cried because they had been so scared.

But gradually, because they were sixteen and seventeen years old and it was summer and a time for exams and friendships and falling in love, their domestic attentions would become more sporadic. There were crumbs between the sheets, old newspapers and apple cores and crusts of bread on the bedside table, mugs of cold tea and a stained wine glass on the window ledge, damp towels by the door. Connie would lie amid the detritus listening to them downstairs. She heard them laugh with their friends: Zoe's peal and Dorothy's guffaw. She heard the front door open and bang shut.

Late at night music would come up the stairs: rap, sad female ballads, heavy metal. She thought she could smell cigarettes and wine on their breath when they came to say goodnight, leaning over her so that their long, perfumed hair brushed her face. She would lie quite still, keeping her spine straight, imagining crushed bones straightening, cracked bones weaving together again. She stopped hoping that Sid would reappear; she inched her body across the double bed so that she lay plumb in the middle, books and magazines and letters heaped around her. At last, she realized she didn't even want him to come back. He belonged to a different time: the time before the fall.

She would let the window stand ajar and the curtains open, even at night, and spend hours simply noticing the changes in the world outside. The cool grey dawn with its rich chorus of birds, and on a branch near her window a blue tit always sang, puffing out its chest. Every morning she would watch its open beak and pulsing throat. The bleached turquoise of early mornings. She would know by looking at the sky when the mail would clatter through the letterbox; when she would hear Zoe's radio turn on; at what point Dorothy would sit heavily on her bed and fiddle with the rings on her fingers and ask her if she wanted marmalade or honey on her toast. And when the wind fluttered the opened curtains and at last the house was dark and quiet, she would watch the stars out of the top of her window, a tiny cluster of silver pinpricks in the dense fabric of the night. There was a dog that barked in the early hours that she had never before noticed.

On one Saturday afternoon, she would see through

the bottom right-hand frame of the window a thickset young man with his hair tied back in a pony-tail kiss Dorothy, pushing her up against the garden wall. His arms were under her loose white shirt. She would see her youngest daughter tilt her head back to him and clutch his hair in her left fist, and would turn away and close her eyes but still see the picture in her head. And one evening, underneath her window, she would hear Zoe's voice, thick with joy, saying, 'I love you too. Oh I do; I do!'

All her life, she had held hard on to those she loved. She saw that clearly now. But her husband had fallen from her, like water through clenched fists. And Sid, too, returning to the wife and family he'd told her he had left. And now her two daughters, her precious cargo, were slipping anchor. She knew their soft giggles, the tiny subcutaneous spots under their smooth skins, the ink stains on their index fingers, the tiny blemishes that made them more perfect. Is that how it would be, she wondered? Is it? Dawn becoming dusk, night lightening into day, and the year turning. You have to let go, she said to herself. You have to let them go. The scent of flowers was in her nostrils; Bach's sonatas filled her skull. The walls of her room dissolved as she floated above her body, looking down at herself. Her fingers brushed against the horse's flying mane and then were empty. She had let herself go, too; she had fallen out of her own life into a mysterious space and the blue sky hung above her and the spangled sun stroked her face and her bare skin; the warm breeze touched her.

I am in an accident, she thought to herself calmly, as the body hung suspended in the bright air and then dropped like a stone. Her daughters leaned towards her, blocking out the dazzle of the sky, and she gazed up at their beloved silhouetted shapes until pain split the silence like a spade striking into flinty ground, cracking it asunder. Someone screamed, like an animal in agony. Someone called out 'Mummy!' and she thought to herself: that used to be me.

Karen Gunning is a Londoner living in Somerset. She works with people who have learning disabilities, and is currently writing her second novel. *Looking for Perfect Peony* won the *Woman & Home* Short Story competition in 2002.

Looking for Perfect Peony

Do you know what I've just realized? What it's taken me, oh, twenty-two years to realize? No? Well, it's this: you can be a bloody good Twankey even without Perfect Peony by Lady C. And if Mother thinks that's me blowing my own trumpet, then she can go and do the other thing, except of course she can't because she's dead.

I've got a decent dressing room for once. They're usually glorified broom cupboards, but there's even a kettle and a basket of fruit in here. There was half a sausage roll and a pair of knickers in the last one. I'm a bit worn out this year; it's the first time I've really noticed it. Especially Saturdays, with the matinees and the evening performances, but then, as Kevin always reminds me, I am sixty-two years old. Kevin's my Wishee Washee, bless him, he's a lovely lad. He's my surrogate son this season. His mum's so proud of him; she's been in to see him twice so far.

Right then, time for Sandy to exit stage left and Twankey to enter stage right. I've only been Sandy Blake since 1978. I was Alexander Blake when I was waiting for Godot in Bath; perhaps you remember me?

My old mother never once saw me as the Dame; she

wouldn't come, she said it turned her stomach to see me done up like this. Not even when Princess Fishface brought her little darlings to see us. I thought Mother would have loved the chance to meet royalty after the show, but did she turn out? Not on your life. She said she had to wait in for the Avon lady. It was the night when Mother didn't come to see me perform for the royals that I decided to base my next dame on her.

Then, a year to the day, I opened in *Babes in the Wirral*, as Nurse Nora from Knotty Ash. The review in the local paper said, 'Nurse Nora from Knotty Ash is not a dame you'd want to meet in a dark alley', and I thought to myself, that's my mother you're talking about.

I've kept that review ever since. I could have it framed now, couldn't I?

If I tell you what Mother was like, you'll have a fair idea of what I'm starting to look like at this very minute. She was a tiny little thing, her hair dyed bright ginger, except for a patch round the back where she couldn't reach. (I've even kept that in – I've got a grey bit on the back of my wig, but not many people notice it.) Pale skin and blue eyes, like mine. But then there was this blessed make-up; it had to be seen to be believed.

Green eyeshadow, and I mean bright green; reddy-pink rouge in two great big circles on her cheeks, and the lipstick . . . well, I'm calling it lipstick, but Mother was never one to confine it to her lips. Up to her nostrils, down to her chin, anywhere she fancied really, but it was the colour that did it, a sort of orangey coral. I can't compare it to anything to give you a clearer idea of the colour. There's nothing like it in nature; I don't know what they made it from. I reckon the people who created it sat around and said

138

to themselves, 'What's the brightest and least flattering colour we can come up with for British ladies?'

And then a young boffin with his eye on the main chance stands up and says, 'Ladies and gentlemen . . . I give you Ada Blake', and there sitting behind a glass partition would be Mother with this revolting lipstick smeared halfway across her face.

Tell you what though, that 'look' of Mother's made me my fortune, such as it is. I rarely have to audition nowadays; every panto producer knows Sandy Blake. I've even been asked over to Italy, and they invented pantomime. What an honour that was, except of course I couldn't go because Mother was coughing all sorts up, and they thought she wasn't going to last. She was eighty-one at the time. She lasted another eleven years, so I could've gone, couldn't I?

I use proper theatre make-up for the most part, because it's brighter and it stays put longer than normal ladies' stuff, plus it gives me an excuse to go up to London once a year. I buy it in a little stage-supplies shop in Covent Garden. I go in there because the lovely lady who owns it remembers me from my days in Rep. She saw my Bottom, and she wrote me a couple of letters, but I only had eyes for Laura at the time, so, sad to say, nothing came of it.

I do like to keep in touch, though, and I think there's still a little spark there, but it's difficult to impress a lady when you're buying glittery false eyelashes for yourself. It was her that made me my first padded do-dah to go under my frock. It was a bra stuffed with old stockings, sewn onto an orthopaedic corset.

She tried for years to mix Mother's lipstick colour for me, but she could never get that radioactive look. Mother, you see, would never tell me what it was. I tried everything to find out; I phoned for an Avon catalogue but I couldn't see anything like it; I looked in her bag while the nurse had her in the bath, but it wasn't there. You name it, I tried it.

God knows where she hid it, and He wasn't telling.

Sometimes I wonder if Mother knew why I wanted to know what lipstick she used. I wonder if she knew she had a face that launched a thousand pantomime dames?

As soon as I got home from the hospital after she'd, you know, I turned the place inside out, but no joy. She'd been plastered in it when she was taken in three days before, for pity's sake.

I hate seeing myself at this stage, when I'm half done. I'm wearing padding, the stocking that goes on under the wig and full make-up. I look like a guilty bank manager trying on his wife's things while she's at a bridge party. I'm locking my dressing room door this year, because there are certain people who should never, ever see you wearing a 44DD bra and stripy tights.

It's funny, but I've ended up doing *Aladdin* right round the corner from the pub where I grew up. The Queen's Arms it was then, and this theatre wasn't even here – it was a bombsite in my day.

I went back to the pub for my dinner when we started rehearsals, but it's called Jinty's Theatre Bar now, and all they had left to eat was something called Fun-Gi Polenta, which was like a load of slugs on a bath sponge. Billy Whitt – he was the landlord when we first went to the Queen's Arms – would never have messed about with Fun-Gi Polenta; it was all sausages and mash with him, when he could get the sausages, of course.

He was good to us in his way, was Billy Whitt. My

140

father left us, you see, and he took pity on Mother and gave her a job and a room above the pub.

He was a poor old sad really, a widower, and he'd lost both his legs, but not because of the War; he'd had blood clots from smoking about sixty a day. I don't know if artificial limbs were rationed or what, but he used to have two bar stools strapped on over his trousers.

I thought it was normal until I realized all the kiddies who had to wait outside while their parents had a drink were terrified of him. They used to dare each other to poke their heads in and cheek him, so he'd try to chase them away.

He was a miserable old so-and-so was Billy, but he thought the world of Mother for some reason, and he absolutely loved Variety. He booked a different act every Saturday night – singers and magicians and whatnot – but my favourites were the comedians because everyone was in such a good mood after they'd gone. Well, not Mother, obviously, but everyone else.

I wouldn't be doing what I do now if it wasn't for those comedians; I've pinched half their jokes over the years.

I get a bit of a funny feeling, looking at myself like this now Mother's gone. It's when the wig goes on mainly, the ginger hair next to the blue eyes.

I thought she'd go on for ever. It felt like for ever, living with her all those years. She died three months ago, a week after her ninety-second birthday. Smoked like a chimney, drank like a fish, did the other thing like a rabbit in her day, but there we were, me sixty-two nearly and her over ninety, still digging at each other over the breakfast table. I shouldn't really say this, but I was glad to see the back of her.

I always thought I'd be married with children and

grandchildren by now. I love kiddies, I love the racket they make when the baddie comes on stage and how they laugh like drains at all my terrible jokes.

Thinking about it, I should be celebrating my, what, ruby wedding anniversary by now. And do you know the worst part of it? You don't change as you get older, not one bit, so I'm still hoping, same as I did when I was twenty. Every morning I wake up and wonder if this is the day when I'll meet Miss Right.

So imagine how I felt when I got the letter inviting me to meet the production team at this theatre, and one of the names on the list was Laura Morgan.

Now Laura Morgan was Juliet opposite my Romeo back in 1954 and she was very nearly my real-life sweetheart as well. Nineteen we were, and I was more or less on my home ground, Taunton. She was from Leeds, so I took her all round Somerset in our free time; we had days out in Cheddar, Bath, Weston-super-Mare, anywhere the bus would take us.

On our last night, I was all ready to propose to Laura, but I took her home to meet Mother, and that was that. It was all going well, or so I thought, but then I went outside to get some coal, and when I came back in, Laura had gone. Mother said she'd let it slip that I wanted to pop the question, and Laura had been so horrified by it she'd run off in tears.

When I think of it now, it was so out of character for Laura; it was ridiculous but, stupid me, I believed Mother. She was quite nice to me for about a week after Laura went and I thought it was because she felt sorry for me.

I suppose a lot's happened between then and now, but I can't think of much off hand. Did some telly, a few adverts, a lot of theatre. Then, later on, teaching at the drama college. Mother came around the country with me at first; it was always me and her in all the guesthouses, she had a rare old time. We must have been in every tea shop in the country.

In her later years I bought the house I'm in now and only took on local work. I always kept an eye out for Laura, but she seemed to have retired from the business prematurely.

Ooh, look, there goes our Abanazer. I just saw his turban go by my window. He's not very tall for a panto villain.

I wish mother could see him now. She thought he was the best thing since sliced bread when he was on telly, but then the soaps were Mother's religion, bless her. Never mind that he had affairs with all the female characters, killed his wife and had a secret second family, he was still the bee's knees.

If she could see him now, she'd call him a fart in a colander. He's marching up and down the corridor doing his vocal warm-ups, the silly sod. He's not doing Lear. I'm not keen on these productions with sacked soap stars in the lead, but I've got a mortgage to pay.

I already knew Laura was married to Abanazer. Well, strictly speaking, they're separated. His name's Gerard Walsh, but his on- and off-stage performances blend in, so she might as well have been married to Abanazer. He's not a nice man, and I'm not just saying that because of her.

Mother told me about the wedding in 1962. It was in the paper, not because of Laura but because of Gerard, who was already quite well known by then.

'Ooh, look at this,' she said. 'My bit of lush has got married. Look at the state of the bride – it's not a bad dress but she can't fill it out properly.' She made out like she didn't know who the bride was, but she knew full well.

Imagine, I have to make eyes at him every night – the Dame always fancies the villain. It makes me sick.

Laura usually comes here for the performances, but it's a bit awkward with Gerard about. We don't talk very much. I'd love to know exactly what Mother said to her all those years ago.

I was at a bit of a loose end this Tuesday just gone. I know the town too well to look round it, even though I don't live here any more, and anyway I didn't really want to walk down that particular memory lane, but I did catch sight of a poster advertising an 'Afternoon of Clairvoyance with Audrey Herring'. Did you expect me to say there was something fishy about her? Well, I thought there was at first.

She was a type, Audrey Herring, I'm telling you. Long nylon frock like Joseph's Technicolor Dreamcoat, only less Amazing. Diamanté necklace that could sink a ship and a big blonde wig in the old beehive style. There was enough nylon on her to power the national grid, although that might be necessary in order to contact the Other Side, I wouldn't know. She looked like a sparkler when the lights went down.

We started the proceedings with a hymn; she said her native American Indian spirit guide wanted 'Oh Love That Will Not Let Me Go', which struck me as a bit odd. You'd have thought he'd have preferred a native American Indian song, wouldn't you?

Then the business started. Old Diamond Lil got up behind this lectern thing and bellowed out, 'I call for the silver cloak of protection.'

I thought, as long as it covers that bloody dress, you can call for the black cloak of Batman if you want. Then she starts coughing and clutching her neck and I thought someone had poisoned her pre-show Snowball, but she said, 'I've got a gentleman who passed over with a throat problem, does anyone recognize him?'

There was a bit of murmuring, but no one said anything, so she carried on, 'I think he's missing a limb, a leg or something.' I thought of Billy Whitt, but then she said, 'He's quite an educated young man with a gentleman's way about him and he's wearing a dinner suit.' That was Billy Whitt out for a start. It was only when she said this character was offering her a plate of fish and chips that a woman stood up and said, 'That's my brother Alfie.'

How could a plate of fish and chips make that much difference? She didn't recognize a one-legged man with Neck-upon-the-chest and a penguin suit, but the bell rang as soon as he produced a spectral fish supper.

I'm laughing by now, as you can imagine. All the old dears are shooting daggers at me over their knitting, but then Madam says, 'I've got a tiny little lady with bright ginger hair and she's wearing a light-blue bed jacket.'

I bought Mother that for her birthday, but I didn't say anything. Then, 'This lady is telling me that she's got a well-known and well-respected son and she's got a special message for him.'

Well, I stood up for that. Wouldn't you have? I took a few little bows, but I don't think anyone recognized me.

'Ah, thank you, darling,' said Audrey Herring. 'Your dear old mum's telling me that the lipstick you've always wanted is Perfect Peony by Lady C.'

One of the old biddies in my row said, 'Dirty beggar.'

I felt such a fool.

Today, I plucked up the courage to ask Laura out. Well, strictly speaking, I just asked her to help me find

Perfect Peony, but she told me that Lady C went out of business years ago.

Mother must have stockpiled it; I wonder where it all went? Perhaps she flushed it down the toilet and there's a fluorescent coral oil slick in the Bristol Channel as we speak.

Anyway, Laura said, 'Tell you what, we'll go out tomorrow and I'll help you find the closest match. See if you can find a photo of your mum for reference.'

So that's going to be our first date, I hope, shopping for lipstick. I bet not many men can say that.

I'm going to dig out the photo of Mother hanging the washing out the year we moved into this house. It's the one where she looks most like Widow Twankey.

Ooh, that's my five-minute call, I must be away. I gave Audrey Herring two complimentary tickets for tonight, so I'll be looking out for her. You never know, she might bring Mother along with her.

Maeve Haran shot to fame with her best-selling novel *Having It All*. A former journalist and television producer, she took up writing after the birth of her second child. She lives in north London with her husband and three children.

Aunt Margaret's Visit

'Damn and blast it, not bloody Aunt Margaret!' Three heads swivelled in Fiona's direction. Kirsty, her bolshie sixteen-year-old, smiled in sullen superiority that her mother was losing her rag. Jamie, the anxious middle child, fixed his reproachful blue gaze on her, and Archie, only six but already adept at ignoring the swirling tensions of his family, tried to feed a Cheerio to the cat.

Her husband Hamish remained behind his copy of the *Telegraph*.

'She wants to come for a real Scottish Hogmanay,' Fiona read out.

'Tell her we don't celebrate it,' Hamish grunted. 'Hogmanay's for tourists and people who like kilts and the White Heather Club. Tell her to stay in a hotel in Edinburgh and go to a dinner-dance.'

'I won't be in anyway,' Kirsty announced, knowing this might finally persuade her father to put down his paper. 'I've been invited to a rave in Auchtermuchty.'

Hamish put down his paper, unaware his strings were being skilfully yanked by his daughter. 'No, you certainly are not.'

Kirsty's eyes levelled with his. She was the confrontational one, so like her father that it sometimes amazed Fiona. Not only did Kirsty share his striking dark looks, but she was fearless and passionate, just as Hamish had been when Fiona had met him twenty years ago. In those days he'd been the one who was always fighting with his father.

'No,' Kirsty conceded, 'because they don't have raves in Auchtermuchty. But I'll be out anyway.'

Hamish looked as if he might ban Kirsty from going out for the rest of her life, but caught himself in time. 'Why can't she go and stay with your mother?'

'Because Ma's going on a cruise. "New Year in the Fjords".'

'Maybe she'll hit an iceberg,' murmured Hamish. 'What's this Aunt Margaret like? And how come I've never met her before?'

'She emigrated to America when I was about three and she hasn't kept in touch with Ma. I've no idea what she even looks like.'

'I suppose she's one of those fanatics who goes to church all Sunday and never touches a drop. Perfect company for New Year. She'll probably make us all promise to give up everything we enjoy for our New Year's resolution.'

'That shouldn't be too tough,' Fiona said before she could stop herself. 'There's not much we do enjoy these days.'

Ten-year-old Jamie stood up abruptly, knocking over his glass of orange juice. Fiona bit her lip, hating herself. He'd probably done it on purpose to create a diversion from his parents' bitching.

'She's coming anyway,' Fiona insisted. 'On the thirtieth. We'll have a party for once.'

150

'Parties cost money. And in case you hadn't noticed, that's one thing we don't have much of.'

Fiona held back her response of 'Whose fault is that, then?'

It wasn't really Hamish's fault they were so broke. It had been the worst year for farming anyone could remember. *Farmer's Weekly* ran story after story of bankruptcies, farm sales and suicides.

Hamish hadn't even wanted to be a farmer. He'd dreamed of being a musician until his elder brother had disappeared to Australia and his father had begged him to take on the farm.

The bribe had been this beautiful house which Fiona loved, but which drained away both their money and energy. After much heart-searching they'd tried to sell it and move somewhere practical, but no one had wanted to buy it. Beautiful but draughty piles were commoner than council houses in Scotland.

'It's up to you,' Hamish shrugged. 'I'll be busy with the shoot anyway.'

Kirsty's eyes were on her mother now, appraising and challenging, daring Fiona to respond. To make some extra money Hamish had organized a shoot with a business partner from Birmingham. The partner had a glamourous wife called Claire. And it wasn't deer or grouse that Claire had in her sights. It was Hamish.

'And I suppose the Caramel will be helping you?' Kirsty enquired, realizing Fiona was, as usual, going to let it pass. The Caramel was Kirsty's nickname for Claire. Claire was sickly sweet, Kirsty maintained, and, where her father was concerned, dangerously sticky.

Kirsty couldn't understand why her mother didn't fight back.

Reading her daughter's mind, Fiona looked away.

What was the point? She'd loved Hamish once, for his passion and his certainty, and the way he'd included her in all his schemes and dreams. But she couldn't remember when he'd last shared those. Or even made love to her. They'd already tried to rescue their marriage once, and Archie had been the result. Now they had the tensions and Archie.

Under the table the cat sicked up a pile of Cheerios. Once Hamish would have laughed. Now he barked at Archie.

'Archie, clear up that mess at once! Why the hell we needed a cat, I don't know.'

I got the cat to take Archie's mind off us fighting, Fiona wanted to yell. Instead she cleared up the Cheerios. The Caramel was welcome to him.

At the airport they studied the stream of bleary tourists who'd flown in overnight and were anxiously looking for friends or relatives.

'Which flight is she on?' asked Kirsty.

Fiona consulted her letter. 'Gosh. It's already come in. It must have been early.'

'Hello,' said a soft voice behind them. 'You must be Archie, Jamie and Kirsty. And, of course, Fiona. You were a little girl last time I saw you. I'm your aunt Margaret.'

Fiona almost gasped. The owner of the voice was a rangy, elegant woman with blonde, sleek hair and a toned, expensively clothed body who could have been anything from forty to seventy.

But the most noticeable thing about Aunt Margaret was her warmth. She exuded it like a kind of glow.

'You're wondering,' Aunt Margaret confided as they piled her bags onto the trolley, 'why I look different. It's thirty-five years of Florida sunshine, plus the

152

belief that old age is for enjoying.' She winked at Fiona.

In the car Aunt Margaret declined the front seat and chose to sit in the back with Archie and Jamie. Kirsty, who usually fought her brother for the privilege of sitting in the front, felt a jolt of disappointment.

'So' – with an instinctive perceptiveness that stunned Fiona, Aunt Margaret turned first to Jamie – 'you must be ten, Jamie, and I bet you like Game Boys.'

She produced the latest model, the very one Jamie had been nagging Fiona for. 'And you, Kirsty, a girl needs a good mobile phone, hmm?' Kirsty gasped at the tiny matt-grey object of desire.

Margaret turned towards Archie. 'Now, I seem to have forgotten. Who are you?'

'I'm Archie,' Archie announced, adding by way of helpful explanation: 'I was supposed to rescue Mum and Dad's marriage. I heard my granny say so.'

Fiona's vision clouded suddenly and she almost drove into the car in front.

'Were you now?' Aunt Margaret answered as if he'd just told her about his A in spelling. 'That's nice, dear. Here's a T-shirt. It's got your name on, plus your new email address.'

'Wow!' Archie grinned. 'No one in my class has one of these.'

'Would you like to see around?' Kirsty asked when they got home, before Margaret had even had time to settle into her bedroom. 'If so, I'd love to show you.'

Aunt Margaret thought that the place was very beautiful. She especially loved the way the old house stood, grey and haughty, above the wide and winding river. 'It's just like a fairy tale,' Aunt Margaret said, and smiled to herself as if at some secret joke.

'Or a nightmare,' Kirsty smiled, revealing the stud in her tongue. 'You don't know how cold it gets here.'

'So,' Aunt Margaret asked, when they were all sitting at the comfortable kitchen table drinking tea, 'a real Scottish Hogmanay. Will you have coal and short-bread? And what about New Year's resolutions? What do you want to change about your life, Fiona dear?'

There was a gaping silence. Kirsty looked at her mother.

'Oh,' Fiona shrugged, avoiding Kirsty's glance, 'we don't believe in that sort of thing.'

'I see. Maybe your life's pretty perfect already then?'

Fiona jumped to her feet. 'Why don't I take your bag up?'

Behind her she distinctly heard Kirsty whisper, 'Perfect, my arse. There's this horrible blonde piece who's trying to get her nails into my dad.'

That night as Fiona lay in their bed, the huge one they'd bought because their children always ended up joining them, she listened to Hamish's breathing. He'd always had the gift of sleep. If she were honest, there was one resolution she wanted to make. She wanted her husband back. The old Hamish. The Hamish who laughed and argued and had made his father despair of him. But admitting that would need courage, because if that Hamish really was dead, then she ought to get out of her marriage now, no matter what pain it caused her children. The coward's option was to hide her head under the duvet and leave things the way they were. And that was just what Fiona intended to do.

When Fiona woke up the next morning she had the curious feeling that something about the house had changed. She put an arm outside the bedclothes. The air was warm. Usually, although they didn't quite have to break the ice in the washing bowl, it was cold enough to make you dash for your clothes. But not today.

There was an unfamiliar scent, too. Spices and lemon peel, a touch of cinnamon, something that took her back to her childhood, when Christmas and New Year had been a season of wonder, not tension and disappointment.

From the other side of the bed Hamish reached out and stroked her back.

Fiona jumped as if she'd been stung.

It was so long since he had touched her with tenderness or loving intent.

She realized her mistake. She turned round, taking in the hurt in his eyes.

'Sorry,' she said. But it was too late.

'Doesn't matter. I better get up. I just wanted to say I know this year's been hard.'

She was about to try to make amends when a small tornado in Pokemon pyjamas suddenly appeared in the bedroom. 'Come on, Mum. Aunt Margaret's making delicious American pancakes!'

Downstairs the warmth and spiciness were palpable. Fiona banned all thoughts of fuel bills and breathed in deeply. 'What is that heavenly scent?'

'An old *pot pourri* recipe of my mother's. I thought it might be nice for your party. Kirsty and I are going to pick some ivy this morning and decorate the place. She says we should aim for Divine Decadence.'

Fiona shook her head. 'I don't know where that child came from.'

'The product of your and Hamish's loins, I assume.' Margaret looked her directly in the eye and Fiona felt herself flush. 'And very nice loins they are. I gather the wife of Hamish's business partner thinks so, too.'

'Kirsty's been gossiping to you.'

155

'Perhaps Kirsty's right. Now,' Margaret swept on as if she were discussing her next dental appointment, 'I gave the others a gift and I wanted to give you one, too. Kirsty and I nipped into town last night and chose it.'

Margaret produced a classy carder bag, the type with a rope handle, tied up with ribbon, that Fiona had always envied when she'd seen ladies-who-shop. Inside, wrapped in tissue paper, was a black taffeta dress with a boned corset and a full skirt. It was irredeemably gorgeous. 'Kirsty says it'll look great with your tartan sash.'

Fiona opened her mouth to protest when Kirsty appeared. 'If you don't wear it I'm taking it straight to Oxfam.'

The day passed in a blur of tidying, cooking and trying to keep Archie and Jamie from helping themselves to Aunt Margaret's shortbread. 'You have to leave some to carry through the door at midnight with a lump of coal,' Fiona explained.

In the end there were only twenty minutes left for her to get changed into the taffeta dress.

Kirsty materialized out of nowhere and insisted on putting Fiona's hair up into a sexily messy French pleat and securing it with a Scottish thistle. 'They're the latest fashion in London. It'll give you courage in battle.'

'What on earth are you talking about?' Fiona demanded.

'Don't blame me.' Kirsty smiled infuriatingly. 'It was Aunt Margaret's idea.'

Downstairs the guests had already started to arrive.

Kirsty had done an incredible job with the decorations. Every door, mantelpiece and staircase was swathed in holly and ivy, the red berries glowing in the richly scented candlelight. In the corner of the sitting room, the Christmas tree twinkled with fairy lights and peeling gilt angels.

Jamie and Archie had sacrificed their football gear for lace jabots and kilts in honour of the occasion and a friend of Kirsty's had launched into an Eightsome Reel on the accordion.

It does look like I've got a perfect life, Fiona thought; if only people knew the truth.

'Fiona, hen, have a glass of my special punch.' Fiona turned to find Aunt Margaret proffering a glass of fragrant liquid. The older woman looked dazzling in a long outfit in ivory velvet with fur-lined sleeves. A tiny gold tiara nestled in her blonde hair. 'What an amazing dress, Aunt Margaret. You didn't get that in Haddington?'

Aunt Margaret shook her head. 'No, I brought it with me. Specially for the party.'

Fiona took a sip. The strangest feeling crept through her, heady and disorientating. She hadn't even talked to Aunt Margaret before she came, so how did she know there'd be a party? Maybe she'd just assumed everyone had New Year's Eve celebrations.

Fiona took a second sip of the punch. It tasted like nothing she'd ever drunk before. 'Is this another of your mother's recipes?'

Margaret simply smiled. 'No, this one's all my own. One day I'll tell you what's in it.'

Jamie appeared, looking happier than she'd seen him for months. 'Hi, Mum. Mrs McLaughlan wants to know should she serve dinner?'

The evening flew past and Fiona had to check her watch when someone called out it was almost time for the bells.

'Where's Hamish, by the way?' asked Aunt Margaret, glancing round.

Molten anger, repressed ever since this thing with Claire had begun, suddenly sizzled through Fiona. 'Just let me guess.'

Hamish stood in front of the big fire in the hall, silhouetted against the firelight. It made him seem even taller than usual. Next to him was a tiny woman who was smiling up into his face. With her fair hair and small feet in extremely high heels, she reminded Fiona of a ballerina on a jewel box.

Fiona took another quite long sip of punch. The sensation was really extraordinary, as if someone had lit a fuse in her veins and the whole world was standing back, waiting for the explosion.

'Excuse me, Claire' – Fiona made sure her tone was firm, but friendly, as if she were talking to a rather thick child – 'but that's my husband you're borrowing.'

Behind her she could hear the sudden stop in conversation as the party suspended itself, listening. Probably these people had known about it for months.

'I'm just about to make some New Year's resolutions.' Fiona stood in front of Claire, separating her from Hamish. 'First, that I want Hamish back. And, next, that I want you out of my house. Now.'

She noticed Aunt Margaret standing just behind Claire holding our a pashmina. How on earth had she known that Fiona was about to chuck her out?

'Is this your stole dear?' Aunt Margaret took Claire firmly by the arm and led her towards the big front door. 'Such a pretty colour. Matches the steel of your eyes.'

Fiona looked up into Hamish's face. Had it really been she, fearful Fiona, who'd just sent The Caramel packing?

Hamish looked solemn, but there was the ghost of a smile in his eyes. 'I didn't know you cared. Even this morning you seemed to find me more of an irritation than a husband.'

From the cosy sitting room they could hear the countdown to the New Year beginning – 'ten, nine, eight, seven, six, five, four, three, two, one . . .' and she felt Hamish crushing her into a bear-hug that left her in no doubt of his New Year's Resolution.

Later on, in bed, when all the guests had gone, she buried her face in his bare chest. 'It's funny, isn't it? We were dreading Aunt Margaret's visit, but everything seemed to get better when she came.'

Next morning, when Kirsty saw their door was shut, she smiled and kept Jamie and Archie downstairs in front of the television.

There was still no sign of her parents by 11 o'clock when the front door bell rang.

Kirsty stared out of the window at a departing mini-cab. Who on earth could be arriving on New Year's Day?

She answered the door, still wearing her Snoopy nightshirt.

A very small, white-haired woman stood on the doorstep. She looked Kirsty up and down, narrow-minded disapproval stamped all over her face. 'Hello there, dear. Stay inside or you'll catch your death. Just tell your mother that Aunt Margaret's here and she hopes it's better late than never.'

Kirsty held on to the doorframe and stared, then glanced up at her parents' closed door.

'Could you hold on a minute, please?'

She ran upstairs and burst into the spare room. The bed was made and the room empty except for the tiny tiara.

Kirsty stood on the landing, staring. She didn't know what the hell was going on, but she was clear about one thing. Life had taken a turn for the better and she didn't like the look of that person down there one bit.

'I'm really sorry,' Kirsty began to close the front door politely but firmly, 'but I'm afraid you must have got the wrong address.'

Wendy Holden was a journalist prior to publishing her first novel, *Simply Divine*, in 1999. She has since published four more novels, the latest being *Azur Like It*. She is married with a son.

The Perfect Village

When James and I moved to the countryside, we were determined to do it properly. Not like our weekend-cottage-owning friends, sweeping down in the Saab from SW7 every Friday night. For one thing, we didn't have a Saab. For another, we disapproved of second homes, which were, we believed, fundamentally unfair. When we moved, it would be a permanent commitment. We would make friends locally and get involved in the village, not import half of Chelsea to make up our social life.

'Trust you bloody muesli eaters to be so bloody pious,' snapped one cottage-owning friend, Celia, an upmarket party organizer, when we said this.

I replied that I didn't entirely see what our choice of breakfast cereal had to do with anything. The health and well-being promoted by the regular intake of oats, dried fruit and skimmed milk was in any case a well-known nutritional fact. Our point, James and I told Celia, was the casual way she and everyone else we knew used their country places. Wouldn't a greater commitment to the local community be a better idea?

'But I've got to go back to London,' Celia groaned. 'It's called making a living. There's not much call for miniature Peking duck and coriander-scattered baby shrimp skewer in Slack Bottom, you know.'

Given such attitudes, it seemed a miracle that Celia had apparently never suffered any of the dreadful things disgruntled locals were supposed to do to city migrants. Shoving dung in their exhaust pipe, pouring concrete in their drains and so on. Heaven only knew how she had escaped so far.

'They must think your job's very frivolous,' I ventured primly.

Celia shrugged. 'Can't say I care if they do. You know country people,' she added airily. 'They like nothing better than to laugh at townies. So why deny them their fundamental human right?'

James and I exchanged sidelong looks of horror. It was impossible to think of a more blatantly ridiculous excuse for unapologetically elitist behaviour. Typical of Celia, though, we agreed on the way home. Her outlook on life had always been lamentably frivolous.

Our own opportunity to up sticks for rustic bliss came soon after this conversation. The liberal-intellectual, left-wing broadsheet for which James worked as deputy news editor and I as cookery editor (using organic and smallholders' produce whenever possible, naturally) suddenly changed proprietors and, with it, political persuasions. James was replaced by a thirty-something fogey with a monocle and I, in deference to our once-proud organ's demeaning new obsession with celebrity culture, by the ex-wife of a famous pop star who had probably once boiled an egg. We decided to cut our losses, sell up, go freelance and move to pastures new.

We looked at and discounted various options. The Cotswolds were struck off straight away – too gin and Jag and generally far too smug, not to mention expensive. We also researched Suffolk but discounted that too after Hugo, a schoolfriend of James's with a weekend cottage in Walberswick, revealed with delight that he hadn't even met a local yet. Politely, we tried to conceal our horror. A village full of people from London was the last thing we wanted. When in Rome, etc.

But in the end it wasn't Rome. In the end it was Redithick, a small village on the north Cornish coast. It was exactly what we required: small, pretty, unspoilt, comprised of delightfully plain cottages straggling up a green hillside towards some picturesque abandoned mine workings. Best of all, there wasn't a Londoner, or any other kind of incomer, in sight.

Having located the village, we found buying somewhere in it more of a struggle than expected. With the money from our Clapham house we could have afforded somewhere sizeable, but we decided small was beautiful on the grounds that anything big might alienate the locals. We also wanted something as collapsing as possible, so we could democratically redistribute wealth by using Redithick labour to refurbish the place. No one was going to accuse us of bringing in our own workmen and cheating local people out of jobs. The type of concern, we thought smugly, that never occurred to the likes of Celia.

The tiny tumbledown cottage we eventually chose had a small garden, one part of which I intended to devote to vegetable growing. Not only would this allow James and I a degree of self-sufficiency, but would demonstrate our willingness to join in with the village by entering the annual horticultural show.

Most of the locals were regulars at the low-roofed eighteenth-century pub, The Engineer, built of the same pink Cornish granite as the cottages. Entering it was an intimidating experience. The landlady was old and unsmiling and her clients entirely of the unblinkingly staring variety. The most grumpy-looking of all was the old man propping up the bar, who seemed to go by the name of Dick Dour. 'Do you think I should grow carrots or potatoes?' I asked him one day in my pleasantest voice. He looked at me, twisted his face in disgust and tipped the rest of his pint down his throat. Did that, I wondered, mean onions?

Yet James and I did not give up. We enrolled for classes in Cornish and policed ourselves rigorously for any references to our urban roots. Desperate not to remind anyone we had at one time lived in London, we never mentioned the L word outside of whispers in bed. The green Range Rover James had driven in London, which bore the label of a Hampstead garage, was quickly swapped for a beaten-up Ford bearing the insignia of a Padstow car dealer. We even worried about that because of the middle-class-urban Rick Stein associations.

Yet despite the constant purchasing of rubber Cheddar, Mother's Pride and either bullet-hard or bashed tomatoes in the local shop (rarebit was becoming the centrepiece of our diet), the shop still fell silent whenever I walked in. The pub was little better, despite me mugging up on a few country sayings. 'Spare at the spigot and spoil at the bung,' I observed brightly one evening to Dick Dour, but his only response was a look of disgust. As for the landlady, no matter how many pints of the near undrinkable local bitter I ordered in pointed avoidance of the urban gin-and-tonic trap, she never failed to ask where exactly it was we'd lived in London.

London seemed to come up in every conversation (admittedly these were few) we had with a local. It was as if to remind us we'd never be accepted. A month after our arrival, I was still checking our exhaust pipe for dung, our drains for concrete and the collapsing lean-to for smouldering, petrol-soaked rags.

We were thrilled, therefore, when Cheryl and Ken arrived on the scene. The claret metallic Jaguar parked outside The Engineer with plates from a Kensington garage had augured well. But the couple in the pub were beyond our wildest dreams. Flashily dressed, powerfully perfumed and apparently in their early forties, they blazed out of the murky gloom of The Engineer like a pair of illuminated plastic Santas.

The lavishly lipsticked woman, hair dyed a brilliant brass blonde, had perched her red-leather-trousered bottom on a bar stool and was listening to her bristle-haired consort cheerfully regale Dick Dour in broadest Sarf Lunnon about their search for 'some lickle week-end place round 'ere. Roomy though. Six bedrooms – a couple ornsuite, natch. I'm Ken by the way. This is Cheryl.'

'High Street Ken!' I whispered to James in delight, remembering the Jaguar's numberplates. It seemed the perfect nickname.

Sitting, almost invisible in our oatmeal jerseys and dingy tweeds, we delightedly awaited Dick Dour's response. He did not, however, have time to make it before High Street Ken interrupted again. 'Wiv a huge gardin, obviously. Not for plants, mind – can't stand growin' things meself. And Cheryl don't wanna break her nails. But we need somewhere to land the 'elecoptah.'

I sniggered to myself. Hee hee. Redithick was about to discover just how lucky it had been with us. It was now finding out what real incomers were like. Brash, loud and unapologetic about their origins.

Or perhaps I'd got the last bit wrong. 'We're finking of buyin' a title as well,' Ken announced to The Engineer's landlady. 'Might be noice. Lord and lady of the manor an' all that.'

I was desperate to hear the landlady's response, but by now my suppressed laughter was proving too painful to contain. We edged out past the bar, where Cheryl bared blazing white teeth in a rictus grin and Dick Dour gave us a look of withering contempt.

No doubt he had done the same to Cheryl and Ken, but equally no doubt they both had hides like rhinoceroses and didn't notice. The red Jaguar, anyway, was back the following weekend. A week later, I entered the village shop to hear someone saying that High Street Ken had snapped up the local manor house.

'Manor house!' I scoffed to James. 'Just for weekends? Talk about flash gits.' We had no doubt whatsoever that Ken and Cheryl's comeuppance was just a couple of petrol-soaked rags away.

It certainly deserved to be. The new arrivals, after all, couldn't have handled things more insensitively. Take the builders. We entered The Engineer one evening to find Cheryl plastered in make-up and poured into the usual tight leather and to hear Ken loudly declaring, through mouthfuls of (admittedly delicious-looking) pie and chips, that he'd been using London brickies, having no intention of waiting for a load of rustics to get off their arse.

I saw my opportunity. In no uncertain terms and before the entire Engineer, I haughtily reminded Ken that local building firms had to get what work they could, and if that sometimes meant not turning up for weeks while they finished another job, then so be it. Instead of approbation, however, there was silence from the pub when I had finished.

Doubtless, I decided, they were inwardly digesting my brave stand. High Street Ken, meanwhile, stared at me as if I was insane.

We were thrilled to hear, via the army of cockney builders that subsequently colonized the village, about High Street Ken's swimming-pool-sized hot tub, thermo-nuclear central heating, power shower installed in the priest hole and the halogen down-lighters in the Jacobean central beams. There were also rumours of a Fort Knox-style security system but that sounded too ridiculous for words. What would be the point, in Redithick?

'It all sounds so naff,' I sniffed to James. 'Just what you'd expect from' – I wrinkled my nose – 'someone making his living from musicals full of people from *Pop Idol*.' We had discovered that Ken was a theatrical impresario.

'But comfy,' James replied rather wistfully, shuffling in one of the hard-bottomed, second-hand Windsor chairs comprising our authentic seating arrangements.

'Not very in keeping, though,' I stressed.

James shrugged. 'Maybe not. But apparently the vicar's been in the tub twice and he loves it.'

'That,' I said, 'tells you all you need to know about the evils of organized religion.'

Worse was to come when it emerged that Ken had compared The Engineer's shepherds pie to that of The Ivy – to the detriment of The Ivy. 'Ken goes there all the time with his showbiz contacts apparently,' added the landlady, with what sounded suspiciously like pride.

I found relief for my feelings in kicking the usual puddles as we walked home in the usual rain. 'How low can you go?' I raged to James. 'I mean, we've been to The Ivy. And The Caprice. I've even been to Nobu, for Christ's sake. But would we ever dream of boasting about it? Never!'

'Perhaps that's where we've been going wrong,' ventured James. I stared at him in utter fury.

As the summer wore on, Cheryl and Ken wore on our nerves. Mine in particular.

'What really gets me,' I fumed to James, 'is the way they're not even trying to blend in with the rest of us. Just look at them – flying down from Battersea heliport every Friday night in that disgusting red chopper of theirs. How vulgar can you get? The locals ought to be disgusted.'

'But they're not,' mused James. 'They love it. Dick Dour even went up for a spin in it the other day. Or so Cheryl told me.'

I shot him a sharp look. 'And she's no better. Showing off in that stupid speedboat of hers. Talk about nouveau riche. Even named the damn thing after herself.'

'It's a joke,' James said.

'You're telling me it is. All dressed up in her gold braid and navy blue. Who the hell does she think she is? Ellen MacArthur?'

James sighed. 'No, I mean the name of the boat's a joke. She called it Cheryl so everyone who sails in it is "all in Cheryl on the sea".'

I stewed on this for a few minutes.

'So vulgar, too, having that huge place in Knightsbridge as well,' I burst out. 'Isn't the Manor big enough for them or something? Why two homes? Can't they leave London behind them once and for all? Or just go back there, preferably.'

'Well,' James sighed, 'they'd disappoint a lot of people if they did. The village has got very keen on these shopping weekends in London – have you heard about them?'

'No,' I said, my stomach tensing. 'I thought it took days to get to London from here.'

'It used to. Which is why no one ever went. But now they go in the helicopter – Ken's personal pilot takes them. Then they take in a show and stay overnight at Cheryl and Ken's place just off—'

'High Street Kensington, don't tell me. You're joking!' I stared at him in horror. 'What – for free?'

'No. He charges them. He's making a fortune by all accounts. He's certainly hit a demand. But then, he is an impresario.'

I was stunned. I wanted to weep. This was outrageous. This wasn't fair. This wasn't playing by the rules. This could not be tolerated. The presence of Cheryl and Ken began to weigh inside me like one of the Cornish pasties I still hadn't quite got the knack of making. Who the hell did they think they were, these vulgar people? Ruining the peace of our pretty village with their garish, loadsamoney, incomer ways?

Finally, I could bear it no longer. I decided to act.

It took me a day or so to do my recce and get everything together. We went to bed that night as usual, but once certain that James was asleep, I crept downstairs where I had laid out a set of dark clothes and the bag containing my equipment. Quietly, I let myself out into the night.

The village was in darkness as, keeping to the wall, I slunk down the main street and up the slight incline to the manor house. I edged along the estate wall to the old stables at the back, which Ken had apparently turned into a vulgar garage complex complete with his own Formula One-style pit and car wash. I shinned to the top of the wall and looked down into the stableyard for the first target on my list. Just then, the moon slid out from behind the clouds and shone full on my goal.

There was the Jaguar, its two gleaming chrome exhaust pipes simply begging to be stuffed with the horse manure in my carrier bag. And behind them, buildings which would look infinitely less brash and new following the application of a few petrol-soaked rags. Grinning, I jumped down.

And that's when it all went wrong. Simultaneously a thousand lights flashed, ear-splitting bells rang and hooters sounded like the scenes in James Bond when Dr No's secret lair is about to explode. People, including Ken (and Cheryl in an oyster silk peignoir), appeared from all directions. My mistake, for all my careful planning, had been to dismiss the rumours of the Fort Knox security system as having any basis in fact.

A week later, I picked up the phone for the first time in days. Calls from the local newspapers, national newspapers, Radio 4 and the BBC breakfast news inviting my contribution to items about 'incomer wars' I had left to the answerphone.

'Surprise!' Celia trilled.

'Really?' I said sourly. I'd had enough of surprises lately. Admittedly, Ken's decision not to prosecute had been one of the more pleasant. Less pleasant was the discovery that this was because he felt sorry for me on the grounds of my obvious insanity.

'I'm coming down to your village in a fortnight. Reallythick or something?'

'Redithick. Sorry, we won't be here, Celia.'

'But I was hoping to bum a bed off you,' said Celia, disappointed.

I wiped an arm over my sweaty brow and looked around at the array of half-packed cardboard boxes and the floor scattered with the different estate-agents' details we were considering. 'Sorry,' I repeated.

'What a shame,' said Celia. 'Because the reason I'm coming down is because I'm doing a party.'

I blinked. 'A party?' This seemed unlikely. The annual WI outing was Redithick's biggest jamboree and it had gone the week before to Tintagel.

'Stinking rich chap,' Celia gushed. 'No expense spared. Top-of-the-range canapes – or can-apes, as he calls them. Foie gras and passion fruit. And gallons of Bolly. Hang on a minute, I'll get the address.'

'No need,' I said heavily. Can-apes had given me all the clues I needed. 'It's Ken and Cheryl at the manor house, isn't it?'

A rustle of paper. 'That's it. Giving a bash to thank the village for welcoming them so warmly. Isn't that sweet?'

'Adorable,' I snarled.

'I must say,' Celia mused, 'this Reallythick of yours sounds a great place. Friendly and sophisticated and all that. I'll be interested to have a look round when I come down. Wonder if there's anything for sale?'

David Lodge is a critic as well as the author of eleven novels, including *Thinks* . . . Emeritus Professor of Modern English Literature at the University of Birmingham, he has also written for theatre and television. His most recent book of criticism is *Consciousness and the Novel*, and a new novel, *Author, Author* will be published in September 2004.

Pastoral

DAH DAH DAH, dah dah dah, dada dada dada . . .
I never hear the opening strains of the Shepherds'
Song from Beethoven's Pastoral Symphony without
remembering my scheme to embrace the Virgin Mary.
That is to say, Dympna Cassidy, who was impersonat-
ing the Virgin Mary at the time. The time was one
Christmas in the 1950s and the occasion a Nativity
play I produced for the Youth Club of Our Lady of
Perpetual Succour in south London. And when I say
produced, I mean I wrote the piece, directed it, cast it,
acted in it, designed the set for it and, of course, chose
the music for it. The only thing I didn't do for it
was sew the costumes. My loyal mother and resentful
sisters were pressed into performing that task.

It must sound as if I was already stagestruck, but in
fact I wasn't when I embarked on the project. I was
in the sixth form at St Aloysius' Catholic Grammar
School, studying English, French, Latin and Eco-
nomics, and intended to read Law at university, with
the ambition of becoming a barrister (an idea im-
planted by my father, who was a solicitor's chief clerk,
and had set his heart on my becoming a star of the
legal profession). I never expected to end up as a

director of stage musicals anywhere from Scunthorpe to Sydney – mostly touring productions of golden oldies like *Oklahoma!* and *The King and I*. I did direct a new musical in the West End a few years ago, but you probably never heard of it – it folded after three weeks. Still, I have great hopes of my new project, a musical version of *Antony and Cleopatra* called *Cleo!* I've written the book myself.

But I digress. Back to the Nativity play, *The Story of Christmas*, as it was rather unimaginatively entitled. I wanted to call it *The Fruit of the Womb*, but the parish priest, Father Stanislaus Lynch, wouldn't have it – the first of many battles we had over the play. He said my title was indecent. I pointed out that it was a quotation from the Hail Mary: 'and blessed is the fruit of thy womb, Jesus'. He said that, taken out of context, the words had a different effect. I said: 'What you mean is that in context they have no effect at all, because Catholics recite prayers in a mindless drone, without paying any attention to what they're saying. My play is designed to shock them out of their mental torpor, into a new awareness of what Christmas is all about: Incarnation.' I was a fluent and arrogant youth – at least in intellectual debate. In other areas of life, such as girls, I was less assured.

But Father Stan, as we called him, replied: 'That's all very well, but there'll have to be a poster advertising it. I won't have the word "womb" stuck up in my church porch. The Union of Catholic Mothers wouldn't like it.' At home I complained bitterly about this example of philistine ecclesiastical censorship, until one of my sisters said that 'Fruit of the Womb' reminded her of 'Fruit of the Loom', in those days a trademark for cotton underwear, and I decided to abandon the title without further resistance.

Dah dah dah dah dah dah . . . There were other pieces of music in *The Story of Christmas*, played while the scenery was being changed behind the curtain, and setting the mood for the next scene. I chose Gounod's *Ave Maria* for the Annunciation, a theme from Rimsky-Korsakov's *Scheherazade* for the Three Kings, and the *Ride of the Valkyries* for the Flight into Egypt. My father had a decent collection of classical music on 78s and used to let me play them on our radiogram, a walnut-veneered monolith that stood in the bay window of the front parlour. But it's the Shepherd's Song that triggers memories of the play and of Dympna Cassidy.

I chose it to introduce the scene where the shepherds of Bethlehem come to venerate the infant Jesus, but it spread into other parts of the play in the course of rehearsals. It all started one Sunday in November at the youth club hop. Father Stan and I were sitting on folded chairs on the edge of the dance floor, if one might so dignify the splintering floorboards of the parish hall, watching couples shuffling round to Nat King Cole groaning 'Too Young' from a portable record player.

I was sitting down because I didn't dance, couldn't dance, pretended I didn't want to dance, though truly it was a reluctance to look silly while learning to dance that made me a wallflower. I attended these events on the pretext of being Secretary of the youth club committee, drawn by a secret need to behold Dympna Cassidy, exquisite torture though it was to watch her swaying in the arms of some other youth.

Fortunately most of the boys in the club were as shy as I was and the girls were compelled much of the time to dance with each other, as Dympna was doing with her friend Pauline that evening to the syrupy strains of

'Too Young'; and even when she had a male partner, club protocol prohibited close contact. That was why Father Stan was there: to make sure light was always visible between them.

> They say that we are much too young.
> Too young to really be in love . . .

She was beautiful and buxom, with jade-green eyes and copper-coloured hair, which, freshly washed for social occasions, surrounded her head in a shimmering haze of natural curls. Her complexion was a glowing, translucent white, like the surface of a fine alabaster statue, and her underlip had a delicious pout. When she smiled, two dimples appeared in her cheeks, which I associated with her first name. Cassidy was rather lacking in poetic resonance, but Dympna – it was eloquent not only of her dimples, but of her whole person. The syllables had a soft, yielding, pneumatic quality that I imagined her body would possess when clasped in an embrace. And how I longed to embrace it! How I yearned to squeeze that voluptuous form like a cushion against my chest and press my lips on the pouting perfection of her mouth, in the manner I had observed in a thousand cinematic love scenes. But I didn't love Dympna Cassidy. Nor was I prepared to pretend that I did. And in that time and place the only way you would get to kiss a girl like her was to do one or the other. That is to say, I would have had to declare myself publicly as her steady boyfriend.

And here I have to make a rather shameful confession: I thought I would be lowering myself if I courted Dympna Cassidy. It wasn't simply that she came from the wrong side of the tracks, though she did; her large and slightly raffish family lived in a tenement flat on a council estate, whereas we owned our own home, a dignified Victorian terraced house. It wasn't that she dropped her aitches occasionally, and tended to elide the middle consonant of 'butter' and 'better'. I could have lived with these handicaps if Dympna Cassidy had had some qualities of mind to compare with the attractions of her body. But her mind was conspicuously empty. There was nothing to be found in it except a few popular songs, the names of film stars, fashion notes and anecdotes about her teachers. She attended a technical school, having failed the 11-plus examination in which I had distinguished myself, and was following what was called a commercial course. She was being trained to be a shorthand typist, though her own inclination was to be a sales assistant in a dress shop. I knew all this because I took the opportunity to chat to her – outside church after Sunday Mass, while clearing up the parish hall after a youth club evening, or during one of the club's occasional rambles through the Kent countryside. I could tell that Dympna was interested in me: intrigued and attracted by the slightly foppish air I cultivated when out of school uniform, my long hair, green corduroy jacket and mustard waistcoat. I was aware that she had attached herself to no other boy, though she had many admirers in the parish. I felt sure that she would reciprocate, if I would only make the first move.

But I hung back. My future was clearly marked out for me, and Dympna Cassidy had no place in it: study, examinations, honours, prizes; years of effort and self-denial ultimately rewarded by a distinguished legal career. Dympna's kind had a totally different attitude to life: leave school as soon as you could, get a job however repetitive and banal, and live for the hours

181

of recreation, for dancing, shopping, going to the pictures, 'having a good time'. Consuming one's youth in a splurge of thoughtless, superficial pleasure, before relapsing into a dull, domesticated adulthood just like one's parents, struggling to bring up a family on inadequate means.

Becoming involved with Dympna would, I was certain, drag me down into that abyss. I swear that I thought one kiss would do it, one kiss and I would be set on a course leading to a premature and imprudent marriage. And marriage would not be kind to Dympna Cassidy. You could see what she would look like in twenty years' time by looking at her mother: a sagging bosom, a waist thickened by childbearing and hollowed cheeks where the back teeth were missing. Dympna would never again be as beautiful as she was now, so I told myself gloomily, watching her leading Pauline in the foxtrot, chattering away inanely about a pair of shoes that she had seen in a shop window. This topic seemed to engage their interest for the duration of the set; they were still talking about it every time they rotated past me and Father Stan.

'You know Mrs Noonan, who teaches in the Infants,' he said suddenly. I admitted that I did: she had taught me ten years earlier. 'And you know she puts on a Nativity play every Christmas, with the children. Well, she's got to go into hospital next week for an operation and she'll be on convalescent leave until January. I've been thinking, wouldn't it be a fine thing if the youth club took on the job for this year? The Nativity play, I mean. It would be good to have something a little more . . . grown-up, for once. Something the young people of the parish could relate to. D'you think you might be able to organize something, Simon?'

'All right.'

'Well, that's grand,' said Father Stan, somewhat taken aback by the speed of my assent. 'Are you sure you've got the time? I know they work you very hard at St Aloysius.'

'I'll manage, Father. Leave it to me.'

'Well, that's very good of you. I'll see if the Catholic Truth Society publish a suitable play. I don't think the one Mrs Noonan uses would be quite the ticket.'

'I'll write the play myself.'

As soon as he had mentioned the Nativity play a tableau had formed in my mind's eye: Dympna Cassidy as Our Lady, stunningly beautiful, her copper filigree hair shining like a halo in the footlights, and myself as St Joseph supporting her on the road to Bethlehem, my arm round her shoulders, or even her waist. I had found the perfect alibi for getting into close physical contact with Dympna Cassidy, without incurring any moral or emotional obligations.

'You'd have to show me the script before it's performed, just to make sure there's no heresy.' Father Stan exposed his irregular, nicotine-stained teeth in a wolfish grin.

I wrote the play, believe it or not, over two weekends. I didn't bother with auditions, partly because there wasn't time, and partly because nobody would have turned up for them. There was no thespian tradition at the Youth Club of Our Lady of Perpetual Succour. I picked out the likeliest members of the club for my cast and, as we say in the profession, made offers without asking them to read. Naturally I approached Dympna Cassidy first. When I told her I wanted her to play the Virgin Mary she went pink with pleasure, but shook her head and said that she had never acted in her life. I told her not to worry. I had some experience acting in school plays and I would help her. I looked forward to intimate coaching sessions in the front parlour at home, with the radio-gram providing some suitable background music. Dah *dah* dah, dah *dah* dah . . . Did I already have that piece of music in mind?

I deferred showing Father Stan the script on the grounds that we were continually revising it in the course of rehearsals. But eventually he got suspicious and borrowed a copy from another member of the cast and there was the most almighty row. He came round to our house one evening, fortunately when my parents were out, grasping the rolled-up script in his fist like a baton. He waved it furiously in my face.

'What's the meaning of this filth? What do you mean by soiling the spotless purity of our Blessed Mother?'

I knew at once that he was referring to the stage direction at the end of Act I, Sc. i: '*JOSEPH and MARY embrace.*'

Admittedly, there wasn't a great deal of Biblical authority for this scene. It was an imaginative attempt to evoke the life of Mary when betrothed to Joseph and before she had any idea that she was to become the Mother of God. I was aiming at a contemporary style in my play – 'relevance' it would have been called a decade later. No pious platitudes and Biblical archaisms, but colloquial speech and natural behaviour, that modern teenagers could relate to. I imagined Mary as a rather merry, high-spirited, even skittish young girl at this stage of her life, engaged to an older and rather serious man. I wrote a scene in which Mary calls in at Joseph's carpentry shop and tries to persuade him to go for a walk. Joseph refuses, he has a job to finish, and there is a kind of lovers' tiff, which is soon made up. And their reconciliation is sealed with a kiss.

Several members of the cast questioned the propriety of this scene at the first read-through. But I argued that it was natural behaviour between an engaged couple who didn't at that stage know that they were going to bring the Messiah into the world. Dympna herself didn't contribute to this discussion. She kept her eyes down and her lips closed. I think she had a good idea of the real motivation for the scene.

After a couple more read-throughs, I started blocking out the moves, starting from the top, but I found that when I came to the curtain line of Act I, Sc. i –

JOSEPH: Mary, I can never be cross with you for long.
MARY: Nor I with you.

– my nerve failed me. I simply said, 'Then Joseph and Mary embrace and the curtain comes down.'

'Aren't you going to rehearse the kiss?' said Magda Vernon, who had volunteered to be stage manager. She was an odd girl, tall and skinny, with glasses that kept falling off her snub nose and spiky hair that stuck out in all directions, as if she had just got out of bed. She favoured long, dark-hued sweaters that she pulled cruelly out of shape, tugging the hem down low over her hips and stretching the sleeves so that they covered her hands like mittens, as though she were trying to hide herself in the garment. It was rumoured that she had had some kind of nervous breakdown and tried to run away from home and that her parents had made her join the youth club so that she would become more normal. But she didn't seem to enjoy it much. The Nativity play was the first event that had aroused the slightest flicker of interest in her. She had supported me in the discussion about the propriety of the embrace, for which I was grateful. But now I wished she would not interfere.

'There isn't time to rehearse everything at this stage,' I said. 'Could we move on to scene two?' But the next time we ran the first scene, I stopped it again just short of the final kiss.

'Shouldn't you have decided what kind of kiss it's going to be?' Magda insisted. 'I mean, who kisses who? And is it a kiss on the lips or on the cheek?'

'It'd better be on the cheek,' said the boy playing Herod, 'or Father Stan will have a fit.' There was a general titter.

'I really haven't thought about it,' I lied, having thought of little else for days. 'I think we should leave it till we have the costumes.'

Later, when the cast had gone home and Magda and I were alone, going through a list of props that would be required, she gave me an arch look: 'I don't believe you know how to.'

'How to what?'

'How to kiss a girl. I'll teach you if you like.'

'I can manage perfectly well on my own, thank you.'

But later, walking home in the cold December night, I rather regretted having turned down the offer and mentally rehearsed various strategies for reviving it. But the very next day Father Stan exploded, the first scene of my play was scrapped and I had no further pretext for requesting Magda's tuition.

So I never did get to embrace Dympna Cassidy. I got my arm round her waist on the road to Bethlehem, but she was wearing so many layers of clothes in that scene that it was no great tactile experience. By this time, in any case, I'd rather lost sexual interest in Dympna and was much more preoccupied with her shortcomings as an actress. The manic, obsessive quest

186

for perfection that possesses those who make plays had me in thrall. Dympna kept forgetting her lines. And when she remembered she delivered them in a flat and barely audible voice. If I criticized her she sulked and said that she'd never asked to be in my stupid play anyway. The only thing to be said for her was that she looked sensational. So what I did was to cut her lines to the bone and make her part consist mostly of silent action with background music. I noticed that she liked the Shepherd's Song and would hum it to herself when she was in a good mood, so I decided to use it as a kind of leitmotif, whenever Mary appeared. This required some nifty work from Magda in the wings – she had to operate the gramophone and act as prompter at the same time – but it proved highly effective. I had stumbled on one of the primary resources of musical theatre: the reprise. No prizes for guessing what the audience were humming as they filed out of the parish hall. Our play was a hit. I walked Magda home afterwards and we kissed in her front porch until our lips were sore.

Magda became my first girlfriend, until we both went to different universities the following year and drifted apart. I read law as planned, but spent all of my time mucking about in the Drama Society and the Opera Society, scraped a third class degree, and to the great disgust of my father went straight to drama school. Curiously enough, Magda had been bitten by the same bug. She did theatre studies at university, became an ASM at various provincial reps and finally went into television, where she has done rather well as a production manager. We meet occasionally at showbiz occasions and when we embrace each other, as showbiz people do when they meet, she always teases me by saying, 'Lips or cheek, darling?'

And Dympna? Well, she didn't become a typist or a shop assistant. And she didn't lose her figure or her teeth. Somebody spotted her potential as a photographic model and she had a successful run in the late 1950s, appearing on the front covers of several women's magazines, until the Jean Shrimpton look put her out of fashion. According to my mother, she married a rich businessman and retired from modelling. They live in a manor house near Newmarket and own a string of racehorses . . . I've been thinking I might write and ask if they'd like to invest in *Cleo!*

Angela Lambert, a former TV reporter and journalist, began writing in 1979 and published her first novel in 1986. Her third novel, *A Rather English Marriage*, was televised by the BBC in 1998 to critical acclaim. Now the author of seven successful novels, including *Kiss and Kin*, which won the Romantic Novel of the Year award in 1998, Angela also writes for a number of national newspapers. She is currently working on her first biography.

Second Honeymoon

So here she was, nine months to the day after George's death, Geraldine Rathbone, dutiful wife and mother, all on her own and becalmed by the afternoon heat in a scruffy cafe in Arles. Except. Except that George had died on the first of January. First disloyal thought: such a difficult date. It meant she'd had to ring everybody cut across their New Year wishes and hear their voices do a 180-degree turn as they hoisted in that what she'd actually said was, 'I'm sorry to have to tell you that George died in his sleep last night.' After the stock condolences they kept assuring her that for someone so full of vigour as George a heart attack was a marvellous way to go and she kept replying, 'Yes, he would have hated to *decline* . . .' The months since then had been an exhausting journey through different emotional climates, from the public dignity of the funeral, into states of mind that made her feel like an ocean-going yacht, veering within hours from half-mad, tempestuous anger to motionless, robotic grief. This stage – the worst – was followed (second disloyal thought) by a kind of shameful secret glee because finally she could put her own needs first. The journey had ended in lonely, stunned acceptance. 'You're so *brave,*' people said. She wanted to retort, 'What else can I be? I can't exactly drum my heels and *scream.*' Several of her friends had softly mentioned counselling, but Geraldine didn't want to be counselled. She wanted George. Or did she?

The hardest thing about being widowed was learning to think for herself again. George wouldn't have wanted her to come to Arles, she was pretty sure of that; but having established how much money she had to live on and discovered that despite his dire warnings there was quite a lot, she decided to do what *she* wanted. George, after all, was dead, not her. Third disloyal thought.

'Why on earth are you going to Arles?' her younger son had asked when she told him she planned to spend a week there. 'Why not Polzeath or Skye? That's where we've always gone. Or you could visit Robbo in Montreal. But *France*?' She couldn't possibly have told him the truth . . . that aged nineteen she'd wanted to spend her honeymoon in Arles, having fallen in love with Van Gogh and his work, its hectic beauty and un-English colours. George had, of course, overruled her. George thought the south of France was either sex-mad (Bardot) or savage (gypsies and wild horses). Was that another disloyal thought?

He'd compromised, as he saw it, by taking her to Jersey for their honeymoon. He liked to be near the sea. They'd walked the long beaches and swum in the waves and once she had nearly died of terror when he underestimated the current in St Ouen's Bay and it took the uttermost limits of his strength to get him back to the beach safely. She'd clasped him in her arms and sobbed against his shivering wet shoulder. 'I thought you were going to die. I thought you were *drowning.*' She wrapped a towel round him and rubbed his hair and he huddled inside its warmth and let her revive him. That night they'd made love successfully for the first time, and for the first time she had felt like his wife.

For the ten-thousandth time Geraldine wondered why, of all the wives he could have had, George had chosen *her*. She had been chastely, hopelessly in love with him from the moment they met. He was the perfect junior officer, devastatingly handsome in his uniform, tall and broad-shouldered, with an uncomplicated loyalty to Navy, Queen and country. She herself had been – she realized now, though she hadn't at the time – pretty enough, maybe more than that; far from stupid, and given to unexpected shafts of wit, not something the other girls seemed able to manage. On the other hand, they'd been better off, better bred, far better dressed and a good deal more determined in their pursuit of 'Gorgeous Georgeous', as he was known to the chatterers in the Ladies'. Yet on her eighteenth birthday, with her father's permission, he had proposed – to the surprise and delight of her mother, who hadn't expected her shy, bookish daughter to make nearly such a good catch.

Geraldine spent her first day in Arles pursuing the shade of Van Gogh. Not a building was left that he had painted or lived in just over a century ago, the local tourist office told her, nor did the town possess a single one of his works. Yet the people he had painted were everywhere. Sturdy, swarthy, their black eyes set in emphatic faces, they could have been descendants of M. Roulin, the double-bearded postman, and his stout wife, while the young man who sold her postcards was the image of their scowling son, Armand. The chambermaid at her hotel looked exactly like La Mousme, the ruddy-faced, healthy young peasant whom Vincent had also painted in her best blue-and-red striped bodice, the one that showed off the voluptuous curves of her bosom and waist.

How the respectable bourgeoisie of Arles had hated him! They had got up a petition and presented it to the mayor, demanding that he should be driven out of town. Poor Vincent . . . eccentric in manner, with a funny foreign accent, aching for kindness, had 'given himself up to alcoholic excess, after which he gets in a state of overexcitement to such an extent that he no longer knows what he does or says, which is very upsetting for the public', the petition spelled out disapprovingly. Send him home or put him in an asylum, they meant. Geraldine planned to go to St Rémy to see the hospital where he had been looked after by nuns and had at last encountered someone who cared about him – M. Rey, the young doctor whose gentle eyes gazed out of Vincent's portrait with a compassion that still lingered. But for now her feet hurt and her face burned and she needed to sit down.

She found a scruffy café just off the main square and ordered coffee and a *pain aux raisins*. She combed her dusty hair, picked an empty table, put her handbag down on the red-tiled floor and looked around. A couple of bull-fighting posters were stuck onto the whitewashed walls and behind the counter hung two wire baskets of bedraggled plants that looked as if they'd been watered with the dregs from the coffee machine. The blackboard displayed the day's menu scrawled in chalk. *Omelette aux fines herbes*, *jambon du pays*, *piperade*, *pâtes au pistou* . . . George would have dismissed it as a slovenly tourist trap and given it four out of ten. (He awarded marks for everything . . . state of the lavatories, other people's driving, music in shops or restaurants – and few earned more than six out of ten. George, a perfectionist, expected his own high standards from everyone else. Did that count as a disloyal thought?)

George hadn't spoken French, or any other foreign language for that matter, so they'd spent their holidays in Scotland or Cornwall. He would lead them at a brisk pace across cliffs and mountains, or plunge into the sea ahead of them. Robin and Andrew were so desperate for his approval that they'd follow until they were drooping with exhaustion. George never noticed, so she had to make sure he didn't push them beyond their endurance.

'Do them good! Build them up!' he'd say if she tried to protest as her small sons emerged from the freezing water with pinched faces, blue with cold. 'Fit bodies . . . that's what we want, isn't it, boys? Clean minds and fit bodies.'

'Yes, Daddy,' they'd say.

'There you are! Stop fussing, Mummy.'

He'd hold out a hand and towel his sons dry until their tender young skin turned from blue to purple, while Geraldine watched the muscles in his arms and shoulders ripple with energy. Other women had watched her husband too, not that George seemed to notice.

His manly vigour and air of authority had been attractive, just as – in a quite different way – the young man at the opposite table was attractive to the six or seven girls surrounding him. Drawn by the sight of them laughing, Geraldine had brushed aside the plastic ribbons that fluttered across the doorway, wanting a share of that young laughter for herself. How long was it since she had *laughed*? The girls were gesticulating, tossing their thick black hair, competing for the handsome youth's attention. 'Philippe!

Philippe!' they tweeted, like a flock of birds. After drinking her coffee and a glass of cold water, she burrowed in her handbag for the paperback copy of Van Gogh's letters. The young women reminded her of a phrase he'd used, and she searched until she found it: 'That sun-steeped, sun-burnt quality, tanned and swept with air.' Perfect! They were swept with air, their skin burnished, buoyed up with airy vitality. For the first time, she noticed the quiet girl on his left. Shy and modestly dressed, she was easy to miss. A relative . . . his sister, perhaps, or a cousin? Maybe she was a classmate who'd been secretly in love with him for years and this was his way of setting her free to find a husband properly suited to her rather than pining futilely for him: the first choice of every girl in the *quartier*.

Geraldine knew all about the private agony of being young and yearning for beauty . . . though now, in her mid-fifties, she thought all young women were pretty, with the shining skin, taut limbs, clear eyes and glossy hair that no beauty products could reproduce. She wished she'd known *that* in the days when she'd gone to teenage parties in the school holidays. Cheeks and throat crimson with embarrassment, big feet doubly conspicuous in the elongated, pointed shoes that were fashionable at the time, Geraldine had always been convinced she looked a freak.

When she left school she'd been terrified of the opposite sex, paralysed into shyness by her mother's warnings. Boys seemed like wild animals barely held in check. One touch of her breast might unleash forces beyond their control, ending in seduction, pregnancy, humiliation, illegitimacy or a shotgun wedding. In 1963, aged seventeen, it was still possible to believe the old myths, and most well-brought-up girls did.

Trained by her parents never to push herself forward or seek praise, she felt she lacked any social skills, virginity her only asset. Mam'selle at school had encouraged her to try for university, but her father said girls didn't need qualifications; shorthand and typing would tide her over till she got herself married. So off she'd gone to Miss Judson's secretarial college and from there to a job at the Ministry of Defence (Naval Section), which was how she'd first met George. The liberation of the late sixties had not quite begun, and she married just ahead of its breaking wave.

Freed from parental disapproval and still fairly unaffected by George's, she'd developed a quick and original sense of humour. She discovered she could make her husband laugh by inventing a range of caricatures to share their lives. They were headed by the Admiral, whom she called the Admirable. From his puffed-up chest, in a deep authoritarian voice, issued a stream of nonsensical orders ('All hands to the anchor – grasp it firmly – AND all together now: one, two, three . . . *jump!*). Then there was the nippy little cabin boy, forever ducking away from the grasping hands of lecherous officers; and the sad wives waiting on shore. These characters, each with a different, preposterous voice, made George roar with laughter – a series of explosive barks quite unlike his controlled laconic speech. She missed having someone to appreciate her jokes.

George was a man of his word. He had made a vow before God and this congregation to keep himself only unto her and, as far as she knew, that's what he had done. Had it been an effort? She hoped not. As for her, providing she kept his home and his sons clean and tidy and comfortable and accepted his undemanding love-making, that seemed to satisfy him. The melodrama of her friends' marriages – their arguments, intimacy, never mind their claims of rollicking sensuality – was unknown to her and George. Yes, but had he loved her? Not in the way she'd loved him, that was certain. Throughout their married life Geraldine had pitched and soared on an emotional roller-coaster, driven by longing for his approval, fear of his rebukes, and the bliss of those moments when he was helpless with laughter at her absurd, inventive jokes.

Pretending to write postcards, Geraldine settled down to eavesdrop on the festive group opposite. Her French was still pretty fluent. Once the boys had gone off to prep school (at the age of eight, poor darlings), she'd taught French at the local comprehensive, but only as far as GCSE. George said she wasn't nearly good enough to get her pupils through A level. Her mind would keep wandering back to her husband. Former husband. *Dead* husband. It couldn't be disloyal to think that. Even after this many months it still shocked her to realize that George was dead.

Tomorrow, Geraldine thought, she'd go and look at the canal bridge Van Gogh had painted: the Pont de Langlois, now renamed Pont Van Gogh. Pity she couldn't have come in the spring when the orchards were in full bloom, when she might have recaptured some of the ecstasy the painter had felt upon seeing them. 'I am in a mad whirl of work,' he wrote in a letter to his brother Theo, 'because the trees are in blossom and because I want to do a monstrously gay orchard.' Wonderful word: monstrously gay! It reminded her of Dennis Potter in his last television interview, glittering-eyed and visionary as death stalked towards him over the hills of his childhood. 'The blossomest blossom,' he'd called it. Live in the present, they had both meant.

Van Gogh had also written, 'After a while one's sight changes, you feel colour differently. I am convinced that I shall set my individuality free simply by staying on here.' Was that why she had come to Arles . . . to set her individuality free? In thirty-seven years of marriage her nature had become so moulded to George's needs and wishes that she had forgotten how to be the person he had first met, that girl whose interior life was both deeper and freer than her modest demeanour suggested. Even at seventeen Geraldine had known that the person inside her was more interesting than the twinset-and-pearls girl she was groomed to be.

The quiet girl put her hand on Philippe's arm, revealing for the first time a shiny new ring. For a moment he glanced down at her and his vivid expression softened into tenderness. He lifted his glass and said, '*À toi, petit lapin!*' and all the others lifted theirs too and said in unison, '*Bonheur à Philippe et Josette!*' Good heavens, Geraldine thought – how extraordinary – *she*'s the one! What could have made him choose the least vivacious of the girls when by the look of it he could have had his pick? The plainest one of all – no, not exactly plain, but not a great beauty either.

The cheerful mob opposite went on celebrating, cracking salted pistachios and expertly spitting out the shells, capping each other's stories, laughing and reminiscing. They had already drunk a second bottle of red wine and were calling for a third. She sensed they'd known one another since childhood . . . been to the same school, made their first confirmation together, groaned through the rigours of the Baccalauréat, gone on trips abroad crammed into the school coach and pressed hotly against one another's urgent throbbing bodies in discos and nightclubs. Why did he pick *that* one, Geraldine puzzled; was it for the same reason that George picked me? Perhaps he thought the subtle, composed Josette was most likely to be a good wife and a good mother to his children – good not only in the sense of efficient but *virtuous*. Did anyone care about virtue, probity, honesty, goodness, any more? It struck Geraldine suddenly why the girl held herself apart. Her love was private; too important to be twirled above her head like a cheerleader's flag. And it would last for ever. Had George, too, sensed a different girl in her and was that why he'd asked her to marry him? She had always wanted desperately, passionately, to know whether her husband really loved and needed her. His English reticence had prevented him from confessing to such weakness, and by dying so suddenly he'd left it too late.

The animated young women were getting to their feet. They huddled at the counter, rooting in their purses, working out how much they owed, dividing it up between them. Left alone for a moment, Philippe bent to kiss his fiancée and suddenly she wasn't plain at all, she was radiant, her face alight and filled with joy. At last Geraldine saw what Philippe found in her; what Vincent had seen in La Mousme, and George must have seen in her . . . the vulnerability and hopefulness of youth along with a seriousness that promised lifelong love. Idiot that I am, she thought – of *course* he chose her! The others crowded round begging to be noticed but she just quietly got on with loving him. And that was me, too . . . my God, that was *me*!

She looked steadily across at Philippe until she caught his eye, then raised her coffee cup to him and mouthed, *'Félicitations!'* He gave her a conspiratorial grin and Geraldine Rathbone flashed back a smile that blazed like a tiara.

The Wagon Mound

Nothing destroys the quality of life so much as insomnia. Ask any parent of a new baby. It only takes a few broken nights to reduce the most calm and competent person to a twitching shadow of their normal proficiency. My wakefulness started when the nightmares began. When I did manage to drop off, the visions my subconscious mind conjured up were guaranteed to wake me, sweating and terrified, within a couple of hours of falling asleep. It didn't take long before I began to fear sleep itself, dreading the demons that ripped through the fabric of my previous ease. I tried sleeping pills, I tried alcohol. But nothing worked.

I never dreamed that I'd rediscover the art of sleeping through the night thanks to a legal precedent. In 1961, a ship called *The Wagon Mound* spilled oil in Sydney Harbour. The oil fouled a nearby wharf, and when the wharf's owners began welding work, it burst into flames. In the resulting court case, it was finally decreed that the ship's owners weren't liable because the type of harm sustained by the plaintiff must be reasonably foreseeable. When Roger, the terminally boring commercial attaché at the Moscow embassy, launched into the tale the other night in the bar at Proyekt OGI, he could never have imagined that it would change my life so dramatically. But then, lawyers have never been noted for their imagination.

Proximity. That's another legal principle he raised. How many intervening stages lie between cause and effect. By then I was the only one listening, and only because he'd summoned up the starting point of my sleepless nights.

Although the seeds were sown when my boss in London decided to invite the best-selling biographer Tom Uttley on a British Council tour of Russia, I can't be held accountable for that. The first point where I calculate I have to accept responsibility was on the night train from Moscow to St Petersburg.

I'd been looking after Tom ever since he'd landed at Sheremetyevo airport two days before. I hadn't seen him smile in all that time. He'd lectured lugubriously at the university, glumly addressed a gathering at the British Council library, done depressing signings at two bookshops and sulked his way round a reception at the Irish embassy. Even the weather seemed to reflect his mood, grey clouds lowering over Moscow and turning April into autumn. Minding visiting authors is normally the part of my job I like the best, but spending time with Tom was about as much fun as having a hole in your shoe in a Russian winter. We'd all been hoping for some glamour from Tom's visit; his Channel 4 series on the roots of biography had led us to expect a glowing Adonis with twinkling eyes and a gleaming grin. Instead, we got a glowering black dog. Over dinner on the first evening, he'd downed his vodka like a seasoned Russian hand, and gloomed like the most depressive Slav in the Caucasus. On the short walk back to his hotel, I asked him if everything was all right. 'No,' he said shortly. 'My wife's just left me.'

Right, I thought. Don't go there, Sarah. 'Oh,' I think I said.

The final event of his Moscow visit was a book signing, and afterwards I took him to dinner to pass the time until midnight, when the train would leave for St Pete's. That was when the floodgates opened. He was miserable, he admitted. He was terrible company. But Rachel had walked out on him after eight years of marriage. There wasn't anyone else, she'd said. It was just that she was bored with him, tired of his celebrity, fed up of feeling inferior intellectually. I pointed out that these reasons seemed somewhat contradictory.

He brightened up at that. And suddenly the sun came out. He acted as if I'd somehow put my finger on something that should make him feel better about the whole thing. He radiated light and I basked in the warmth of his smile. Before long, we were laughing together, telling our life stories, swapping intimacies. Flirting, I suppose.

We boarded a train a little before midnight, each dumping our bags in our separate first-class compartments. Then Tom produced a bottle of Georgian champagne from his holdall. 'A nightcap?' he suggested.

'Why not?' I was in the mood, cheered beyond reason by the delights of his company. He sat down on the sleeping berth beside me, and it seemed only natural when his arm draped across my shoulders. I remember the smell of him: a dark, masculine smell with an overlay of some spicy cologne with an edge of cinnamon. If I'm honest, I was willing him to kiss me before he actually did. I was entirely disarmed by his charm. But I also felt sorry for the pain that had been so obvious over the previous two days. And maybe, just maybe, the inherent *Dr Zhivago* romance of the night train tipped the balance.

I don't usually do this kind of thing. What am I saying? I never do this kind of thing. In four years of chasing around after authors, or having them chase after me, I'd not given into temptation once. But Tom penetrated all of my professional defences, and I moaned under his hands from Moscow to St Petersburg. By morning, he swore I'd healed his heart. By the time he left St Pete's three days later, we'd arranged to meet in London, where I was due to attend a meeting in ten days' time. I'd been out of love for a long time; it wasn't hard to fall for a man who was handsome, clever and amusing, and who seemed to find me irresistible.

Two days later, I got his first email. I'd been checking every waking hour on the hour, wondering and edgy. It turned out I had good reason to be anxious. The email was short and sour.

Dear Sarah, Rachel and I have decided we want to try to resolve our differences. It'll come as no surprise to you that my marriage is my number one priority. So I think it best if we don't communicate further. Sorry if this seems cold, but there's no other way to say it. Tom.

I was stunned. This wasn't cold, it was brutal. A hard jab below the ribs, designed to take my breath away and deflect any possible comeback. I felt the physical shock in the pit of my stomach.

Of course, I blamed myself for my stupidity, my eagerness to believe that a man as charismatic as Tom could fall for me. Good old reliable Sarah, the safe pair of hands who second-guessed authors' needs before they could even voice them. I felt such a fool. A bruised, exploited fool.

Time passed, but there was still a raw place inside me. Tom had taken more from me than a few nights of sexual pleasure; he'd taken away my trust in my judgement. I told nobody about my humiliation. It would have been one pain too many.

Then Lindsay McConnell arrived. An award-winning dramatist, she'd come to give a series of workshops in radio adaptation. She was impeccably professional, no trouble to take care of. And we hit it off straight away. On her last night, I took her to my favourite Moscow eating place, a traditional Georgian restaurant tucked away in a courtyard in the Armenian quarter. As the wine slipped down, we gossiped and giggled. Then, in the course of some anecdote, she mentioned Tom Uttley. Just hearing his name made my guts clench. 'You know Tom?' I asked, struggling not to sound too interested.

'Oh God, yes, I was at university with Rachel, his wife. Of course, you had Tom out here last year, didn't you? He said he'd had a really interesting time.'

I bet he did, I thought bitterly. 'How are they now? Tom and Rachel?' I asked with the true masochist's desire for the twist of the knife.

Lindsay looked puzzled. 'What do you mean, how are they now?'

'When Tom was here, Rachel had just left him.'

She frowned. 'Are you sure you're not confusing him with someone else? They're solid as a rock, Tom and Rachel. God knows, if he were mine I'd have murdered him years ago, but Rachel thinks the sun shines out of his arse.'

It was my turn to frown. 'He told me she'd just walked out on him. He was really depressed about it.'

Lindsay shook her head. 'God, how very Tom. He hates touring, you know. He'll do anything to squeeze out a bit of sympathy, make sure he gets premier league treatment. He just likes to have everyone running around after him, Sarah. I'm telling you, Rachel has never left him. Now I think about it, that week he was in Russia, I went round there for dinner. Me and Rachel and a couple of colleagues. You know, from *Material Girl*, the magazine she works for. I think if they'd split up, she might have mentioned it, don't you?'

I hoped I wasn't looking as stunned as I felt. I'd never thought of myself as stupid, but that calculating bastard had spun me a line and reeled me in open-mouthed like the dumbest fish in the pond. But, of course, because I'm a woman and that's how we're trained to think, I was still blaming myself more than him. I'd clearly been sending out the signals of needy gullibility and he'd just come up with the right line to exploit them.

A few weeks later, I was still smarting from what I saw as my self-inflicted wounds at the Edinburgh Book Festival, where us British Council-types gather like bees to pollen. But at least I'd finally have the chance to share my idiocy with Camilla, my opposite number in Jerusalem. We'd worked together years before in Paris, and had become bosom buddies. The only reason I hadn't told her about Tom previously was that every time I wrote it down in an email, it just looked moronic. It needed a girls' night in with a couple of bottles of red wine before I could let this one spill out.

Late on the second night, after a gruelling Amnesty International event, we sneaked back to the flat we were sharing with a couple of boys from the Berlin office and started in on the confessional. My story crawled out of me; I realized yet again how foolish I'd been from the horrified expression on Camilla's face. That and her appalled silence. 'I don't believe it,' she breathed.

'I know, I know,' I groaned. 'How could I have been so stupid?'

'No, no,' she said angrily. 'Not you, Sarah. Tom Uttley.'

'What?'

'That duplicitous bastard Uttley. He pulled exactly the same stunt on Georgie Bullen in Madrid. The identical line about his wife leaving him. She told me about it when I flew in for Semana Negra last month.'

'But I thought Georgie was living with someone?'

'She was,' Camilla said. 'Paco, the stage manager at the opera house. She'd taken Uttley down to Granada to do some lectures there, that's when it happened. Georgie saw the scumbag off on the plane and came straight home and told Paco it was over, she'd met someone else. She threw him out, then two days later she got the killer email from Tom.'

'The bastard,' I said. For the first time, anger blotted out my self-pity and pain.

'Piece of shit,' Camilla agreed.

We spent the rest of the bottle and most of the second on thinking of ways to exact revenge on Tom Uttley, but we both knew that there was no way I was going back to Russia to find a hitman to take him out. The trouble was, we couldn't think of anything that would show him up without making us look silly, credulous girls. Most blokes, no matter how much they might pretend otherwise, would reckon good on him for working out such a foolproof scam to get his leg over. Most women would reckon we'd got what we deserved for being so naïve.

I was 30,000 feet above Poland when the answer came to me. The woman in the seat next to me had been reading *Material Girl* and she offered it to me when she'd finished. I looked down the editorial list, curious to see exactly what Rachel Uttley did on the magazine. Her name was near the top of the credits. *Fiction editor, Rachel Uttley*. A quick look at the contents helped me deduce that as well as the books page, Rachel was responsible for editing the three short stories. There, at the end of the third, was a sentence saying that submissions for publication should be sent to her.

I've always wanted to write. One of the reasons I took the job was to learn as much as I could from those who do it successfully. I've got half a novel on my hard disk, but I reckoned it was time to try a short story.

Two days later, I'd written it. The central character was a biographer who specialized in seducing professional colleagues on foreign trips with a tale about his wife having left him. Then he'd dump them as soon as he'd got home. When one of the victims realizes what he's been up to, she exposes the serial adulterer by sending his wife, a magazine editor, a short story revealing his exploits. And the wife, recognizing her errant husband from the pen portrait, finally does walk out on him.

Before I could have second thoughts, I printed it out and stuffed it in an envelope addressed to Rachel at *Material Girl*. Then I sat back and waited.

For a couple of weeks, nothing happened.

Then, one Tuesday morning, I was sitting in the office browsing BBC Online News. His name leapt out at me. '**Tom Uttley dies in burglary**', read the headline in the latest news section. I clicked on the <more> button.

Best-selling biographer and TV presenter Tom Uttley was found dead this morning at his home in north London. It is believed he disturbed a burglar. He died from a single stab wound to the stomach. Police say there was evidence of a break-in at the rear of the house. Uttley was discovered by his wife, Rachel, a journalist. Police are calling for witnesses who may have seen one or two men fleeing the scene in the early hours of the morning.

I had to read the bare words three or four times before they sank in. Suddenly, his lies didn't matter any more. All I could think of was his eyes on mine, the flash of his easy smile, the touch of his hand. The sparkle of wit in his conversation. The life in him that had been snuffed out. The books he would never write.

Over a succession of numb days, I pursued the story via the internet. Bits and pieces emerged gradually. They'd had an attempted burglary a few months before. That night, Rachel had gone off to bed, but Tom had stayed up late, working in his study. Tom, the police reckoned, had heard the sound of breaking glass and gone downstairs to investigate. The intruder had snatched up a knife from the kitchen worktop and plunged it into his stomach, then fled. Tom had bled to death on the kitchen floor. It had taken him a while to die, they thought. And Rachel had come down for breakfast to find him stiff and cold on the kitchen floor. Poor bloody Rachel, I thought.

On the fifth day after the news broke, there was a large manila envelope in my post, franked with the *Material Girl* logo. My story had come winging its way back to me. Inside, there was a handwritten note from Rachel.

Dear Sarah, Thank you so much for your submission. I found your story intriguing and thought-provoking. A real eye-opener, in fact. But I felt the ending was rather weak and so I regret we're unable to publish it. However, I like your style. I'd be very interested to see more of your work. Gratefully yours, Rachel Uttley.

That's when I realized what I'd done. Like Oscar Wilde, I'd killed the thing I loved. And Rachel had made sure I knew it.

That's when my sleepless nights started.

And that's why I'm so very, very grateful for Roger and the case they call Wagon Mound (No. 1). And for an understanding of proximity. Thanks to him, I've finally realized I'm not the guilty party here. Neither is Rachel.

The guilty party is the one who started the wagon rolling. Lovely, sexy, reckless Tom Uttley.

The Clean Slate

About 11 o'clock this morning – after the nurses had tidied her up, as they put it, and she'd fixed her eye make-up – I sat down by my mother's bed and coaxed her to do the family tree with me. Considering how self-centred she is, it worked out surprisingly well. She would like to write VERONICA in the centre of the paper and strike lines of force running outwards from herself. But, although she thinks this would give you an accurate picture of the world, she does have a grasp on how these things are done. She has seen the genealogy of the kings and queens of England, their spurious portraits glowing by their names, stamp-sized and in stained-glass colours: their plaits of flaxen hair, their crude medieval crowns with gems like sucked sweets.

She has seen these in the books she pretends to read. So she understands that you can also do a family tree for us, the poor bloody infantry. The pictures by the names will be equally spurious. A woman once told me that there was no family so poor, when the nineteenth century ended, that they didn't have their photographs taken. It might be true. In that case, somebody burned ours.

I began this enterprise because I wanted to find out something about my ancestors who lived in the drowned village. I thought it might provide a reason for my fear of water – one I could use to make people feel bad when they advise me that swimming is good exercise for a person of my age. Then again, I thought it might be a topic I could turn into cash. I could go to Dunwich, I thought, and write about a village that slipped into the sea. Or to Norfolk, to talk to people who have mortgaged houses on the edge of cliffs. I could work it up into a feature for the Sunday press. They could send a photographer, and we could balance on the cliff-edge at Overstrand, just one rusting wire between us and infinite blue light.

But Veronica was not interested in the submerged. She twitched at the ribbons at her bosom – still firm, by the way – and eased herself irritably against the pillows. The veins in her hands stood out: as if she had sapphires, and wore them beneath the skin. She hardly listened to my questions, and said in a huffy way, 'I really can't tell you much about all that, I'm afraid.'

The people from the drowned village were on her father's side of the family, and were English. Veronica was interested in matriarchies, in Irish matriarchies, and in reliving great moments in the lives of matriarchies by repeating the same old stories: the jokes that have lost their punchlines, the retorts and witty snubs that have come unfastened from their origins. Perhaps I shouldn't blame her, but I do. I distrust anecdote. I like to understand history through figures and percentages of these figures, through knowing the price of coal and the price of corn, and the price of a loaf on the day the Bastille fell. I like to be free, so far as I can, from the tyranny of interpretation.

The village of Derwent began to sink beneath the water in the winter of 1943. This was years before I was born. The young Veronica was no doubt forming up thoughts of what children she would have, and how she would make them turn out. She had white skin and green eyes and dyed her hair red with patent formulations. It didn't really matter what man she married – he was only a vehicle for her dynastic ambitions.

Veronica's mother – my maternal grandmother – was called Agnes. She came from a family of twelve. Don't worry, I won't give you a run on each of them; I couldn't, if I wanted to. When I ask Veronica to help me fill in the gaps, she obliges with some story that relates to herself, and then hints – if I try to bring her back to the subject – that there are some things best left unsaid. There was more to that episode than was ever divulged, she would say. I did find out a few facts, none of them cheerful. That one brother went to prison for theft committed by another. That one sister had a child who died unchristened within minutes of birth. She was a daughter whose existence flickered briefly somewhere between the wars; she has no name, and her younger brother to this very day does not know of her existence. Not really a person: more a trick of the light.

The village of Derwent didn't die of an accident, but of a policy. Water was needed by the urban populations of Manchester, Sheffield, Nottingham and Leicester. And so in 1935 they began to build a dam across the river Derwent. Ladybower was the dam's name.

When Derwent was flooded it was already flattened, already deserted. But when I was a child I did not know this. I understood that the people themselves had left before the flood, but I imagined them going about their daily work until the last possible moment: listening out for a warning, something like an air-raid siren, and then immediately dropping whatever it was they were doing. I saw them shrugging into their stout woollen coats, buttoning in the children, tickling smiling chins and picking up small suitcases and brown paper parcels, trudging with resigned Derbyshire faces to meeting points on the street corner. I saw them laying down their knitting in mid-stitch, throwing a pea pod half shelled into the colander; folding away the morning paper with a phrase half-read, an ellipsis that would last their lifetime.

'Leicester, did you say?' Veronica beamed at me. 'Your Uncle Finbar was last seen in Leicester. He had a market stall.'

I shuffled my hospital armchair forward, across the BUPA-contract carpet. 'Your uncle,' I said. 'That's my great-uncle.'

'Yes.' She can't think why I quibble: what's hers is mine.

'What was he selling?'

'Old clothes.' Veronica chuckled knowingly. 'So it was said.'

I didn't rise to her bait. All I want from her is some dates. She likes to make mysteries and imply she has secret knowledge. She won't say which year she was born and has told a blatant lie about her age to the admissions people, which could, of course, jeopardize her insurance claim. Also, I am conjoined to the same insurance scheme, and they might begin to wonder about me if they ever compare files and see that, by their records, my mother is only ten years older than me.

A man once told me that you can date women by looking at the backs of their knees. That delta of soft flesh and broken veins, he swore, is the only thing that cannot lie.

'They were a wild lot,' Veronica said. 'Your uncles. They were,' she said, 'you must remember, Irishmen.'

No they weren't. Irish, yes, I concede. But not wild, not nearly wild enough. They drank when they had money and prayed when they had none. They worked in the steamy heat of mills and when they knocked off shift and stepped outside, the cold gnawed through their clothes and cracked their bones like crazed china. You'd have thought they would have bred, but they didn't. Some had no children at all, others just one. These only children were precious, wouldn't you think? But one failed to marry, and another spent much of his life in an asylum.

So far, so good: what sort of family do you expect me to come from? All singing, all-dancing? You'd just know they'd be tubercular, probably syphilitic, certifiably insane, dyslexic, paralytic, circumcised, circumscribed, victims of bad pickers in identity parades, mangled in industrial machinery, decapitated by fork-lift trucks, dental cripples, sodomites, sent blind by measles, riddled with asbestosis and domiciled downwind of Chernobyl. I assume you've read my new novel, *The Clean Slate*. I was working on the first draft at the time I decided to tackle Veronica. I had the theory that our family was bent on erasing itself, through divorce, elective celibacy and a series of gynaecological catastrophes. 'But I had children,' Veronica said, bewildered. 'I had you, didn't I?' Yes, Miss Bedjacket, you bet you did.

*   *   *

Probably the one thing you couldn't guess would be that I come from the drowned village. As a child, I could hardly realize it myself. There is such a thing as portent-overload. Of course, I had the whole thing wrong. I misunderstood, and was prone to believe any rubbish people put my way.

Suppose that in Pompeii they had been given an alert: time, but not much of it. They would have left what – their oil-jars, their weaving shuttles, their vessels of wine, dashed and dripping? I can't really picture it. I have never been to Italy. Suppose they had taken the warning and cleared out. That was how I thought Derwent would be: a Pompeii, a *Mary Celeste*. I thought that the waters would rise, at first inch by inch, and creep under each closed door. And then swill about, aimless for a while, contained by linoleum. The first thing to go would be the little striped mats that people dotted about in those days. They were cheap things that would go sodden quickly. Beneath the lino would be stone flags. They would hold the water, like some denying stepmother, in a chilly embrace: it would be the work of a generation, to wear them down . . .

And so, thwarted, the water rises, like daughters or peasants long denied, and plunges hungry fingers into the cupboards where the sugar and the flour is kept. The colander, resting on the stone sink, goes floating, the water recirculating through its holes. The half-attended pea pods bob, and egg cups, pans and chamber pots join the flotilla, as the water rises to the windowsills. A street's worth of tea brews itself. Cakes of soap whirl twelve feet in the air, as if God were taking his Saturday soak. Gabbling like gossips on a picnic, the water surges, each hour higher by a foot, riser by riser creeping up the stairs and washing about the private items of Derbyshire persons, about their crisply ironed bloomers floating free of lavender presses, the lapping of wavelets hemming their plain knee-bands with lace. The flannel bedsheets are soaked, and the woollen blankets press on the mattresses like the weight of sodden sin, until the mad gaiety of the waters takes them over and buoys them up in the finest easy style. The beds go sailing, tub chairs are coracles; the yellowed long johns with their attached vests wave arms and legs, cut free from conjugal arrangements, and swim like Captain Webb for liberty and France.

This was what I imagined. I thought some up-river valve was eased, and the flood began.

But in fact, the Ladybower dam was down-valley from Derwent village. There was no flood. Derwent died by drips. The rain fell and was bottled. The streams flowed and were contained. Ladybower closed her downstream valves and gradually the valley filled, in the course of nature, from the hillside streams and the precipitation of Pennine cloudbursts. It filled slowly: as tears, if you cried enough, would fill a bowl.

Veronica is old now. She does and does not under-stand this. She could always entertain what they call 'discontinuities'. That is to say, slippages in time or sense, breaches between cause and effect. She can also entertain big fat sweating lies, usually told either to mystify people or make her look good. I cannot tell you how many times she has misled me.

I take the map of the Derwent valley to the light. I look back at her in bed. I am sorry to say it – I wish I could say something else – but the plan of the reservoirs looks very like a diagrammatic representation of the female reproductive tract. Not a detailed one: just the kind you might give to medical students in their first year, or children who persist in enquiring. One ovary is the Derwent reservoir, the other is Hogg Farm. This second branch descends by the school and the church, through the drowned village of Ashopton to the neck of the womb itself, at Ladybower House and Ladybower Wood; from there, to the Yorkshire Bridge weir, and the great world beyond.

What I know now is this: they demolished the village before they flooded it. Stone by stone it was smashed. They waited until the vicar had died before they knocked down the vicarage. I think of Derwent Hall and the shallow river that ran beside it, the packhorse bridge and the bridle path. They knocked down the hall and sold what they could. The drawing-room oak floorboards went for £40. The oak panelling was sold at two shillings and sixpence per square foot.

The village of Derwent had a church, St James and St John. There was a silver patten and an ancient font, which the heathens at the hall had once used as a flowerpot. There was a sundial, and four bells, and 284 bodies buried in the churchyard. Nowhere could be found to take in these homeless bones, and the Water Board decided to bury them on land of its own. But the owner of the single house in the neighbourhood raised such objections that the project was called off. It seemed they would have to go under the water, the dead men of Derwent.

But the churchyard at Bamford offered to house them, at the last push. They were exhumed one by one and their condition recorded – complete skeleton – together with the nature of the subsoil, the state of the coffin and the depth at which they were found. The

Water Board paid £500 and it was all settled up. A bishop said prayers.

Through 1944 the water rose steadily. By June 1945, only a pair of stone gateposts and the spire of the church could be seen.

When I was a child, people would tell me AS A FACT that in hot summers, the church spire would rise above the waters, eerie and desolate under the burning sun.

This is also untrue.

The church tower was blown up, in 1947. I have a photograph of it, blasted, crumbling, in the very act of joining the ruins below. But even if I showed this to Veronica, she wouldn't believe me. She'd only say I was persecuting her. She doesn't care for evidence, she seems to say. She has her own versions of the past, and her own way of protecting them.

Sometimes, to pass her time, Veronica knits something. I say something because I'm not sure if it has a future as a garment, or if she'll be wearing it anywhere out of here. She has a way of working her elbows that points her needles straight at me. When the nurse comes in she drops her weapons in the fold of the sheets and smiles, nicey-nice.

Every Saturday night, in the village where Veronica grew up, the English fought the Irish, at a specified street, called Waterside. As a child, I used to play on this desolate spot. Bulrushes, reeds, swamps. (Be home for half past seven, Veronica always said.) I expect they were not serious fights. More like minuets with broken bottles. After all, next Saturday night they would have to do it all over again.

No, it was the Derbyshire people who were the wild bunch, in my opinion. Two brothers used to go around

223

the pubs and advertise each other: my brother here will fight, run, leap, play cricket or sing, against any man in this county. The cricketer destroyed his career by felling the umpire with a blow in his only first-class match. Another brother, making his way home by moonlight, manslaughtered a person, tossed him over a wall and took ship for America. Another walked the bridle path from Glossop to Derwent in the company of a man who described himself as a doctor, but was later discovered to be an escaped and homicidal lunatic.

I like to imagine cross-connections. Perhaps this 'doctor' was my psychotic Irish relative, whom I mention above. I tried to run my theory past Veronica, and see if the dates fitted at all. She said she knew nothing about the bridle path, nothing about a lunatic. I was about to take her up on it when a nurse put her head around the door and said: 'The doctor's here.' I had to stand in the corridor. 'Coffee?' some moron said, gesturing to two inches of sludge on a warm plate. I just ignored the question. I put my head on the clear, clean plaster of the wall, which was painted in a neutral shade, like thought.

After a time, a doctor came out and stood by my elbow. He did a big act of ahem to attract my attention, and when I continued to rest my head on the restful plaster, he percussed my shoulder until I looked around. He was smaller than me, in fact, and trying to impart news of some sort, almost certainly bad. As I write, the average height of an Englishwoman is a hair's-breadth below 5ft 5in. I barely scrape 5ft 3in, and yet I tower over Veronica. A tear stings my eye. *So small*. Within the space of a breath, I witness myself: tear is processed, ticked and shed.

*   *   *

The Ladybower Reservoir has a surface area of 504 acres. Its perimeter is 13 miles approximately. Its maximum depth is 135 feet. One hundred thousand tons of concrete were used in its building, and one million tons of earth. I am suspicious of these round figures, as I am sure you are. But can I offer them to you, as a basis for discussion? When people talk of 'burying the past', and 'all water under the bridge', these are the kind of figures they are trading in.

Edna O'Brien made her literary debut in 1960 with *The Country Girls*, and since then has written fifteen books. Her most recent novel is *In the Forest*.

Forbidden

In the dreams, there is always a kidney-shaped enamel spittoon, milk white, and a gleaming metal razor such as old-fashioned barbers. My mother's hand is on the blade, and then her face comes into view, swimming as it were towards me, pale, pear-shaped, about to mete out her punishment, to cut my throat. Then, with a glidingness that eludes me, the dream is over and I wake shaking, having escaped death not for the first time. In dream my mother and I are enemies, whereas in life we were so attached we could almost be called lovers. Yes, lovers insofar as I believed that the universe resided in her being. She was the hub of the house: the rooms took on a life when she was in them and a death when she was absent. She was real mother and archetypal mother. Her fingers and nails smelt of food, meal for hens and chickens, gruel for the calves, and bread for us, whereas her body smelt of drifting things, depending on whether she was happy or unhappy, but the most pleasant was a lingering smell of perfume from the cotton wad that she sometimes tucked under her brassiere. At Christmas time it was a smell of fruitcake soaked with grog and the sugary smell of white icing, stiff as starch, which she applied with the rapture of an artist.

Anything that had mystery attached to it was inevitably transposed on to her. For instance, when in the classroom one learnt that our vast choppy lakes have the remains of cities buried beneath them, it seemed that in her, too, there were buried worlds. At mass when the priest turned the key of the gold-crested tabernacle door, I had the profane thought that he was turning the key in her chest. As if reading my mind, she would pass her prayer book for me to read, solemn words in Latin, which neither of us understood. Her holiness seeped into me along with her nightly ejaculations and her scalding sense of self-sacrifice. We lived for a time in such symbiosis that there might never have been a husband or other children, except that there were. We all sat at the same fire, ate the same food, and when a gift of a box of chocolates arrived, we looked with longing at the picture on the back, choosing in our minds the flavour we preferred. That box might not be opened for a year. Life was frugal. It was on a farm in Ireland, the harvest and hay subject to the hazards of rain, and always hovering over her and instilled into us, was the spectre of debt. Yet there were touches of grandeur, three silver cloches stationed along the sideboard, and mirrors with cupids kissing and cuddling. In drawers upstairs were folds of silk from the time when she worked, long before, in the silk department of a store in Brooklyn, the name of which ranked second only to Heaven. On Sundays, for mass, she would hurriedly don her good clothes that had been acquired in those times, or clothes sent by relatives, voile dresses cut on the bias, which curved over the stomach. I would beg her to re-don them in the evening so that we could go for a walk and, in summer, to enjoy the evening intoxication of stock in other people's gardens. We did not have a garden; we had ploughed fields and meadows. Somehow I thought that a garden would be a prelude to happiness. The only flowers I had occasion to study were those painted on china cups and plates, splotches of gentian in cavities of moss, and, on the wallpaper, rosebuds so compact, so life-like, one felt that one could pluck them off.

Those walks bordered on enchantment, what with the notion that we might walk out of our old sad existence and the certainty that in the eyes of neighbours she was beautiful. She had beautiful hair, brown with bronzed glimmers in it, and blue, blue eyes that held within them an infinite capacity for stricture. To chastise one she did not have to speak, her eyes did it with a piercing gaze. But when she approved of something everything seemed to soften and the stream of bluish light was like stained glass melting. On those walks she invariably spoke of visitors who were bound to come in the summer and the dainty dishes she would prepare for them. There was a host of recipes she had not yet tried. Sometimes her shoes hurt and we had to sit on a wall while she rolled down her stockings and mashed and massaged her poor reddened toes. Once, a man we scarcely knew, came and sat down beside us. He wore a torn flannel shirt and sang a questionable song.

She laughed afterwards and said he was a yahoo. I often think she would have liked a city life, a pampered life where she could wear those good clothes and her court shoes that glittered like filigree. With a buckle of diamante. Yet at heart she was a countrywoman, and as she got older, the fields, the bog, her dogs and her fowl became more important to her, were her companions once I had left. I had always promised not to leave. I promised it aloud to her and alone to myself as I looked at the silver cloches on the sideboard and the about-to-burst rosebuds on the wallpaper. Our house had quarrels in it, quarrels about money, about drinking, about recklessness, but, not content with real fear, she also had to summon up the unknown and the supernatural. A frog jumped into the fire one night and she believed it was the augury for a sudden and accidental death, all the more so because when she cleaned out the ashes the next morning there was no trace of a frog, not even a charred skeleton. Likewise a panel of coloured glass above a vestibule door broke again and again and she insisted that it was not wind or storm, but a message from the world beyond. One evening, sitting in the kitchen in some dreaded suspense, she conceived the thought that a man, a stranger, had come and was standing outside the window preparing to shoot us. We moved to the side of the window and sat side by side on two kitchen chairs, barely breathing, waiting for our executioner. We sat there until morning when the phobia was replaced by a real one, her husband, home from some all-night card game, still half drunk and vexed at having to return to us, vented his rage. She and I were mendicants together, cooking, making beds, folding sheets, doing all the normal things in the so-called normal times and in the opposite times cowering out of doors, under trees, our teeth chattering in a mad musical duet. We were inseparable.

I cannot remember when exactly the first moment of the breach came. There were tiffs with her over food that I refused to eat and questions about nonsensical slides that I put in my hair. I began to write – jottings that had to be covert because she would see in them a sort of wanderlust. She insisted that literature was a precursor to sin and damnation, whereas I believed it was the only alchemy there is. I would read and I would write and she, the matrix of what I was writing, had to be banished, just as in a fairy tale. One day she lost her temper completely when I read aloud to her a quotation of Voltaire's which I had copied – 'Illusion is the source of all happiness'. She looked at me as if I was the next candidate for the lunatic asylum twenty miles away. Many had gone there, and we had seen them go, dragged by their relatives, fighting and shouting to be let out of a car or else sitting in a state of numbness.

'Illusion!' she said, and went on with her task. She was pounding very yellow oatmeal mixed with boiling water and the vehemence with which she did it was so great she might have been pounding me. From literature to worse wickedness. Those passions, those liaisons that were in novels, that were in Tolstoy, the recklessness of a Natasha willing to elope through a window, was the life I now craved. She sensed the impulse in me the way a truffle hound sniffs the fawn spores buried beneath. She searched my eyes, she searched my clothing, she searched my suitcase when, as a student, I returned home from Dublin. The few books I had brought with me she deemed foul and degenerate. The battle was on, but we skirted around it. I wrote and she silently seethed. She would tell me what others – neighbours – thought of what I really wrote, tears in her voice at my criminality.

Flings, youthful love affairs, were out of the question. I eloped with a man I had known for only six weeks. Though hating him by merely seeing a photograph of him, she nevertheless insisted on my marrying him to give the seal of respectability to things, and there followed a bleak ceremony, which she did not attend. With uncanny clairvoyance she predicted the year, the day, even the hour of its demise. Ten years and two children later when it happened she wrote her ultimatum. It was sent poste restante and I read it in a street in London. She enjoined me to kneel down on the very spot as I was reading and vow to have nothing to do with any man in body or soul as long as I lived, adding that I owed it to God, to her and to my children. She lamented the fact of my being young and therefore still in the way of temptation. She reclaimed me. Then came years and years of correspondence from her. She who professed disgust at the written word wrote daily, bulletins that ranged from the pleading to the poetic, to the philosophic and the apocalyptic. I never fully read them, being afraid of some greater accusation, and my replies were little niceties, squeezed in with bribes and money to stave off confrontation.

Yet there was something that I wanted to ask her about in some inexplicable way. I sensed the ghost inside her. An infant before me had been born prematurely and had died, and I believed it was caused by some drastic measure. Why else was its name never uttered, prayers for it never said and never did we visit the grave where even the four letters of its name were not inscribed on the tombstone underneath that of distant forebears. She had not wanted another child. Three children and waning finances were hardship enough and by being born two years later I had in some way usurped her will.

For twenty-odd years I had postponed opening the bundle of letters, which lay in a mildewed leather trunk, silent enjoinders that I often meant to destroy. Then one day, deluding myself into the belief that I needed, to revisit rooms and haunts that had passed into other hands, I lifted the little bronze latch. It was like being plunged into the molten seas of memory. Her letters were deeper, sadder than I had remembered, but what struck me most was their hunger and their thirst. Here was a woman desperately trying to explain herself and to retie the cord that had been summarily cut. There were hundreds of them or maybe a thousand. They came two, three a week, always with an apology for not having written in the intervening days. I read them and stowed them away. She would wonder whether I was at home or away, wonder how soon we would meet again, wonder what new clothes I had got, or if any piece of furniture in my house had been moved about. She would reiterate that it was hard work to earn a living in the event of attraction or distraction. She would swear to cross the sea to England even if she had to walk it and strenuously I postponed those visits. She would send things from her linen press and the letter which preceded the parcel went like this: 'I sent you yesterday 18 large doyleys, 18 small ones and 4 centre ones, I didn't get to wash and starch as it takes so long to iron them properly, when starched.' The next letter or the one following would be about toil – she had drawn a hundred buckets of water and sprayed the entire avenue with weedkiller to kill off the weeds and the nettles. One Sunday she had gone for a walk, further than she had ever gone before. It was a scorching day, as she said, and she felt a strange kind of energy, exhilaration as when she was young.

Up there on the slopes of the mountain there were ripe blackberries, masses of them on the briars, and not wishing to have them rot she began to pick them to make blackberry jelly. Without basket or can she had to remove her slip and put the blackberries inside it, where they shed some of their purple juices. Her letter kept wishing that she could hand me a pot of clear jelly over a hedge and see me taste and swallow it.

I had no intention of going back to buy a house or a plot of land, but nevertheless she had her eye out for holdings that might suit me. One was called Gore House, named after an English landlord, long since dead. She said it was a pity I had not bought it instead of the German who not only never set foot in it, but had bought it when he saw it from the air, travelling in his private jet. Continentals loved the place and therefore why not I.

The letters about her dogs were the most wrenching. She always had two dogs, sheepdogs, who sparred and growled at one another throughout the day, apart from when they were off hunting rabbits, but who at night slept more or less in each other's embrace, like big honey-coloured bears. They had a habit of following cars in the avenue, and one, either one, got killed, while the other grieved and mourned, refused food, even refused meat as she said, kept listening to the sounds of dogs barking in the distance and in a short time died and was buried with its comrade. She would swear never to get another pair of dogs but yet in a matter of months she was writing off to a breeder several counties away and two puppies in a cardboard box with a nest of dank straw would arrive by bus and presently be given the same two names – Laddie and Rover. She gloried in describing how mischievous they were, the things they ate, pranks they were up to. She looked out one May morning and thought it was snowing, but when she went outdoors she found that they had bitten the sheets off the clothes line, chewed

236

them into small pieces and spat them out. Her life got increasingly hard, there were frosts, floods and heating oil got costlier each year while the price of cattle went rock bottom. People were killing their own beef but, as she said, for that, one needed a deep freezer, which she did not have. A mare that my father loved and had despatched to a trainer was expected to come first in a big race, but merely came third and the difference in the booty was that of a few pounds as opposed to several hundred pounds. Then there was the tip to the jockey. The mare, as she said, could have come first, but that she was temperamental, could be last in a race, then out of the blue, pass them all or purposely not. Not having the means, she nevertheless lived for a day when she could afford to get me a chandelier and to have it so carefully wrapped that not a single crystal would get broken.

As she got older she admitted to being tired and sometimes the letters were in different inks where she had stopped writing or maybe fallen asleep. Death was now a big factor, the big question mark that could not be answered. She was bewildered. She began to have doubts about her faith. One morning for a moment she went blind and from that day onwards she hated night and hated dark and said she lay awake fearing that dawn would never come. Life, she maintained, was one big battle, because no matter who wins, nobody does. She began, as things grew darker, to forgive implicitly my transgressions, whatever they might have been.

I was going to America and she asked me to track down a gentleman at an address in Brooklyn. He must have been a sweetheart. She had written to him the previous summer at an address which someone had given her, but the letter had been returned after many months and much handling. She believed that it had been opened and read. It was like finding a phantom room in a house I thought I knew. I remembered something that as a child I had squirmed at overhearing. We were in the hire car, my mother, a newly married woman called Lydia and myself, waiting outside a hospital for a coffin to be brought out to the hearse. My father and the driver had gone inside. Lydia chain-smoked, laughed a lot and was overfriendly. Normally guarded with neighbours, my mother began to tell this stranger of her adventures in Brooklyn, the style she had, the dances she went to, the men she met. Pressed on that point she said that yes, there was one in particular, dark, handsome and with a beautiful reserve. He had been such a gentleman, had given her little gifts and on their Sunday outings had seen her back home to her digs and shook her hand on the doorstep. Yet one night, passing a house of ill repute with its red lights and its tasselled curtains, he had nudged her and said that maybe they should go in there and see what went on. She did not say if the friendship had been broken off abruptly, but what was clear, by a little shiver in her body in which desire and disgust overlapped, was that she had probably loved him and would have gone through that forbidden door with him.

She was taken ill at home and brought to a hospital in the city, hundreds of miles away and like many another in the time of reckoning, she decided that she wished to change her will. She wished to give me her house. Her son, fearing that he was about to be disinherited, came in high dudgeon and they quarrelled in the hospital hall. She had some sort of fit there and was brought back to bed, her mind rambling. Late in the evening she began her last letter – 'My hand is shaking now as well as myself with what I have to say.'

It remains unfinished and so I wait for that dream that leads us from the inner room and that ghastly white spittoon, up to the mountain, that bluish distance, half earth, half sky, towards her dark man and the zest of her youthful ways.

Imogen Parker has published six novels with Black Swan. She lives on the south coast with her husband and eight-year-old son.

Not the End of the World

War has started and we are on our way to Eden. There are bombs raining down on dusty cities far away, and it feels almost banal to be walking up and down a coach aisle in bright, white, morning sunshine, making sure the children have their seat belts on.

'No, Shane, it's not the same if you just hold it . . .'

'Are we nearly there, Miss?'

'We haven't left the school car park yet.'

'Miss, how many minutes will it take to get there?'

'About two hours. How many minutes is that?'

'Two, Miss?'

'Anyone else got any ideas?'

A chorus of voices. 'Three, Miss? Fifty, Miss? A centrillion, Miss?'

Where did this centrillion stuff come from? When I was at school the biggest number known to man was a trillion, and no one really believed that existed. A billion, yes. That was a proper word. You heard it occasionally on the news.

'Well, there are sixty minutes in an hour . . . Two times sixty is . . . ?'

'Twelve, Miss.'

'Almost right, Alice.'

'Thirteen, Miss?'

'The answer is one hundred and twenty minutes.'

Several troubled faces who'd been earnestly trying to get their head around the mental arithmetic smile at me.

'I thought so, Miss.'

'Miss?'

'Yes, Jack.'

'How many seconds?'

Is it the fact that I drank a bottle of Frascati by myself last night, or because we're in an even more confined space than usual, that the frequency and shrillness of the Miss quotient seem higher today.

I hate the prefix 'Miss'. It makes me think of Miss Take, Miss Demeanour, Miss Anthropy and, particularly, Miss Thomas, who is sitting at the front of the coach with her class a noiseless, seated crocodile behind her.

'We're not going until you sit down, Shane,' I warn ineffectually as the coach driver, who smells like an ashtray, chooses this moment to lurch off. The engine is as loud as a generator on a building site.

'Sit down, Shane!' I summon my extremely un-amused look. Normally I save it for later in the day, but now I've deployed the ultimate weapon in my disciplinary arsenal and it's only just gone nine o'clock in the morning. I toy with the idea of keeping my extremely unamused face on all day. But we're going to Eden. We are going to understand and celebrate the world we live in – that's what it says in the guidebook – so we might as well enjoy it. While we can.

'Shane, sit down this minute!'

Miss Thomas has spoken and he obeys.

Miss Thomas is a real Miss. She commands respect as proper Misses should. I might as well just let the children call me Lydia. I probably would if I thought they would stick to it and not come up with some dirty rhyme after five minutes. We did rhymes last week. Miss Thomas's class wrote little verses about cats and mats and dogs and frogs. I tried to liven it up with a few limericks with the children's names in.

'Bit of a Pandora's box, limericks,' said the headmaster, after the second parental complaint.

'Miss?'

'Yes, Shane.'

'You smell funny, Miss.'

Frascati, sour cream and onion Pringles, Eternity and Listerine. Even though I ate a whole packet of Tic Tac mints on the way to school, my mouth still has that not-enough-sleep sourness in it.

'Out on the piss!' Shane informs Alice, knowledgeably.

Miss Thomas sits stiffly in her seat like someone who's afraid of flying – and who isn't nowadays? – but this is a bus. I know she's itching to lecture me on the wisdom of seating a naughty boy next to a nice girl, but she daren't in front of the parent helpers.

'My mum sometimes smells like you, Miss,' Alice confides reassuringly.

I wonder if there's some trouble at home that makes Alice's mum drink, or maybe she was up late last night like me. Perhaps there are millions of us dotted over the sofas of England when bad news is breaking. Perhaps we all find ourselves at two in the morning with the strange sensation that we've seen the same footage of a cruise missile taking off from the same boat many times, and wondering where the Frascati, the Pringles and the last three hours have gone.

*   *   *

245

'You won't be any wiser watching it on TV,' Andy says.

'It may be the end of the world and I want to feel I'm there.'

'Well, wake me up in the event of a nuclear attack. I've got an important meeting in the morning.'

'I've got to take a coachload of six-year-olds to the Eden Project.'

Beat that on the stress ladder.

I fall asleep eventually, and wake with a cricked neck and a thigh that's got pins and needles because the sofa's too narrow to stretch out on. I drag myself into the kitchen where Andy's eating a large bowl of Sugar Puffs. The distinctive sweet smell of puffed wheat makes me nostalgic for the innocence of childhood breakfast times, almost weepy.

Andy's listening to Radio 4 and now knows more about the war than I do.

I have a vague memory of John Simpson against a backdrop of anti-aircraft fire popping in some foreign sky, speaking in his weary, nothing-new-to-me voice just slightly out of sync with the pictures. Ever since we were told that he was smuggled into Afghanistan wearing a burka, I haven't been able to absorb what he is saying because I'm concentrating so hard on trying to picture him in it. Why didn't his feet give him away? Was the garment black, or that incongruously pretty lavender shade the women of Afghanistan seem to wear?

There are articles in the broadsheets about the death of trivia, but my brain seems incapable of processing anything else at the moment. When I see the woman journalist who's with the Northern Alliance, I wonder how many changes of clothes she's brought and whether she has a rucksack or one of those little pull-along suitcases like an air hostess. I watch the telethon of American celebs, preoccupied by what I would say to Jack Nicholson if he were to answer my pledge. Here's ten quid, Mr Nicholson, and can I just say I thought you were really great in *The Shining*, but my absolute favourite is *Terms of Endearment* . . .

Andy says that I should be crisis correspondent for *Hello!* magazine.

Why was it that my first thought when I saw the news on September 11th was: Does this mean that we'll have to cancel the wedding?

'Miss?'

'Yes, Jack.'

'Are we still in England?'

It's an unseasonally beautiful day. The fields of Dartmoor are green and pleasant. We have each taken our designated group of children to the toilet without major incident. Momentarily, it seems like all's right with the world.

'Yes, we are.'

'Is Afghanistan in England, Miss?'

'No, Jack. It's a long way away. Now, who can tell me something about Eden?'

'It's got apples, Miss.'

'And there's this snake, Miss.'

'You're not allowed to eat the fruit, Miss.' Emma clearly goes to Sunday School.

'Yes, well, that's the Garden of Eden. That's in the Bible. The place we're going today is named after that, and it's also a type of garden—'

'Miss?'

'Yes, Alice.'

'My mum put an apple in with my lunch.'

Suddenly half the class are brandishing apples like

247

miniature eco warriors demanding their right to eat fruit. Only last week we were learning that we must eat our five portions a day.

'You can eat your apples. It's just that Adam and Eve weren't allowed to eat theirs.'

'Who's Adam and Eve?'

'Can anyone tell Jack who Adam and Eve were?'

'The first people invented,' says Shane.

Panic. They're going to ask me why it was wrong for Adam and Eve to eat the fruit, and either I've forgotten or I've never known. I can't really ask Miss Thomas or the parent helpers. Andy would know the answer, but it's too late now to ring him from the loos on my mobile.

Andy's brain stores proper facts as effortlessly as mine stores the ridiculous names the stars give their children. We are a virtually unbeatable pub quiz team.

Andy and the Lovely Lydia.

That's what we call ourselves. My idea. I'm not really lovely. In fact, I'm quite plain. I'm the sort of person of whom people say, 'She has a nice smile,' but that is what the pub quizmaster called us on the occasion of our first victory, which was also the first time we met. It stuck, and so did we.

'The Eden Project,' I say, kneeling up against the back of my seat, 'is like the whole world in a great big greenhouse.'

'You haven't got your seat belt on, Miss.'

'No, we're still in the service station, so I don't think I'll come to much harm, thank you, Shane.'

The coach driver has so recently extinguished his cigarette that a puff of smoke comes out of his mouth when he grunts, 'Ready?' and closes the coach doors with a sigh of compressed air.

'The Eden Project,' says Miss Thomas, 'is about man's relationship with plants.'

In the seat behind us, Alice informs Shane, 'My dad's having another relationship.'

'My mum has loads of relationships,' Shane tells her, as if they're talking about lipsticks or shoes.

I suddenly remember the dream I had last night as I lay with my face stuffed against the sofa and that cruise missile taking off again and again on the telly screen. I dreamt that at my last fitting my wedding dress had turned into a cake. A great white stiff wedding cake with lots of tiers, and, frankly, it looked rather wonderful, like something by Hussein Chalayan, but was incredibly heavy and restrictive, and as I started to sweat the icing on the tier beneath my armpits melted. I woke with a big wet patch next to my face where I had dribbled on one of Andy's scatter cushions. I think it's a washable cover.

The countryside surrounding the Eden Project is disappointingly nondescript and barren. My mind tries to grasp at reasons why it was a good idea to come in case Miss Thomas says something acid, or the parent helpers start exchanging looks, but then we get our first glimpse of the biomes, rising like giant glassy mushrooms that have sprung up overnight in a great inhospitable hole in the ground. Unexpected and beautiful, exceeding all our expectations. The dull throb of non-specific anxiety disappears from my head as the children shriek and bounce in their seats.

'Miss . . . they're like spaceships . . . they're like mega soap bubbles . . . Miss, they're like alien frog-spawn . . .'

Silk banners in natural earthy colours, ochre and rust and plum, flap gently on flagpoles that line the zig-zag path down to the entrance. They make me feel as if we are on our way to some wonderful outdoor production of *A Midsummer Night's Dream*.

'Almost theatrical,' I venture, trying to sound intelligent and grown-up, to Miss Thomas, who's walking beside me.

'Is it?'

For a moment, her expression reminds me of someone, and I realize with dismay that it's Andy. Andy is never tentative. Andy's opinions come well formed out of his mouth. He knows exactly what he thinks, for instance, about the morality of bombing Afghanistan.

'Can anyone read that sign?' I ask my group.

'Welcome to the living the— the— theatre of plants and people.'

Tiny smirk in Miss Thomas's direction.

Should we have banners at the wedding? 'So simple, yet so instantly celebratory . . .' In my head, I've adopted the slightly patronizing, cajoling voice of any one of the army of people now involved in organizing 'my big day'. The caterers, the florists, the dressmaker, the cake maker, the make-up lady – Look! It takes years off you! – the photographer, the balloon man, the woman who'll give me false nails with pearls stuck on them, which I thought looked a bit like growths at the free trial, but are apparently what everyone's having this year. All these people I keep thanking and booking as they gently erode my confidence and point me towards further necessary ephemera. I did draw the line at a liveried toastmaster.

'Imagine building a world from nothing.'

All the signs are carved in wood, bringing a natural effect to this totally artificial construction.

'It feels a bit surreal, doesn't it, being here . . . I mean, with all that's going on in the world?'

'Does it?' says Miss Thomas.

'Who can give me an example of what we use plants for?'

We have eaten our lunch al fresco and we are gathered in front of a sculpture of a giant bee.

'Trees?'

'Yes, trees are plants. What do we use trees for?'

'Climbing.'

'OK, yes, that's one thing. Shane, get off the bee!'

'But it's made from trees, Miss.'

'Yes, very good, but this is not a theme park.' Extremely unamused face.

'Anyone else got any ideas about what we get from plants?'

'Apples, Miss?'

Oh, please, not apples again. 'How about what we're wearing?'

Mistake. Most of the children are dressed in blue fleece and grey polyester. I pinch the sleeve of my cardigan. 'Where do you think this comes from?'

'M and S?' Sophie guesses. She has pierced ears, and sometimes forgets to remove her nail polish after the weekend.

Designers at Debenhams, as a matter of fact. 'It's made from cotton, which comes from . . . ?'

'Plants!' they all chorus. I've finally bored them into learning something.

'Can we have an ice cream, Miss?'

'No, Shane, you can't.'

'But it's made from plants, Miss.'

'How's that?'

'Because the cows eat the grass, and cream comes from cows.'

'Well done, Shane. Perhaps we'll all be able to have an ice cream later.' I couldn't help noticing that one of the flavours was strawberry and clotted cream, which sounds almost irresistible.

'Seen it on the Anchor advert,' Shane confides to Alice.

I said to my mother last week, 'What if I didn't marry Andy?' and she replied, 'It wouldn't be the end of the world,' which I took to mean that in her view it would, because frankly who else was I going to find, and if I wanted to settle down and have children of my own, I'd better not leave it much longer.

'Miss, it feels like a swimming pool in here.'

'That's right. It's warm and damp. What's a word that describes warm and damp?'

'Rain?'

'Good, Jack. But I'm thinking of an adjective, you know, one of those words that describes things.'

'Is it hummid, Miss?'

'Well done, Shane. Humid.'

'There's a sign where we came in,' he whispers to Alice, as if he's come by the information fraudulently.

She beams at him.

'Can we play Tarzan, Miss?'

'As long as you don't break any of the trees.'

Sophie and Emma pretend to cook a meal of rice in the Malaysian house.

'There are wonderful vegetables out here,' I tell them, attempting to entice them back onto the path, because I'm not sure they're allowed to go in the bamboo construction on stilts. 'Okra, paprika, spinach . . .'

'Why don't they have proper food?'

I'm transfixed by a short poem on a stick which says:

> A cup is made of bottom and sides
> But it's use lies in its emptiness
> *Lao Tsu*

Which seems profoundly relevant, although I'm not sure why. As I read it again in my head, I'm suddenly aware of a small, familiar voice reading out loud some distance away.

'Please take care. Steep slopes and water.'

Then there's a splash.

By the time I arrive, sweating from the tropical heat and the uphill sprint, the words 'risk assessment' screaming just behind my forehead, Shane and Alice are in a pool, stripped to their knickers and frolicking like a miniature Adam and Eve before the fall. I feel my face morph from completely terrified to extremely unamused, but I can't hold it, and suddenly our laughter is gurgling through the rainforest.

'We are going to get married,' Shane says, as I dry him in my cardigan, 'when we're old enough.'

'Why's that, then?'

'Because we love each other,' he says, looking at me like I'm crazy.

'Why do you want to marry me?' I asked, when Andy proposed.

We'd just represented our pub in the regional quiz and won. We were riding a great wave of victory and Stella Artois.

'We make a good team,' he replied.

At the very top of the rainforest, where the signal is just strong enough, I ring Andy on my mobile.

'I can't go through with the wedding . . .'

'Can't hear you. You sound like you're standing under a waterfall or something.'

'I'm in the Humid Tropics Biome—'

'The largest conservatory in the world with a height of 55 metres—'

'I DON'T WANT TO GET MARRIED.'

'Oh. Why?'

Because balloons and nail extensions are no substitute for love, and Frascati and trivia do not make the war go away. Actually, I just say, 'I don't think I'm old enough.' The children probably wouldn't stop calling me Miss anyway.

'Is this the end of the world?' Alice asks.

We've roamed through banana and pineapple plantations, seen coffee and Cola plants, and a treasure trove of spices.

'No, it's not.'

I push open the door. There's still the Warm and Temperate biome with grapes and cork and scented flowers ahead of us, and then strawberry and clotted-cream ice cream. There's the gift shop, and the passionate belief in an optimistic future for mankind. At least, that is what it says in the guidebook.

Julie Stradner is a teacher and teacher trainer in Cambridge. She has lived in Turkey and Sweden, and has recently started writing. *Barley Sugar* won the *Woman & Home* Short Story competition in 2001.

Barley Sugar

'I hate you, Mummy! I hate you!' Katie spits out the words like drops of green poison, fizzing in the hot air. The hate is so huge and heavy in her chest that she can't speak any more. Mummy reaches out to touch her face, but Katie can't bear it. She slaps the hand away, opens her mouth in a snarl of rage. She turns to run out of the room, but Mummy catches her in her arms.

'Katie, we can't have a kitten right now. They're too small to leave their mother. And Grandad's so ill. Perhaps later.'

But Katie won't listen to her. Her skin is slick with sweat and she slides out of her mother's grasp, runs and hides under the sofa where it's dark and safe and smells of dust. She hears her mother sigh. She can see her mother's trainers and the bottoms of her jeans. There are tiny beads of glossy dark brown on the shoes where Mummy has spilt some of Grandad's medicine. Suddenly, Mummy hits the back of the sofa, once, very hard; she's still for a moment and then she goes out, back upstairs to Grandad's room.

Katie crawls out from under the sofa. The velvet curtains are nearly right across the windows, but in the patch of sunlight motes of dust whirl and fall slowly, glittering. Everything in Grandad's house is dusty now. It smells heavy and sweet, a nasty sweetness, the odour of the medicine Katie sniffs on her mother's clothes. Katie doesn't like it here any more. They've been here for ages and she wants to go home. She wants Grandad to come downstairs and bounce her on his knees like he used to. When he kisses her he smells of clean lemon soap and his jacket is scratchy, but fragrant with the spicy scent of pipe tobacco.

She and Grandad have a secret: he gives her hard sweets, barley sugars, which she's not supposed to have. She likes to peel off the crackly yellow Cellophane and look through it; when she pops the sweet in her mouth and moves it round with her tongue it gets as smooth and slippery as glass. If Mummy comes when she and Grandad are eating barley sugars, he winks at her and she keeps the sweet very still in her mouth until she's full of sugar juice and has to swallow.

Thinking all this makes her mouth water. She gulps a little and it's as if there's a hard stone in her throat where the hate has lodged. She can't see Grandad and Mummy's always busy, so why can't she have a kitten? It's not fair. Mrs Brown's cat next door has five babies. Mrs Brown put them all in a basket in Grandad's shed so Katie can look at them while Mummy is busy. If she asked Daddy for one he'd probably grunt at her from behind his newspaper and say yes, but he's far away in London, and he's always at his office anyway. It's not fair.

Outside the house the heat is fierce. It prickles Katie's skin like the blast from a hairdryer. She has to wrinkle her eyes against the glare that shines red against her eyelids. In the distance an ice-cream van tinkles. For a moment, Katie hesitates. A lolly would be good, a green one, slightly sour and cold enough to make your teeth ache. But more than a lolly she wants to see the kittens.

The shed is at the back of the garden near the tomato plants. She can smell the sharp tang of creosote, and when she opens the door there's the faint mildew of the deckchairs stacked in a corner. Mrs Brown has put the cat basket in the shade and an old cushion on the floor so Katie can sit and watch the kittens. She's been told not to touch in case it makes the mother cat cross, and she knows Mrs Brown will take them all back to her own house in the evening.

She sits cross-legged on the cushion. The kittens are curled up round their mother, all drowsing in the warm afternoon. They're very tiny. Katie watches the soft rise and fall of their breathing. Four are tawny and ginger, like their mother, but one is a dark, rich amber, the colour of Mummy's hair, the colour of barley sugar. In her heart, Katie feels sure this is a girl kitten and, because she is the sweetest and prettiest, she has named her Sugar.

A bluebottle buzzes angrily against the windowpane. Sometimes the kittens squirm and wriggle as they dream, or bat a tiny paw. The mother cat regards Katie with wide and empty eyes of palest citrine. And as Katie watches, her breathing slows and the hard lump in her throat melts and fades away. There's nothing in the world for her except the warm wooden shed and the little creatures slumbering through the summer afternoon.

Sugar stretches and opens her eyes. She yawns, and her tongue is like a little pink petal. For a moment she seems to look at Katie, but then her attention is caught by the bluebottle. She worms out of the basket and plops on the floor. Katie holds her breath, but the mother cat proceeds only to clean her paws. Sugar waddles to the wall, gazing at the window where the fly is bumping against the glass. Katie stretches a finger to touch her fur, just a finger, and the little cat is as soft as the fuzz of a dandelion clock before the wind takes the seeds. She lifts the kitten onto her lap; she is light and warm, infinitely precious. Sugar pats Katie's fingers with her paws and the claws sharp as tiny rose thorns. She snuggles up to Katie with total trust, and the child can hardly breathe for joy.

After a time the bluebottle finds the hole in the glass that Grandad was going to mend last spring. The tinkle of the ice-cream van is much closer. Soon Mrs Brown will come to take the cats back to her house. Mummy will spend the night in Grandad's room, as she always does these days. Katie will sleep alone in the small bedroom, watching the strange shadows move on the wall.

Sugar has fallen asleep in her arms. Carefully Katie stands up, cradling the kitten as tenderly as she does her favourite doll. 'I'm only going to borrow you,' she whispers into the warm fur that smells of sunshine.

Outside the garden is thick with heat, but the glare has gone and the sky is like a thick grey blanket thrown over the world. Her hair sticks to her face and her arms itch, and when she looks down she sees dozens of moving black specks, thunderflies Mummy calls them. She brushes them off impatiently and her movements cause Sugar to stir and struggle. 'Shhh,' she says. 'I'm going to put you somewhere safe until night-time, and then I'll come and get you.'

Her doll's pram is by the rose bushes. From the open window above, she can hear Mummy reading the newspaper to Grandad. There's a click of the gate next door. Soon Mrs Brown will come to take the cats away. Sugar is getting restless and squirms in her arms. Hurriedly, Katie kisses Sugar's head and tucks her under the quilt with her teddy bear. She's careful to tuck the corners in well so she won't fall out. 'I'll come back soon,' she whispers. She can still see the covers wriggling a little, but she knows she'll go to sleep soon. She wipes her sticky hands on her dress and pushes her hair out of her eyes. She'll have her tea, and then come back for Sugar.

Mummy's made egg sandwiches. Katie doesn't really want them – the egg is slimy and salty in her mouth. She takes a little bite and pushes the bread round on her plate. She glances up at Mummy to see if she's cross about the wasted food, but she's gazing out of the kitchen window, holding a cup of tea that's getting cold, running a finger round the rim of the cup, over and over.

'Can I go and watch television?'

Mummy nods and starts to clear away the dishes. Katie lolls on the floor watching cartoons, letting the bright colours and jerky action slide over her eyes, thinking of nothing. She doesn't hear Mrs Brown come in until Mummy switches the TV off. Mrs Brown is smiling, but Mummy's mouth is creased in a thin, tight line.

'Mrs Brown says one of Sheba's kittens is missing. She only had four kittens in the basket when she went to collect them. Did you take one, Katie?'

Katie says nothing. Mrs Brown bends down and gives her a liquorice allsort. It's a black tube with a white middle. Katie turns it round and round in her fingers. She can't imagine how they get the white bit inside the black. Mrs Brown is mumbling something, but now Mummy is crouching down so that her face is level with Katie's. Her eyes are pink and swollen and the fox-coloured hair is loose and wild. She looks like a witch. 'Tell the truth, Katie, or you'll go to bed right now!' She puts her hand on her daughter's shoulder, but the child jerks away and races out of the house.

She's running down the garden path. The sky is storm-lit yellow, like looking through an amber Cellophane sweet wrapper. Thunder rumbles far off. Everything looks slightly distorted in this light, the flat, eerie landscape of a dream. She reaches the pram and flings off the quilt and teddy. Instantly she sees something very wrong. The kitten is a damp streak of fur that doesn't move, her mouth and eyes horribly open. Thunder again, nearer now, a long, low growl. When she turns round, Mummy and Mrs Brown are standing still, looking down, and Katie has no idea how to interpret their faces. They loom very tall and dark against the sky.

For a moment, the child feels caught, pinned, pathetically small. Then she's running again, back to the house, nicking her arm on a rose thorn, yelping but not stopping as the sky splits in a white gash and heavy drops of rain sting her face. She can hear the grown-ups calling her name as she reaches the house. She flings open the door and heads for the stairs. She has to see Grandad. Grandad will look at her with his kind eyes and he'll hold her in his strong arms. She'll kiss his cheek that smells of lemon soap and everything will be all right again, everything will be all right.

The stairs are very steep. The door of Grandad's room is open and spills yellow light. The sickly sweet medicine smell is strong and when she steps into the room there's another odour, a thick stench of illness faintly overlaid with synthetic floral. There's a shape under the pink candlewick but the face is turned away. A sound comes from it, a rhythmic rattle and a gasping sigh. She doesn't like it. Thunder again, and a rumbling: Mummy's running up the stairs. Katie stands very still. Mummy comes in and goes to the bed, strokes the face that Katie can't see. She whispers across to Katie: 'Grandad's very ill. Do you want to come and say goodnight?'

The little girl shakes her head, slides her thumb into her mouth. Mummy always warned her about hard sweets, told her how she might choke. She feels as if she's swallowed one now, as if something sharp and hard has caught in her throat. She loved Grandad and she loved Sugar, but dark and terrible things have taken their place. She lets Mummy lead her into the little bedroom and get her ready for bed. Mummy smoothes her hair and tucks her in. 'Everything will be all right,' she says, and turns off the light as she leaves the room. There's a blue-white flash of lightning and Katie feels as if she's being spun out of her body into a cold and desolate universe. She sucks her thumb and gazes unblinking into the darkness.

When she wakes the scent of rain is in the room, very cool and lovely. The nets flutter pale against the open windows and she can hear cars hissing by in the streets below. The storm is over. She turns.

There's a young man sitting in the chair beside her bed.

She lies quite still. The young man comes and sits on her bed. He bends to kiss her and his cheek smells lemon-soap clean. She sits up and puts her arms round him, stroking the rough jacket that's spicy with tobacco scent. Suddenly she can be silent no longer. The pain of the day rises up in a shudder from her belly so that she gasps and sobs bitter tears.

'I've been so bad, Grandad! I'm so bad!' She tells him about Sugar and about how lonely she's been. He rocks her gently, whispering her name and stroking her hair like he used to. Gradually the shudders and tears stop. She feels light and clean and sleepy. She's safe, she's loved, everything is all right. Grandad smooths the pillow as she lies down in bed. Katie basks in the warmth of his smile, drowsy, and then she notices a fuzzy little head the colour of barley sugar peeping from Grandad's jacket pocket.

'Sugar!' she breathes and Grandad nods. He lifts the kitten on to his lap and scratches her behind her ears.

'I'm taking her with me,' he says. 'Give her a kiss, now.' Katie does so, and the kitten licks her hands. Grandad whispers goodnight and Katie turns over. She's heavy and ripe with sleep, making the sweet drop into dreams like a plum falling from the tree into soft grass.

When she wakes again, the rain is still falling, tapping its wise and ancient code against the windowpane. She can smell Mummy's perfume, and when Katie sits up in bed she can see her sitting in the chair, silvered by rain-light, her head bowed like a sad princess in a fairy tale. She's weeping softly in the rain-soaked night.

Katie creeps out of bed and on to her mother's lap. It's beyond strangeness to see Mummy cry. Mummy whispers only, 'Grandad!' into Katie's hair and there are more tears. Katie nods. 'Grandad's gone to heaven with Sugar,' she says, and Mummy starts to sob harder. Katie tries to soothe her, but she doesn't understand her sadness. After all, everything is all right now, everything is finally all right.

Mary Swann was born in England but brought up in Australia. She is married with a 23-year-old son and she teaches seven-year-olds at a private school. She lives in Knebworth, Hertfordshire, and has written two musicals which were performed in the village. *Mrs Hamilton's Garden* won the *Woman & Home* Short Story competition in 2003.

Mrs Hamilton's Garden

The disappearance of Mr Hamilton from his pleasant, detached house at 52 Mallard Rise caused a froth of excitement and speculation among the neighbours, which bubbled gently through the adjacent streets and trickled along the avenues of the village as far south as the station.

For it was along these unexceptional chequered pavements and beside these bijoux front gardens that he had for the past nineteen years made his way, caught the 8.05 to Kings Cross and, from there, the Piccadilly Line to the offices of the firm of stock-brokers where he earned his living. Briefcase in one hand, mobile phone in his pocket, it was his habit to purchase the *Telegraph*, and, occasionally, half a pound of sherbet lemons at Nathan Hall's on the corner of Duck Street. For the last three days in September, no such journey had been made, no such purchases had been made and Mrs Hamilton, red eyed but self-contained as befits an Englishwoman, reported him missing.

Although a familiar and respectable figure, little was known of his life behind the doors of Number 52. Childless, there was no occasion for him to be seen on the touchline of the frozen football pitch or self-consciously participating in the school fathers' race. He belonged to no clubs and would have been a stranger at the bar of the picturesque Breast and Beak on the corner of Heron Lane.

More surprising was that no one was sufficiently intimate with his wife to feel comfortable in calling to offer comfort, or perhaps be in a position to assuage the curiosity of those who longed to know how she was taking it. The Hamiltons were on no one's dinner-party list.

Days passed and the pages of the *Cornet* were furtively and eagerly scanned for news of his mangled remains. However, interest dwindled as the only tangible facts worth reporting were that his mobile phone had remained firmly switched off and that his colleagues, when interviewed, had deplored the loss of a valued employee. Most readers required company-fund embezzlement, blood, or at the very least a sixteen-year-old temptress to sustain their interest, and of these journalistic treats they were disappointed.

The feelings of Mrs Hamilton remained unconfirmed. She had cultivated no friends within the village and now reaped the reward. Attempts to involve her in coffee mornings or the local rambling group had met over the years with firm but civil rejection. But whether motivated by shyness and a lack of confidence or contentment with her own company was a matter of conjecture. Until the news of his unexplained departure had seeped through the social strata of the community, no one had very much cared. The Hamiltons had paid their rates and kept themselves aloof. Fêtes, cricket matches and local sponsored walks had passed them by.

It was recalled in the shower cubicles of the

Aromatherapy Club that men in their early forties have long been known to suddenly awaken to the fact that they are now unlikely to open the batting for England or become proficient on the bassoon. There was happy debate among the lady members, several of whom had completed elementary psychotherapy courses, as to whether Mr Hamilton had merely gone off to find himself. Many a light lunch of organic salmon and rocket was enlivened by hushed talk of how they themselves would have foreseen and forestalled this defection in their own partners.

Mr Hamilton may or may not have found himself. It is certain no one else did. Weeks passed, no accident was reported and the police declined to interfere in the departure of a grown man in full possession of his senses and where no foul play was suspected.

As Mrs Seraphina Luchins remarked between her rinse and conditioner at Snippets, 'Only time would tell.' And this was generally felt to be true.

As the season of Advent approached, the gentle and deeply religious Mallinson sisters from Number 23 discussed with Father Greenhedge after eight o'clock communion whether Mrs Hamilton should be offered grief counselling. That kindly cleric had called, a little nervously it was true, for he had been ordained only the previous year, and sat for half an hour on Mrs Hamilton's brown velveteen settee. The Hamiltons were not of his flock (or anyone's) but he was anxious to offer the grace of God to any who might show signs of benefiting from it. She had been polite and seemingly grateful for his time, offered him Earl Grey tea and plied him with ginger biscuits. They had talked of the proposed plan for restocking the village pond. This watery attraction, only a few bucketfuls short of a small lake and home to a variety of indigenous wildlife, had been sadly depleted by herons. They touched briefly on the problems that had arisen since the fruit shop off Grebe Street had been forced to close, and a pause ensued long enough for both to become aware of the ticking of the wall-mounted clock.

'I'm afraid that this must be a very difficult time for you.' Father Greenhedge bit hard into his second biscuit. It was not an easy thing to eat while conveying sympathy and concern. The biscuits were like chipboard and it was important to swallow the bite so as to be ready for whatever she might need to share with him. Mrs Hamilton sipped her tea, crossed her ankles and generally seemed more concerned with her guest's welfare than her own recent tragedy. Her cream cotton blouse, tweedy skirt and sensible shoes seemed designed to preclude intrusion. Yes, it was totally uncharacteristic behaviour. Her husband's disappearance was extraordinary. She was living in the hope that all would shortly be explained by a bout of amnesia, and no, since their bank account had not been touched, she herself was not in any immediate financial need. Old Mrs Hamilton had been informed but now thankfully senile was suffering no distress. The vicar was on the whole glad when he could decently rise, reach for his umbrella (the day was drizzly) and say, 'Well, if there's anything, anything at all . . .'

Mrs Hamilton rather wistfully watched him drive away in his little Fiat. What sort of man would he have needed to be, she wondered, to enable her to disclose the details of her marriage? While he, deftly changing the altar cloth from green to purple and ironing his surplice, tried to put from his mind thoughts of uneasiness and inadequacy engendered by the meeting.

Less than generous neighbours, bored at bus stops

and impatient in Post Office queues, wondered whether Mr Hamilton had merely gone to acquire a younger and more attractive replacement for his wife. Excitement was heightened briefly at the news of the almost simultaneous departure from her post and indeed the village of Miss Julie Robotham. Sleek and sweet as a caramel cream, Julie had been wont to serve drinks and dangle her earrings behind the bar of the Breast and Beak each Saturday night and would be sorely missed by its clientele. It was not easy to imagine a romantic intrigue between Miss Julie Robotham, of the outrageous sulphur-yellow hair, tight black leggings and skimpy spangled T-shirts (one of which featured cocktail ingredients in Braille), and Mr Hamilton in his business suits, but the villagers did their level best.

Being thin and nearly forty-two, and with a deeper knowledge of her husband, Mrs Hamilton found it less difficult to imagine. Her own hair, though soft and the colour of a fox, had showed a recent tendency to whiten at the ears. For years, indeed, most of her married life, it had been tied with a thin ribbon and hung down her back not unlike a fox's tail. Wisps detached themselves and framed her pale face. Washed once a week under the shower her hair had lived a life deprived of the advances of modern science that had produced conditioners, gels, anti-frizz agents and styling mousse. Mr Hamilton would have seen these and trips to the hairdresser as unnecessary expense.

As the weeks lengthened into months and the bronzed beech leaves descended to clog the pond that was such a feature of the village, Mrs Hamilton knew in her heart that he would not return. Indeed, had he done so, the effort that she imagined would be

271

required for the repair of their relationship seemed arduous and impractical. She confided in no one, continuing her daily routine of housework, and as she grated cheese and sorted cutlery, considered her position as a possible widow or deserted wife.

To fill her days and calm her anxiety about the future, she began methodically to turn the soil of her medium-sized back garden. Neither Mr nor Mrs Hamilton had ever gardened; the tiny front strip had long ago been neatly cemented over. The back was, as it were, virgin soil. A six-foot paling fence on either side afforded her the solitude and privacy she craved.

She discovered that she enjoyed digging holes. How far down, she wondered, did she actually own? Was the clay layer beneath the topsoil legally hers? Could she dig her way straight through to Australia and claim her legal rights? She pondered the possibility as, unwilling to face these articles every morning, she recklessly interred her husband's toothbrush, flannel and electric shaver.

The silence of the house at first slightly disturbed her. The television had been a necessary background to her husband's hours at home. Now, freed from its demands on her senses, she walked through the empty rooms receptive to the almost imperceptible language of floorboards and plaster. The atonal music of the water pipes insinuated their own dimension to the silence and dust motes jingle-jangled prettily in the October shafts of lemony light. On the fingers of one hand she counted those who now called her by her Christian name and with her forefinger on the old-fashioned sideboard she printed it in capital letters. Neatly she added the word ALONE.

She had always known of her husband's dirty magazines. Concealed under cuttings from the obituary column (why had he been so fascinated by these?), they had lain on the top shelf of the tool cupboard, infecting the hammers and screwdrivers and corrupting the nails and screws. With distaste she dislodged the yellowing pile. His video collection slithered smoothly in beside them and she buried the lot three feet beneath the loamy surface of the soil.

The hours of darkness increased and soupy mists preceded glassy-blue days. The sprinkles of gold in the gutters of the village turned to blackened sludge. A skin of ice splintered beneath the moorhen's feet on the pond. Soon the soil would be crystallized with frost. Hastily, she gathered together his suits and socks, his ties and underclothes. Three large holes, each four feet deep, were required to dispose of them to her satisfaction. Mr Hamilton had always preferred nylon shirts and these, defying the efforts of modern soap powders, had permanently retained a smell of underground stations, busy offices and armpit. These she felt merited a hole entirely to themselves. When she had finished, the garden smiled serenely back at her, neat, smooth, brown and innocent.

The unaccustomed exercise caused her to sleep deeply and without her husband to sweat and snore beside her she woke each morning refreshed. Timidly, for Mr Hamilton would have been scornful and disapproving (their marital bed linen had been white polyester-cotton, a gift from old Mrs Hamilton on their tenth anniversary), she bought two pairs of Laura Ashley cotton sheets sprigged with delicate white violets on a faint clover-green background. When they needed washing she added several drops of lavender essence to the final rinse and ironed them lovingly. It seemed like an act of graciousness, a thoughtful present to herself. The gentle scent greeted and enveloped her and the smooth, delicious cotton cherished her skin.

Energy, she found, begets energy and change enables change. The smooth and fragrant pillowcases deserved a different head.

Snippets, oasis of the gossips, home of the permed, foiled and highlighted of the village, was insufficient for her needs. A trip to London was considered, planned and an appointment booked. So rarely had she travelled that the enterprise felt fraught with the seriousness and purpose of a Holy Quest. Mr Hamilton had seen her single role as his provider of creature comforts. Travel beyond the village had been discouraged and self-improvement deemed unnecessary. Her early secretarial skills had lain dormant and unused. With wonder and admiration she watched the jacketed confident women who went purposefully about their business. On the inter-city train, in and out of shops and offices, their gleaming hair and air of self-sufficiency reproached and intimidated her.

She emerged from the hairdresser's with a jaw-length head of glossy glory that glistened with the depth and glow of amber beads and produced a swishing sensation at the nape of her neck. All the way back on the underground she stared transfixed at the radiant and blurred image reflected in the grimy window. Never before had Mrs Hamilton's hair been known to swish.

A transformation, she decided, should begin at the top and work down. Hair, then what? A dress – surely that would typify the person she could become. Soft, long and silky, the colour of bay leaves, it would cling and caress her bare legs. Where could she possibly wear such a thing in the village? No matter, she would slip it on to bake crusty bread and dance alone in a shaft of moonlight.

Summer, she decided, would be her time for action. By summer she would have exhausted her capital. Summer perhaps would bring the day of the suit (a russet silk and linen blend)? Clad only thus would it be possible to imagine applying for a job. The terror and thrill engendered by the idea of working, leaving the house each day, mingling with the crowds who so casually travelled to offices, so nonchalantly earned a living, gave impetus to her shopping fantasy. The day would come, she promised her emergent self, that the ultimate would be addressed: a pair of impractical, expensive strappy sandals.

The clocks went back, the cricket team drew stumps for their final match and spiders worked all night to produce complicated jewelled necklaces from bird tables and washing lines. Seed catalogues arrived unsolicited and with her hand ready to drop them in the bin some inner prompting held it back and whispered to her of things slyly uncurling and others darkly writhing in the invisible dank underworld. The order form was seductive, offering extra bulbs and two shrubs for the price of one. Was it better to have two shrubs than one? How many bulbs did it take to fill a medium-size back garden? She ordered with abandon.

December came and Mrs Hamilton hibernated. Christmas and New Year passed uncelebrated.

Spring arrived not with a gentle whisper of the possibility of change but with a jubilant and unseemly sudden rush of warmth. Like a giant hole-punch emptied, cherry and pear petals tumbled down and constellations of starry yellow daffodils illuminated dark corners of the village. The air that one week hurt the faces and fingers of school children hurrying home, the next, like angel's breath, caused them to dawdle in the lanes enchanted by a perfumed world they only dimly remembered from the olden days of the previous year.

And in Mrs Hamilton's garden, chemical changes were taking place deep, mysterious and silent beneath the surface of the soil. Where she had buried her husband's sweaty shirts, tulips thrust their grey-green pencil points and unpacked their miniature pink paper party hats. Where the pornographic magazines had rotted, a pearly white rhododendron flourished, each flower a pure and perfect bridal bouquet fringed with its own green edging.

The toothbrush, flannel and shaver knew their duty too. Out of their bathroom remains lilies climbed, promising with spectacular spears to support huge orange bells of powdery sweetness. His socks delivered a clump of purple hyacinths. Their bottle-brush blossoms turned their petals back and under to release a scent that spangled up into the air and saturated the garden.

Like the conductor of some flamboyant floral orchestral piece, Mrs Hamilton encouraged and vitalized the display. As one inspired she augmented the crescendo of bud, bloom and petal. Buoyant and triumphant, seedlings expanded and tendrils extended. The fertile ground in which his business suits had long since lost their city sharpness yielded chubby blue forget-me-nots. The videos sent up shy, satiny mauve anemones. A tangle of sweet peas towered lush like multicoloured ribbon bows from where Mrs Hamilton had buried his ties. And crimson, assertive, belligerent and cruel, giant peonies thrust themselves from the spot where she had buried Mr Hamilton himself.

Sandy Toksvig is a writer and broadcaster. Born in Denmark, she made her name in Britain first in children's television and then on the comedy circuit. She is well known on television for numerous shows including five years as team captain on *Call My Bluff*. Sandi works extensively on radio where she hosts her own daily and weekly shows for LBC and BBC Radio 4. She is a columnist for *Good Housekeeping* magazine and 2005 will see the publication of her thirteenth and fourteenth books.

The Reiki Master

I don't know if I've mentioned my auntie Maureen but she is, and I say this with some pride, Reiki Master to the Cars. No, that's not me making a spelling mistake. I did say cars. Of course, Reiki Master to the Stars might have been a bit more exciting for the family, carrying with it as it would the possibility that we might touch the hand of an aunt who had once laid her palm on George Clooney's chakras, but it was not to be. No, it's cars not stars, and no one could have been more surprised than Auntie Maureen.

To be honest, the whole Reiki thing was rather out of character for the family. We're quite an ordinary bunch, conservative with a small 'c' and not really given to anything 'alternative'. Well, there was cousin Linda who ran off with that saxophonist who turned out to be not quite the man we thought. In fact, not a man at all. I think it's rather a good story, but mother doesn't like me to go into details. Apparently they now run a salsa bar in Sitges in Spain and are very happy, but I'm not to visit.

Anyway, Auntie Maureen. Until the Reiki business there was nothing out of the ordinary about her. She does occasionally listen to those jazz records where everyone involved seems to be searching about for a tune, but nothing else remotely avant garde. She lives on Gosset Street in the same village where we were all born and bred. Everyone always thought Auntie Maureen had done very well. She had married Uncle Joe when he was but a lad working night shifts up at the abattoir on Friendly Street. Auntie M didn't hold with Joe spending his days sending cows to their maker and it wasn't long before she vowed 'never to clean another bloody apron'. I don't think Joe had a choice but to tear himself from the world of the stun gun and the falling heifer. It seems Auntie M knew a man in business through her work with the Legion of Mary (general acts of Catholic charity and Bingo on a Tuesday). Auntie M pulled strings and cleaned Joe up to enter the more sedate world of Upholsterer's Sundries. I can't say I ever understood the detail of the work, but Joe loved it. For some reason, there in the underworld of what makes sofas and chairs tick, he felt he had come home. Generally Joe was a man of few words but he could talk polyester stuffing and wide webbing for an entire evening and, indeed, given enough glasses of porter, that is precisely what he would do. As my Auntie Eileen often says, Joe made 'quite a fist' of the business and before long Auntie Maureen and Uncle Joe had moved to their house on Gosset Street.

It wasn't a grand house but it did stand out. Built in the 1930s, the semi-detached houses on Gosset Street are all of a uniform character, apart from the two in the very middle. These two have a garage each. Perhaps the architects had not foreseen the rise of the motorcar as mobility for the masses. They had envisioned that the vehicle would always remain a plaything of the rich. Perhaps they believed that no more than two families in an area like Gosset Street would ever be able to afford such luxury. To the sometime chagrin of the neighbours, Auntie Maureen and Uncle Joe had a garage. So too did Mr Burns, who lived next door.

Uncle Joe and Mr Burns did not speak. They did not speak for more than twenty years. It seems Uncle Joe overheard Mr Burns at the Silver Jubilee street party saying he thought Auntie Maureen had nice legs. Something close to a row ensued and not another word was spoken between the two men. I believe they even toasted Her Majesty the Queen in silence that night.

Then, sadly, after many years of happy marriage, Uncle Joe passed away. It was an unlucky end. You would have thought that a man of his experience would have known better than to inhale while holding decorative tacks in his mouth. Ironic that a man who had given his life to upholstery went with his insides so firmly nailed into place. Uncle Joe's open coffin was set up in the front room and Auntie Maureen sat beside it, inconsolable. The priest and the family came round to pray with her, hold her hand and tell her how well Uncle Joe looked 'considering'.

'You could devote your life to the Sisters of Divine Compassion now,' tried my mother.

'Why not come and do some work at the charity shop. Help the cats,' asked Auntie Eileen, whose devotion to saving felines has destroyed any hope of her ever having anything decent to wear. She carries the mark of the beast on every item of clothing she possesses.

Auntie Maureen put away her rosary, brushed a cat hair from her lap and declared, 'I'm going to train as a Reiki Master,' and went to put the kettle on.

She might as well have said she was planning to

become a lama in Tibet for all anyone in the family understood.

My mother phoned me immediately.

'Darling,' she said breathlessly, 'Auntie Maureen is going to be a Reiki Master.'

'That's nice, Mum. Look, I can't chat. I've got seven people over for dinner.'

Mum was not interested in my social juggling.

'That's too many people on a school night,' she said, and waited for me to explain about Reiki. I tried to see what I could remember.

'It's a kind of healing system. It's from Japan. You heal people by tapping into the universal life energy. A kind of laying on of hands. I don't think there's any harm in it.'

'Japanese?' exclaimed mother. 'No one in our family has ever done anything Japanese.'

Despite the fact that no one in the family had ever done anything Japanese, Auntie Maureen did become a Reiki Master. She spent her time helping people to reconnect to life, to find their place in the world through a gentle system for restoring wholeness and harmony. It was lovely. It was also done in her garage. Auntie M removed all Uncle Joe's old boxes of upholstery sundries, cleaned and painted the garage and turned it into a place for unblocking your energy flows. It was perhaps the only Reiki massage parlour in the world with an up-and-over door.

It was while Auntie M was attuning a client to the universe in her converted garage that she heard a terrible noise from next door. In the adjacent garage Mr Burns was banging away at something very loud and very metal. The sound reverberated, cutting through Auntie's CD of whale music and her cascading water-fall (Argos catalogue – £14.99 complete with serenity pebbles). It was intolerable. Auntie M covered her client with a golden towel from her Autumn Mist bathroom set, which had been warming on the storage heater, and went next door. She banged loudly on Mr Burns's up-and-over but got no reply. His own banging was far too vociferous for hers to be heard. Exasperated, Auntie pulled up the garage door and stood in a state of barely contained fury.

Certainly the calm aura she adopted for work had gone a very peculiar colour indeed.

'Mr Burns!' she said sharply, and then 'Are you there?' even more sharply, for Mr Burns was not to be seen. The only thing in view was an ancient motorcar marooned on four wooden blocks. It was a beautiful thing in dark racing green with a long front and running boards spreading back across the sides. It looked like a mobster's car. As if Bonnie and Clyde had finally given up the ghost and plumped for the quiet life of Gosset Street. Even standing in the doorway Auntie M could smell the old leather interior. She might have thought it was wonderful had not the non-Reiki banging continued. Auntie M bent down and saw Mr Burns's legs sticking out from underneath the vehicle. She tapped him on the shoe and, startled, he promptly hit his head on the underside of the car. From his prone position Mr Burns looked along the floor. All he could see were Auntie Maureen's legs. Legs he would know anywhere.

'Sorry, sorry, Maureen,' he muttered, pulling himself out and getting upright. 'I'm so sorry, I was trying to fix the . . . sorry.'

Auntie Maureen pulled herself up to her full five foot one. 'I am trying to restore energy flows next door, Mr Burns, and I cannot do it if you are banging.'

'No, of course not. I'm sorry. It's this damn . . . sorry

. . . it's this car. Some cars just fight you. You try to make them happy and healthy and they just keep throwing up problems.' Mr Burns took a cloth from his pocket and began absentmindedly to wipe the bonnet of the car. It was done with surprising affection and gentleness. It reminded Auntie M of her own soothing passes of the hand over her clients.

Slightly taken aback, she asked, 'What kind of a car is it?'

'This beauty is a Morris Minor saloon from 1934. Isn't she gorgeous? But she won't purr for me.'

Auntie Maureen would never know why she did it, but she very slowly began to pass her hands up and over the old saloon. She did not touch the car but allowed her hands to move freely as she sought to tune her mind into the flow of energy it contained. Reiki had taught her that energy holds all matter together and she knew it was here in the car too. Mr Burns stopped his polishing and stood silently. He watched her and seemed to sense a glow around her body. Later, when he had the language for it, he called it 'an aura of peace and tranquillity'.

After a short while Auntie Maureen whispered, 'Try her now, Mr Burns.'

Mr Burns slipped into the seat, put in the key and turned the engine. The old girl purred into quiet life.

It was the beginning of a new era. It seems Mr Burns was quite the hub of the local classic-car enthusiasts. When they heard how his vehicle had been restored to health by Auntie M's hand, they all came to seek her out. Soon she was doing so much business on Austin Healeys and old Jaguars that she had to replace the massage bed in her garage with a hydraulic lift. It was probably just as well. The original Reiki client, who had been left under her golden towel, caught a chill and never did anything alternative again.

Now Auntie Maureen and Mr Burns have a wonderful time going to car rallies, driving to Brighton in open-top roadsters and discussing the finer points of brake-bleeding kits. I know he still thinks she has nice legs but, out of deference to Uncle Joe, I don't believe he ever mentions it.

Barbara Toner is an acclaimed author and journalist. Her novels include *Cracking America*, *All You Need To Know* and *An Organised Woman*. She has also written *A Mother's Guide To Life* and *A Mother's Guide to Husbands*. Born in Australia, she has lived in south London for many years. She is married and has three daughters.

Is Anyone There?

Engadine Square, London SE, is peculiar in that its residents not only know each other to speak to, they live in each other's pockets. Estate agents don't always mention it, guessing so much neighbourliness isn't everyone's cup of tea, but they actually played it down in the sale of Number 40 and that was a mistake. Who doesn't know, in the housing market, that one person's neither here nor there will be another person's be all and end all?

The hideous upshot took everyone by surprise, even Bunty Moxton at Number 23, who should have seen it coming, being a medium. The warning sign everyone missed was the bitterness of the Burtons, who'd wanted Number 40 desperately. Marina Burton looked so sweet, but Marina was beside herself with disappointment and Bunty was almost as upset as she was.

Bunty had introduced the Burtons to the square and predicted that they'd be residents themselves before long. She'd taken it as a huge compliment to herself that the square had embraced them so wholeheartedly, especially Jessica Hargreaves, who ran Neighbourhood Watch and Engadine Against Dirt.

Jessica was adored by everyone, including her own dead relatives. 'And poor Jessie's so adorable!' her late grandmother Elizabeth Jane had remarked to Bunty in the context of her granddaughter's unadorable husband Matthew. The whole world and beyond knew he was a love rat. Bunty only mentioned it to Marina because Marina, depressed about not living in the square, was asking if it was true about him and the Crawshaws' au pair at Number 27.

This was the kind of medium Bunty was, anxious to please everyone. Marina had said would she mind trying to contact dead people from her past for any housing info they might have and she'd been delighted to oblige.

Uncle Jasper, Marina's late godfather, had stepped forward at once and had confirmed to her delight that she would be moving into the square before the year was out. Marina had squealed 'Which number?', but Uncle Jasper hadn't known and it hadn't mattered. Number 40 had come onto the market the very next day and everyone knew it had the Burtons' name on it. No one was more entitled to a coveted deceased estate in a village community just a tube ride from the city. Especially now another baby was on the way.

Unluckily, the word 'entitled' has no pertinence in the world of estate agency, not even at Tinkers, with their excellent reputation for driving a sale along. Oliver Burton was still trumpeting that they were bluffing, there was no other buyer and he wasn't stumping up a penny more than the asking price, when Number 40 was winkled from under his nose by a single mother called Ms Hambrose who drove a Porsche and knew no one. She did this by moving quickly and offering an additional ten K. When Rupert from Tinkers broke the news to Marina, she practically gave birth on the spot.

For three solid weeks she yelled at her husband, screamed at her children, telephoned everyone in the square for support and pleaded with the relatives of the deceased, whose estate was entirely Number 40, as well as with the deceased herself, via Bunty. It came to nought. The deal had been done. Even when she marched on Tinkers and threatened to break her waters all over the floor, Rupert said only, 'Why don't you look at 7 Bishops Lane?'

It was a disaster. Marina had to settle for never forgiving her husband and railing at the only person who had to listen, Bunty, because Bunty had got it wrong. No one else was that bothered. They thought Oliver was an even bigger prat than he looked when Number 40 was clearly excellent value for money even at £10,000 over the asking price. In the face of so little sympathy, Marina turned her heart against Ms Hambrose and, with all her might, she wished her ill.

Ms Hambrose, Zoe, who was something important at Sony, couldn't even have told you under torture the name of the other buyer. In her experience neighbours were numbers, not names. As her solicitors broke all of nature's laws to exchange and complete within the month, she prepared to move, happy as Larry that after months of looking she'd found somewhere suitable. She loved the house. She loved its five double bedrooms, three bathrooms and off-street parking. It was perfect for a growing family, and Zoe Hambrose counted herself, her boy and the nanny as a family.

Marina, in her bitterness, saw exactly what would happen. 'She'll fill that house with fatherless brats.' She and Bunty were sipping green tea in the 33-foot

Moxton garden with timber decking. It was a late spring day and the sun was failing to deliver in warmth what it promised in brilliance.

Bunty shivered. She said, 'Maybe it wasn't Number 40 you were meant to have.'

'And how many other houses are for sale?' Tears seeped from under Marina's contact lenses as she mourned the summer she'd imagined, picnicking among the leafy glades of the square's communal garden. That garden was a miracle of cooperation and clever planting, where children could play as if they'd been born in the 1950s with just an au pair on hand to frighten away strangers. 'Oh God,' she said suddenly. 'You don't think Jessica will ask her to the summer party, do you?'

Bunty fished the tea bag from her cup and wondered if Marina had gone nuts. Of course Jessica would invite Ms Hambrose to her party. Jessica always asked everyone within reason. Her summer party was the high point of the square's social calender.

'She'll ask you as well,' Bunty said. 'Wonder who Matthew will snog this year?'

Marina would not be diverted. 'If she goes, I'm not. How about you?' And it was only to change the subject that Bunty offered her friend another reading to see where things stood.

In the reading room, on the leather armchair opposite Marina on the chaise, Bunty closed her eyes and invited Uncle Jasper to step forward, which he did, within seconds. But how disappointing. He would only list a string of names that meant nothing to anyone, least of all Marina. 'Mary, Consequence, Ethel, Rover, Scarlet, Zoe,' he said to Bunty, who relayed them to Marina. Then, 'Has Scarlet Zoe arrived?'

Bunty rolled her eyes at Marina, who was all ears.

'We're looking for a house number, Uncle Jasper,' Bunty said.

Uncle Jasper replied, 'Has Scarlet Zoe arrived?'

'He said call the baby Scarlet Zoe,' Bunty improvised. Intuited. But then she heard loud and clear from the dead old duffer's ghostly lips two final words which made complete sense. 'Warn Jessica!' It was the kind of moment that made her gift so worthwhile. And it became even more rewarding not two hours later when Liz Wilkins at Number 8, who'd been talking to Mrs Silver at Number 38, passed on the information that Ms Hambrose was a Zoe.

'A scarlet woman,' Bunty said to Marina, who was on her mobile and, as it turned out, at Number 27, having met Sue Crawshaw at the communal garden gate. 'Scarlet Zoe,' Bunty repeated, in case Marina didn't get it.

To be a medium and a gossip is to tread on thin ice, obviously, but Bunty Moxton didn't think of herself as a gossip. In a square like Engadine, everyone expects to know everything there is to know about everyone else and news from a resident's dead relative was no more secret than news from a neighbour. Uncle Jasper had said, 'Warn Jessica,' and Bunty thought she'd better, as did everyone whose opinion she canvassed. So she did, over coffee under Jessica's gorgeous wisteria, and Jessica laughed her head off.

This was another mistake, which the whole square saw the minute it clapped eyes on Zoe Hambrose, who moved in the very next weekend. It was immediately clear that here was a neighbour whose glamour, style, elegance and grace would drive men into a frenzy. 'So is she ugly?' Marina Burton wanted to know when Bunty telephoned her on her mobile during the Monday-morning school run to give her an update.

'Matthew hand-delivered the party invitation himself,' Bunty replied. 'He stayed for an hour. Helping move tea chests.' Marina reversed into the car parked behind her, set off its alarm, and with its urgency ringing in her ears, tore through the back streets of Camberwell as if her future depended on it. She hoped for an early sighting of the object of her bitterness, but she was miles too late. Lovely Ms Hambrose was at her desk by eight as always. And by the time Marina turned into the square, Jessica Hargreaves was already sprawled on Bunty's chaise as Bunty attempted to summon again the spirit of her late grandmother, Elizabeth Jane.

Jessica had only limited faith in Bunty and hardly any in her dead grandmother, but she had even less in her husband who'd exhausted three wives before her with his endless straying. His dalliance with the Crawshaws' au pair had been the last straw. Bunty had offered a reading to put her mind at rest, about the party, she said, but Jessica knew that there was never any rest with a husband like Matthew. 'If you're there, Elizabeth Jane, step forward. Elizabeth Jane? Elizabeth?'

Bunty was calling so long that Marina had time to drive out of the square, find a non-resident's parking spot and walk the half mile back. Many relatives stepped forward to make themselves known, but none that Jessica knew, and she couldn't wait. She had appointments. She was sure the party would go swimmingly anyway. So she left, also a mistake, because Elizabeth Jane pitched up just as Marina flopped onto the chaise.

What she had to say she said to the very person who could make the worst of it. It was so shocking that Bunty wasn't at all sure she should pass it on to anyone. She forced herself. 'Zoe's the slag who will end the Hargreaveses' marriage,' Elizabeth Jane said. These weren't the exact words, but close enough, and they were exactly what Marina wanted to hear. Marina smiled. It was as she had thought, and even prayed.

It took almost no time at all for the residents of Numbers 27, 8, 18 and 12 as well as 23 to agree that Elizabeth Jane was spot on. Their husbands, to a man, fell for the new owner of Number 40 on the most fleeting of glimpses. 'Well, he's not obsessed,' Sue Crawshaw said, because the last thing she wanted was for her chap Lloyd to be mentioned in the same breath as Matthew Hargreaves, 'but he's so drippy, it's tragic.'

It was soon common knowledge that Matthew Hargreaves was at Number 40 every chance he got, having coffee with the nanny if Zoe wasn't home, hanging on pathetically until she arrived. Sue Crawshaw swore it was 3 a.m. when she looked out of her bedroom window two weeks after the move and had seen him creeping back to his house. No one was shocked. It had been predicted. Poor Jessica. Disgusting Zoe. In the absence of solid information, but in no way discouraged by it, the square made its mind up. It was her huge boobs. Did she have huge boobs? It was her age. Get off, she was forty. And a hopeless mother. And a snob. Had she spoken more than two words to anyone not called Matthew Hargreaves? It was touch and go whether she'd even bother with the party. Her acceptance had been vague and Marika, the nanny, who wore far too much make-up, knew only that she was baby-sitting but couldn't say why. 'She should never have been asked,' Marina Burton said furiously.

The big night was less than a week away when the female residents of Numbers 27, 8, 18, 12 and 23 plus Marina collided in the street at tea time. 'I'm amazed they haven't been sprung,' Marina said far too loudly, having listened with racing heart to assorted sightings of MH leaving four-oh.

Bunty invited everyone into her place for comfort as well as discretion and the cork had barely left the Santa Rita when Marina finished what she'd started. 'I don't know how you can sit here and watch it happening. She should be exposed before it's too late.' And stupid as it was, the idea took hold, as something silly can over a bottle or three. An hour and a half later, when the children were hitting each other from fatigue, Bunty agreed she would tackle the cow and let her know that Engadine prided itself on the solidarity of its sisters.

It was only when it came down to it that Bunty decided she couldn't. Not comfortably. It had been ridiculous to think she could. But what she felt able to do, comfortably, was call on Zoe Hambrose in the spirit of neighbourliness, and after a suitable preamble, summon dead relatives to warn her off. That was her plan, braver than it was clever, but thwarted sadly, as so many brave plans are.

Timing failed her, aided and abetted by Ms Hambrose's high-powered job and the demands of her social life. Bunty was obliged to grab her when she could, and the only time she could was well after nine on an evening when driving rain was keeping most people indoors and neighbourliness looked stupid. 'Hi,' Zoe said when Bunty introduced herself. 'If it's something you want from the kitchen you need Marika. Marika!'

Bunty, memorizing every detail of her new neighbour's dark beauty, tried to explain it wasn't anything she wanted from the kitchen. But Zoe kept on hollering for Marika and in the end Marika, all dishevelled, appeared at the top of the stairs. 'Sorry,' Bunty said. And then she went home, which Marina Burton told Sue Crawshaw was just wet. Steel was smouldering in Marina's heart.

That week, Matthew Hargreaves was spotted in the general vicinity of Number 40 on no less than one occasion and Marina decided if no one else had the testicles for it, she did. She adored Jessie Hargreaves. And this wretched house thief was destroying her marriage, for God's sake.

The party was in full swing when she made her move, if you can call full swing that hour after midnight when people who shouldn't bop in public suddenly know how to pole dance and neighbours' spouses are looking far more beguiling than they ever do in daylight. Zoe Hambrose had made her entrance not two minutes before and headed for the only person in the room she recognized, Matthew Hargreaves, who smiled at her sheepishly.

'Vixen!' cried Marina, shouting for two – or five if you counted her whole family. 'Whore, cow, thief!' It brought the room to a standstill. Zoe Hambrose took a second to realize who was speaking and where the words were aimed. Jessica Hargreaves moved towards her husband, but Marina was dragging Bunty to the middle of the circle that was forming around him, hell bent on revenge. Bunty was struggling, appalled at the damage hormones can wreak on a rational mind. But it was worse than hormones. It was hate, and Bunty was implicated in the hate because she had summoned the spirits who had stoked its fire.

It all came out, spilling in a great ugly pool across the marquee dance floor. The gazumping, the seducing, the unfaithfulness, the standoffishness, the Porsche, but towering above it all were the spirits. The spirits whose insider knowledge was all over the neighbourhood. Ms Hambrose didn't hang about, she was back in Number 40 before Oliver Burton had time to explain that his wife had gone into labour and been driven mad by the pain.

Can residents who live in each other's pockets recover from such a party? Rupert at Tinkers wasn't sure. But Marika, the nanny, was sacked within the hour, and next day, solicitors on behalf of Ms Hambrose fired off letters to both Marina Burton and Bunty Moxton threatening legal action if they didn't desist from their slander. A week later, after his wife had forgiven him and extracted promises he'd made many times before, Matthew Hargreaves informed Thomas Moxton that neither he nor his meddling loopy wife would be welcome in his house ever again. Rupert was happy to put Number 23 on the market for the Moxtons. He sold it to the Burtons that autumn.

The very very strange thing was that they never entirely fitted in. Marina was forgiven for the scene she'd caused, as she'd been pregnant and maybe unhinged, but Oliver was a prat. As for Bunty, moving away was a wrench. But what she learnt was that mediums sometimes have to make some sacrifices, and hers was life in a neighbourhood where the residents live in each other's pockets.

Joanna Trollope, a fifth-generation niece of Victorian author and social commentator Anthony Trollope, was born and brought up in Gloucestershire. She is the author of twelve highly acclaimed contemporary novels: *The Choir, A Village Affair, A Passionate Man, The Rector's Wife, The Men and the Girls, A Spanish Lover, The Best of Friends, Next of Kin, Other People's Children, Marrying the Mistress, Girl from the South* and *Brother & Sister*. Under the name of Caroline Harvey she writes romantic historical novels. She has also written a study of women in the British Empire, *Britannia's Daughters*. Joanna Trollope recently won the Booksellers Association Author of the Year award and was appointed OBE in the 1996 Queen's Birthday Honours List for services to literature.

Angel

When I was little, I had this thing about angels. It started soon after my mother died. She died when I was eight, of a brain tumour, and everyone – except my father – thought that it was very sweet and only natural that I develop a fixation about angels. They thought that I thought that my mother was safely with the angels, that they were looking after her. In fact, such an idea hadn't crossed my mind.

The reason I liked angels was because, in the first place, they were kind but impersonal. In the second place, they were sort of nothing, not boy, not girl, and that was peaceful, just as their impersonal kindness was. And in the third place, and very importantly, whether or not they were looking after my mother didn't matter to me as much as that I believed they were looking after me.

I wouldn't want you to think that I didn't love my mother. I did, in the rather casual, unimaginative way that a lot of eight-year-olds love their mothers. And she loved me back in rather the same way. My mother was a scientist. She was a very good scientist, and she worked in a laboratory in Cambridge on all the possible consequences of breaking the links in the

DNA chain. I know she was good at this and I know people admired her. When she died, people were utterly shocked that her brain, that a brain of the calibre of hers, could be susceptible to a tumour. I remember her going off on her bicycle every morning before I went to school – my father took me to school – and coming back after I got back from school every evening with that shuttered look on her face that meant her mind hadn't actually come home with her.

I think it probably was a great surprise to her, to have a baby. It was probably quite a surprise to find herself married to my father, married to anyone. They met in London at some kind of peace rally – I think my father was lying down in Whitehall, in a white T-shirt – and he moved to Cambridge to be near her. He's an engineer. Quite a complicated academic sort of engineer. He used to say that in essence, his work and my mother's weren't so different. But he doesn't have her focus. I rather hope I don't. A focus like that is very luxurious for the person who has it, but pretty bleak for the people they live with. If my father had had it, too, we'd never have had any bread or tea bags or clean socks. As it was, he and I did Sainsbury's together, once a week, down towards the Newmarket Road, which suited me beautifully, as fathers don't make a fuss about crisps and chocolate like mothers do.

Anyway, these angels. I had a postcard that my parents had sent me once when they went away for a weekend in Florence. The postcard showed a fresco of an angel telling Mary that she was going to have Jesus. They both look very young. They are in this empty cell-like room together and Mary is kneeling, and they both look frankly scared. I liked them being young, I liked the angel being without obvious gender, but what

302

I liked most of all was that the angel looked as if it was definitely on Mary's side. It had to deliver this message, it knew that, but it could also imagine how Mary felt having to hear it, and was sorry for her.

I sat on my bed and stared and stared at that angel. I realized that I wanted one too, I wanted one badly. I wanted an angel who would fly gently into my bedroom and say in a calm, kind, unsoppy sort of voice, 'It's OK, Katie, I'm on your side.' And then it might add, 'About everything.' I began to collect angels – pictures, postcards, Christmas ornaments, anything. I had angels in my pockets and on my walls and in my books and drawers. I had winged angel heads under my pillow. I had a very small wooden angel – Austrian probably – which I wore round my neck on a leather shoelace during school tests or exams.

My father thought this was fine. He didn't think I had any remotely sentimental reasons for the angel fixation, but it saved him from having to get a dog, which friends kept telling him I really needed. My father liked dogs, but he knew he wasn't a natural looker-after. Looking after me, in a rather haphazard way, was really all he could manage, so if a flight of angels was a help to me in any way, they were, in his view, most welcome.

I suppose the intensity of the angel phase lasted about three years – at least until the end of primary school. Maybe I felt that I didn't need them so much; maybe I was anxious about the reception my angels might get at my new secondary school. In any case, I stopped having angels absolutely everywhere, I stopped carrying them about. I left the ones on the walls where they were, and I didn't disturb the ones in hibernation among my knickers and sweaters, but I just grew quieter about them all. I stopped feeling, I suppose, that something awful would happen if I didn't have an army of angels physically around me all the time.

Anyway, my father and I were doing fine together. We really were. We bumbled around each other like a couple of old sheep in a field. He went to work, I went to school and somebody called Marge, who also cleaned the place where my father worked, came in and washed the bathroom and kitchen floor. Sometimes she washed our towels and clothes too, and very occasionally ran an iron down the front of my father's shirts. He didn't have any best shirts. He isn't that kind of man. I used to look at him and wonder what it was that made my mother stop beside his prone form in Whitehall and speak to him. He wasn't awful to look at, he just wasn't special. And he was a bird-watcher. I know there's nothing wrong with being a birder, but I also know that it doesn't have sex appeal, and when I started secondary school I got quite interested in sex appeal. I also knew this was one area where no angel could help me.

So, on we went, my father and I, not noticing that the paint was flaking off the window frames, not minding eating pasta or sausages seven times a week, not interfering with each other. I started to go out a bit at the weekend and my father said fine, but never come home later than ten thirty. Mostly I obeyed him because he was not a disciplinarian in general, and when I didn't, he gated me, which meant going with him to Norfolk to watch wading birds.

And then it happened. Three weeks after my fourteenth birthday, and me in a rapture because a boy in fifth year called Grant Ackerly had deliberately stopped to talk to me three times, it happened. My father, holding the ketchup bottle upside down over his sausages and whacking the bottom to get the ketchup out, said that he was going to get married again. At first, I just thought this was an abstract idea, one that he had been turning over in his mind and was now offering for discussion. But no. It was a specific announcement. My father had met someone called Carolyn Mallet and had asked her to marry him.

I screamed. I can see myself now, sitting at that table with a piece of sausage pronged on my fork, and screaming. I screamed about everything. I wanted to know how he dared, who this horrible woman was, what was the matter with our life, and most of all, what about me? Had he thought about me? What was it going to be like for me, having to live with horrible Carolyn? I didn't want her in my house, I yelled. I didn't want her in my life or his or anyone's. I didn't, I shrieked, want anything to be different, ever.

My father watched me. Then he put the ketchup down. 'It'll be fine,' he said. I stared at him. I was out of breath from screaming. 'She plays the cello,' he said, as if that somehow made everything all right. 'She's divorced. She was divorced three years ago. And she has a son.' My father looked pleasedly at me, as if he had given me a lovely present. 'He's about your age. He's called Hal.'

I won't bore you with how I behaved after that. Suffice it to say that my plate got broken and there was sausage all over the floor (such a waste of not having a dog). When I slammed my bedroom door a few minutes later, the force of the slam threw two pictures off the landing wall outside, and the glass broke.

The worst of it was that my father didn't seem to notice. I couldn't say he looked rapturous – he isn't that kind of man – but he looked revoltingly happy. He brought Carolyn Mallet round to meet me. She was quite pretty, with long dark red hair, and she was unquestionably nice and also interesting. I hated her. I hated her so much that I could hardly breathe while she was in the house.

And as for Hal . . . Words fail, really. Hal was fifteen. He was tall and bony and gawky with red hair like his mother's, and joke ears. She was a musician; he was an artist. He drew all day long, on anything. When he wanted to explain something he drew it. I thought of this freak, this jug-eared nerd occupying the guest (except we never had any) bedroom in my house, in the house I had lived in, that had been mine, since I was born, and I was so full of rage and misery that I wanted someone else to suffer. Really, really suffer.

Well, there were three of them that I could make suffer. There was my father and Carolyn and Hal. I had plenty of ideas. I could stop working at school, I could play truant, I could ignore the ten-thirty curfew, I could be very encouraging to Grant Ackerley – who had a bad reputation – and I could simply pretend Hal did not exist, that he was as invisible to me as if he had never been born.

Carolyn set about sorting out the house. She got decorators in, she made new curtains, she dug the garden. She offered to teach me the cello. I said, very distinctly, 'Classical music is gross.' She cooked delicious, varied meals, she put fruit in the fruit bowl and new sheets on my bed. I ate Snickers before meals so that I was too full to eat, and got Biro on the sheets, and raided the fruit bowl at night, leaving cores and peel lying on the table. Every time she spoke, I either ignored her or fell about with derisive laughter. When I made her cry – quite easily – I felt triumph.

I felt enough triumph to stop going to school. I went

with Grant Ackerley to a squat some friends of his had and was given my first spliff. I quite liked it, but I didn't like anything else about that day. I didn't like the squat, or the people in it, or the way Grant was with them. One of his friends tried it on with me, got his hands inside my jeans, and Grant just laughed. He said, laughing, 'You're bloody lucky anyone wants to.'

When I got home, I was thankful there was no one there. The kitchen was tidy; there was no note but there was a cake on the table. I thought about spitting on it, but hadn't the energy. I trailed upstairs instead, planning on a real good howling cry on my bed, and found Hal in my room. He wasn't at all abashed. He turned round when I came in and said cheerfully, 'Hi. I was just looking at your angels.'

'Get out,' I yelled.

'I like angels, too,' Hal said. 'But it's really difficult to draw wings. It's difficult to get the idea of movement into wings.'

'I said get out!'

He looked at me. He said, 'Where have you been?'

'None of your frigging business!'

'No,' he said. He grinned. 'But I'm quite interested.' He came past me towards the door. He said, 'I bunked off school this afternoon, too. I had something I wanted to draw.'

I got into trouble in school, of course I did. I had a session with the head and a session with my father, and my friends, instead of standing up for me, said I must have been out of my mind to go even to Boots the Chemist with Grant Ackerley. I had to do community service the school organized – weeding the garden for an old people's home – and my father gated me completely for a month. When he told me this, I whipped round on Carolyn and shouted, 'Don't smirk!'

307

'I'm not,' she said. 'In fact, I'm rather on your side.' I wanted to murder her. And my father. And Grant Ackerley and the school and Hal. And myself.

Then Christmas came. I was dreading it. Carolyn had finished redecorating the sitting room and I knew she'd want a tree. My father had never been bothered with a real tree. We'd had an imitation one from the garden centre – with electric candles fixed to its branches that you just had to plug in and switch on. I'd made a point, always, of despising my friends' houses with their garlands and wreaths and fairy lights; I told my father I thought it was pathetic – and materialistic – to make such a fuss about just one day, especially in a country where no one believed in religion any more.

My father had smiled at me absentmindedly then and he smiled at me absently now. He looked at the garland along the sitting-room mantelpiece and the candles on the window sills – she lit them every evening – and the real tree in its wooden tub, and he told Carolyn he thought it looked lovely.

'Do you?' I said, sneering.

He regarded me. 'Yes,' he said, quite seriously. 'I do.'

Carolyn made a Christmas cake and mince pies. She wrapped up presents. She filled a bowl with clementines and another with nuts and played Handel's *Messiah* while she stirred things in the kitchen. I wondered what Hal thought of all this carry-on, but he didn't seem at all fazed by it. He drew a huge white and silver angel with its arms full of stars on dark blue paper, and Carolyn pinned it to the front door. I was nearly sick. It was like Mummy pinning up baby's first scribble on the kitchen noticeboard. People passing in the street kept stopping to admire the angel.

I wanted to shout at them that it was all a sham, that I'd been betrayed.

On Christmas Eve, Carolyn and my father said we were all going to have a drink together in the sitting room as a family. Carolyn was going to the carol service at King's College – she said nobody had to go with her, but of course my father did – and then we were all going to start Christmas together with a glass of champagne and all the candles lit and Handel reminding us that unto us a child was born. I opened my mouth to say something and my father said with terrifying quietness, 'Enough.'

They went into the sitting room and shut the door. I could hear Handel beginning. I pictured my father lighting the fire – we'd never lit it, in all our six years together – and the champagne shining in the glasses. I sat on the stairs and wondered if it was possible to feel more miserable, more furious, more neglected. I put my head in my hands and said all the swear words I could think of.

Above me, Hal's bedroom door opened. I heard his feet come along the landing. Then they came down the stairs behind me, then beside me, and I waited for them to go on down, ignoring me as I had steadfastly ignored them. But they didn't. I looked up, squinting, not wanting to raise my head. Hal was sitting two steps below me on the other side of the stairs.

'Hi,' he said.

'Go away.'

He sighed. He had his back to me. 'You're so predictable.'

'I said go away.'

'It's difficult, I grant you,' Hal said. 'All this. It's difficult because it's not the same. But it's not impossible.'

I said furiously, 'Nobody cares what I think. Nobody cares about me.'

He shifted a little on the stairs. 'Oh, I dunno,' he said.

I raised my head a little and said crisply, 'I don't suppose you have any idea whatsoever what it's like to be lonely. What it's like to be alone, really alone.'

He shifted again and then he said, 'As it happens, I have a very good idea. Mum and I are doing OK now, but we didn't. Not when Dad went. I thought it was her fault Dad had gone. I told her so.'

I looked at his back. He was wearing a grey T-shirt, and under it a black polo shirt with the collar rucked up. He was so bony that his frame stuck through the sweatshirt as if it was hanging on a garden rake. I could see the points of his shoulder blades clearly, the points where – well, where his wings might have been attached. If he'd had any. I said, 'Oh.'

'I really went for her,' Hal said. 'I thought it had never happened to anyone before. I couldn't believe they could do this to me.'

I swallowed. I said, gesturing at the sitting-room door – a pointless gesture he couldn't see, 'You going in there?'

He hesitated and then he said, 'If you will.' I heard myself give a tiny gasp. He half turned towards me and said, 'I was waiting for you, in fact.'

I couldn't say anything. I felt completely choked. He stood up and looked down at me. I said, 'In a minute, in a minute,' and shook my head to indicate that I was lost to everything for a while.

'OK,' he said.

He turned away from me and went down. There was a lamp on in the hall – a new lamp – and the light caught his hair and his ears and made them glow.

When he got to the bottom of the stairs he stopped. At first, I thought he was just hesitating before he crossed the hall, but then I realized he was waiting for me. He was waiting for me to gather myself and come down the stairs and join him so that we could go and start Christmas with Carolyn and my father, together. Him and me. I took a breath.

'Wait,' I said. 'I'm coming.'

Lynne Truss is now best known for her bestselling book on punctuation, *Eats, Shoots & Leaves* (2003), but she is also a broadcaster and journalist and the author of three novels including *Going Loco*. She has also written many stories, plays and comedies for BBC Radio 4. She occasionally goes on painting holidays.

The Yellow Door

In shorts and sunhats, long skirts and sandals, Joan
Turner's painting group sat on a rough, low wall in the
dappled, mauve shadows of a spreading pine. An occasional breeze riffled their straw hats and twitched their
linen.

'Look at us,' Gillian thought with a little laugh.
She studied her own long brown skirt, flat shoes and
cardigan, and the effect was so perfectly Virginia
Woolf it was truly a bit startling. The only thing
required to complete the effect, she reflected drily,
would be pockets full of rocks.

Gillian was happy. She felt safe in her Bloomsbury
mufti, holding a fistful of brushes, and she loved
the sort of people who went on painting holidays on
Greek islands off season – people like June and Bill
from Haywards Heath ('Hello, Bill! Hello, June!'), and
that old bat Cicely from Southend, who used to be a
nun. And here we are again, Gillian thought. Our
first day and already it's perfect. Above us church
bells clamour in a whitewashed campanile. To our
right a deep turquoise sea dotted with picturesque
fishing vessels. And directly in front, with an easel
and a large brush newly dipped in a jam jar of water,

our own dear Joan Turner executing a lovely seamless sky.

'Do you see what I'm doing?' Joan said. The group nodded and made sincere wish-I-could-do-that noises. As usual with Joan's painting groups, a range of abilities was represented, but by and large they were a modestly gifted bunch who knew that doing a sky was not easy. 'So. Cobalt and cerulean blue,' Joan summed up with a smile. 'The lightest of washes, tip of the brush, picking up the water from the previous brushstroke – do you see? Does that make sense?'

Joan's question was met with the usual murmur of uncertain agreement and an envious whimper from poor buck-toothed Cicely, who had been painting for twenty years, but still did skies that were heavily striped like a ploughed field and got abruptly darker halfway down. The term 'light wash' meant little to heavy-handed Cicely. Unless it was something she had before going out to dinner.

Unfolding her lightweight stool next morning outside a house with a nice yellow door, Gillian reckoned she had done well booking this holiday. The group was exactly right: eight couples of retirement age who joked about squandering their kids' inheritance; two depressed widows who didn't want to talk about it; a French woman who thought she was a better painter than everybody else; and good old Cicely, who always made Gillian resemble (by comparison) a well-balanced personality. Cicely tended to bring photos of her cats on holiday. To be fair, Gillian did the same. The difference was that she didn't show hers around at meal times.

The French woman (Marie-Louise) was an un-expected bonus. Being uppity and blatantly foreign, she was a natural hate figure for everyone else to talk about. Yesterday she had pointed to some rather nicely executed planks of wood in a picture of Bill's and laughed, 'But zese planks are so pink! Zey are like rhubarb!' And good old Eric from Southampton had said behind his hand to Gillian, 'We've got a right one here.'

Joan came to see what Gillian was doing. It was her custom to visit her chicks as they worked, showing them how to mix grey and yellow to make a decent green, or politely catching up on their news. One year when Gillian had travelled with her to Tunisia, Joan had settled down and inquired, rather innocently, about Gillian's love life, and had been treated to a candid and unedifying reply. The trouble was that Joan (twenty years Gillian's senior) had a rather rose-coloured view of the heterosexual bonding instinct. She thought all physical attraction between men and women was fantastic. In the old days she had been an enthusiastic illustrator for Mills & Boon.

Gillian, impatient with this romantic attitude, had answered her question with brutal truth. She had told Joan all about Gerald, her married boss at the Home Office, their nights in single-bedded Travelodge accommodation, and their episodes in stationery cupboards. It had not made a dent in Joan's world view.

'I'm sure he loved you, Gillian.'

'I know he didn't, Joan.'

'You loved him, though.'

'I shouldn't have.'

At this point Gillian had told Joan a joke she was currently quite fond of. 'How many men does it take to tile a bathroom?'

Joan brightened. 'I don't know. Two?'

'One,' said Gillian. And then, in a low, confidential tone, 'But you have to slice him very thinly.'

But all this was two years ago, and now they were in Greece and they weren't going to talk about Gillian's love life.

'I thought I'd do this yellow door.'

'Lovely.' Joan narrowed her eyes to assess the tonal values of the scene. 'That's lovely. And these shrubs. Yes. But the door will be in shadow soon, don't forget.'

'Oh no. Damn, I didn't think of that.' Gillian dithered. Should she do something else? She rather liked this door.

'See how far you get,' said Joan. 'You can come back tomorrow at the same time.'

'Oh yes.'

'Or another day. We're here for two weeks. I'd like you to finish something.'

'Yes, right.' Gillian was well known for starting pictures and not finishing them.

Joan turned to go. 'I won't ask about . . . you know,' she said, lightly.

'Oh good.'

'Except to say, I'm sure you'll find happiness some time, Gillian.'

'Don't start, Joan. Please.'

'I'd like to see you happy.'

'I am happy, Joan. For the last time, I don't need a man.'

She wanted to say that a woman needs a man like a fish needs a bicycle, but it was too unoriginal. So she arranged her brushes and poured some water in a little jar. Taking a soft pencil, she lightly sketched the outline of the house, its door, its tiled roof. As she became absorbed in her work she found herself wondering idly about the fish and the bicycle.

Actually, when you turned your mind to it, it was quite easy to imagine a fish having a pleasant bike ride. She could picture a salmon bowling along one of those dead straight country roads in France.

She mixed cerulean and cobalt for the sky, a little of one, a dob of the other. Big brush, lots of water, try it out on a spare piece of paper – that's right. In her mind's eye the fish wore a beret and carried a long baguette. As she started to lay the beautiful blue sky, he took his tail off the pedals and freewheeled cheerfully, whistling the *Marseillaise*.

'Scuse,' a deep voice said behind her. She looked up. Damn. A man. A Greek man, moreover. And they were all after only one thing, Greek men.

'Sorry,' she said, half rising but having to sit back down again, what with the picture and her paintbox and everything else she was balancing. 'I'm just . . .' She indicated the half-finished painting of the house. She had left the door for another time.

'Is my house,' the man shrugged. 'Is good.' He produced a pack of cigarettes from his pocket and offered it to her. She waved a no-thank-you.

'OK.' He lit one for himself and curled his face as he took the first drag, looking down at her picture. He didn't move.

'Is fantastic,' he breathed at last.

'No, no, it isn't,' she assured him, with a hollow laugh.

'Yes!' he insisted with a gesture. 'Is good.' He crouched beside her as if to get a better look. Gillian held her breath. Continuing to smoke, he studied the pad on Gillian's lap, his shoulder brushing hers; he looked up and down, comparing the house with the picture, as if genuinely taking it in. Then he turned his face towards hers and smiled. She closed her eyes and stifled a sigh. Why do men always assume we find them attractive, she thought. Why don't they know about body space?

'You come back?' he said, standing up.

She frowned.

'Maybe,' she said. 'There are lots of other things to paint – the sea and the boats and everything—' She stopped. She had spoken too quickly. 'Maybe,' she said.

'You come back,' he said, definitely. He dropped his cigarette and stepped on it. 'Is good,' he said as he departed.

'Yes,' she muttered, 'and you Tarzan, me Jane.'

She tipped her jar of coloured water into some weeds.

It pleased Gillian to be with people who had been married for forty years. It reassured her that she didn't have the temperament for it; that being single and embittered was her ideal state. Over dinner at the open-air taverna that night she sat between George and Evelyn from Frome on one side and Frank and Betty from Derbyshire on the other. All four were testaments to the miracle of long marriage, and none of them was remotely interested in whether she felt the need for a man. Opposite, Cicely was showing snaps of her new kitchen to Joan ('There's little Paddywhack on the windowsill!'), thus effortlessly retaining her claim to Supreme Spinster Saddo. It was only a matter of time, surely, before Cicely produced photos of a tapioca pudding she was particularly proud of.

Joan was just handing the pictures to Gillian when the Greek man walked by and spotted her at the top table. He gave her a wave.

'Who's that?' asked Joan.

Good heavens, this woman was quick to spot any hint of intergender activity.

'Who's what?' said Gillian, obtusely. The man had taken a seat at a further taverna and was discreetly signalling an invitation to join him. 'This stainless steel is effective,' she added, for Cicely's benefit.

Joan peered round, turned back, and pulled a face.

'He's lovely,' she told Gillian, with a twinkle. 'You're a dark horse.'

Gillian snorted. 'Stop it, Joan. Please.'

'You can see he likes you.'

'I mean it, Joan.'

'Why don't you join him for a drink?'

'I'm not a dog to be whistled for, Joan,' Gillian said.

Joan was confused. 'Did he whistle?'

'Could we change the subject?'

Not looking up, Gillian shuffled through the photos and made approving noises about the way Cicely had housed her microwave. When she finally looked up to take a sip of retsina and glance casually at the spot where the Greek man was, he had gone.

'No, I don't think I'll go to the monastery,' Gillian said at breakfast the next day. The air was heavy and she had a headache. The others had hatched a scheme for a walk and a picnic, but she didn't fancy it. Besides, she had spent much of the night thinking about the Greek man and had decided rather angrily that she was not going to let him influence her holiday. She intended to finish the yellow door. People were always on at her about not finishing her pictures.

'You just want to have some time with your mystery man,' teased Joan, as the others collected rucksacks and bottles of water.

Gillian refused to dignify this with an answer.

'Have you seen Cicely today?' asked Joan.

'No.'

'She said she wanted to go to the monastery.'

'Oh, well.'

'I made inquiries about that man. He's the doctor.'

'He should know better than to smoke, then, shouldn't he?'

'I could see he liked you.'

'Joan, it's time I told you something important. I really loathed *Shirley Valentine*.'

Having waved off the group, Gillian climbed the rough steps to the site of the yellow-doored house and arranged her stool. It was hotter today and the air was still; Gillian felt she was stifling. From her rucksack she withdrew the watercolour pad, the paints, the bottle of water, the brushes. Agitatedly, she thought: should I have a plan? In case he comes again? Of course not. She just prayed he wouldn't crouch next to her again. The thought of it made her neck flush and her pulse race. That big arm brushing against hers. The freshly showered smell from his thick black hair.

And so she sat there and mixed a nice light yellow and tried it out on a spare piece of paper. But somehow she couldn't paint the door. Why risk ruining the work she had already done? Such doubts often assailed Gillian when she painted. Now she looked at the picture – the door sketched in but unpainted – and felt a familiar rueful resolve. Yes, better not to botch it. The way she had done the roof was fantastic. She closed the pad and put it back in her rucksack. And anyway, she thought – rummaging for a tissue because she suddenly felt she was going to cry – an hour I've been here and there's no sign of him, is there? Which is the way men always treat you. I don't even want to see him and look what he's done to me. Typical Tarzan behaviour. Not even to send Cheetah with a message.

'Gillian? Are you all right?'

For heaven's sake, thought Gillian. Who is it this time? Of course. Cicely. The woman who could eat an apple through a tennis racquet.

'Hello, Cicely,' she said, trying to sound bright and cheerful. 'Are you looking for the others? They've gone off without you to the monastery.'

'Are you all right, Gillian? You look upset.'

Gillian wiped her eyes and made an effort to smile.

'You can have this spot if you like. But I have to warn you, it's like Victoria Station.'

Gillian hoisted her rucksack onto her back and turned away from the house. The last person she wanted pity from was Cicely.

For the next few days Gillian painted boats in the harbour. She saw the Greek man only twice, first when he called a friendly 'Yiasou!' to June one morning – June having received his doctorly ministrations on a twisted ankle (she said he had lovely soft hands) – and the second time when he came and stood beside her without speaking on the quayside, briefly blowing the back of her neck before going away again. But the holiday was progressing well in many ways. Lots of Metaxa in the evenings, for example. Excellent yoghurt for breakfast. And as a bonus, the maddening French woman had by now so entertainingly offended everyone that Edith from Stratford (with two new hips) had wickedly retaliated by suggesting she go off and photograph a nearby military installation. 'The Greeks really love it if you take an interest in their air force capabilities, Marie-Louise,' Edith had said, revealing a side to her personality that even her husband had never seen before.

It was halfway through the second week when Joan – over a cup of Nescafé – asked Gillian about the unfinished yellow door. They had spent the morning lazily together, cheerfully demolishing Marie-Louise.

'Oh, you know what I'm like,' said Gillian. 'I prefer it the way it is. I don't want to ruin it.'

Joan looked at the picture on the table in front of them. All she could see was the blank at its centre.

'Honestly, Joan,' Gillian persisted. She laughed. 'I like it like this. I like the way it still has the potential to be perfect.'

Joan shrugged as if she had never heard such nonsense. 'Oh well,' she said. She was a woman of remarkable patience. Anyone else would have pushed the French woman off the ferry on the very first day.

'You don't see, do you?'

'No. But then I never have,' said Joan. 'Ever since I've known you I've thought, this woman won't go halfway to meet happiness for fear of making a mistake. Life's too short not to take the odd little risk, Gillian. And I don't mean just not painting this door.'

Gillian was stung. 'I told you about Gerald,' she said quietly. But as she said it, she knew it sounded hollow and self-pitying. It also struck her that the affair with Gerald was ten years ago.

'Look, I shouldn't have said any of that,' said Joan, summoning the waiter. 'But Cicely told me you were upset the other day.'

'Did she?'

'Yes. Bless her.' Joan laughed. 'She said you must be missing your cats!'

The next day was a beautiful one. Gillian climbed to the usual spot, unfolded her chair and set to work. It was time to deal with this thing. It was time to show

Joan a completed picture before she was despaired of altogether. And so she mixed again a fine clear yellow, took the tiniest quantity onto a flat-tipped brush and gently laid it on the paper. A passer-by might have seen her – this watercolourist in her linen clothes bent over her work – and seen an image of serene inner peace. Which just goes to show how little we learn from mere pictorial observation.

She worked on the watercolour for an hour until the sun swung round, and then stopped and held it away from her. The door was all right. It looked . . . it looked pretty much like a door. As for the picture – well, she had to admit the picture had been better before. But she didn't care. As she sat and looked at it a lump of pride rose in her throat and she heard the sound of a person behind her. Oh God. I must be prepared for it being Joan again, she thought. Or Cicely, eating a piece of fruit through an item of sports equipment. Or even the French woman, under arrest for espionage.

But she knew it wasn't any of them.

'You finish,' he said, a note of pleasure in his voice.

'Yes,' she said. She turned round to look at him. Her heart raced.

'Is good now?'

'It's all right.'

He smiled. 'OK.'

He went to the yellow door, opened it, and gestured to come in.

Salley Vickers is a former university teacher of literature and psychoanalyst. She is the author of the bestselling *Miss Garnet's Angel*, *Instances of the Number 3* and *Mr Golightly's Holiday*. She now writes full time and lives in Bath and the West Country.

The Hawthorn Madonna

Each year, at Easter, Elspeth and Ewan stayed in a cottage which had been loaned to them by Mrs Stroud, who had been a schoolfriend of Ewan's aunt Val. Not that the two old ladies ever saw much of each other in the latter part of their days. Still, it was recognizably Edie Stroud in Aunt Val's photo album – the girl with the almost coal-black hair, very bobbed. Unless that was Mary Squires, after all, who died of tuberculosis after her fiancé shot himself?

When Mrs Stroud herself died, the cottage passed to her nephew, who worked in Amsterdam – something to do with diamonds, someone said, though that might have been wishful thinking. And he was glad enough to let it without trouble to a couple who did not mind that there was mould around the window frames, and that you had to hang the bedding before the fire to air each night before you went to sleep. Indeed, they would have missed the nightly ritual, Elspeth and Ewan, if Mrs Stroud's nephew had done what his aunt had always been saying she would do and have a proper damp course laid down.

Luckily, Mrs Stroud herself was now laid down instead, and the fingers of moisture were allowed to settle inside the glass of the windows unhindered and make little feather rivulets down the pane and emanate out into the general air of the place.

Elspeth and Ewan had never had any children. In the early days when they went to 'Brow' they had gone with the plan of serious lovemaking. But anyone who has ever tried knows that 'serious' lovemaking is not the most successful kind – causing perverse longings for a readable book, or even car maintenance. And in the end they tacitly dropped such plans when it became clear that, for one reason or another (they never tried too hard to discover which), they were not going to have children. This did not mean that they were not affectionate with each other. People said of them that they were an exceptionally warm couple – really, it did you good to be with them.

In bed at night they held each other close even years after the lovemaking had been dropped altogether, except for birthdays and Christmas. But it was Easter when they always went to 'Brow' – which seemed not quite to qualify . . .

This Easter was particularly cold – although Elspeth said all Easters were cold these days and she believed that something had happened to the calendar since they were young. Not at all, Ewan said. The Met Office had given out statistics which proved that the weather had been much the same, give or take the odd fluctuation, for the past two hundred years. That was just like men, Elspeth had retorted, to dismiss all the important events as 'fluctuations'. They were driving, as usual, down the M3 and off the A303 past Stonehenge and into the heart of Somerset, if such a promiscuous county could be said to have a heart.

The cottage stood on the brow of a low hill – hardly a hill at all, more a kind of hump. It stood alone at the end of a lane, which fortunately had never been surfaced and discouraged picnickers.

Elspeth unpacked the box of groceries she had brought from London to save having to go too often to Brack, the nearest village, or to Wells for decent wine. Ewan went at once to inspect the woodshed. Yes, plenty of sawn logs stacked – so Tim, the young man who seemed always to be smoking joints but who for all that kept the hedges neatly clipped, had done his stuff. And there were enough candles, too, for when the electricity tripped off. All in order, then. And it never took long to heat up the tank for a bath.

It was still cold the next day when they went for one of the walks which, over the years, they had taken possession of – behind the hill and along the track through the plantation, towards Wells. You could just see the twin honey-coloured cathedral towers in the distance below them. 'Shall we go to Wells tomorrow?' Elspeth asked. 'Tomorrow' was Good Friday. But in the end they decided not to – it wasn't a big thing with them, church at Easter – just that Elspeth liked the pageantry.

'It's going to snow,' Ewan remarked as he opened the wine for supper. They were to have *boeuf en daube*, brought from Highgate in a casserole. Years ago Elspeth had learned the recipe from reading *To the Lighthouse*, but these days she never imagined herself as Mrs Ramsey.

'"Nudity banned until this appears in hedges" – eight letters?' Ewan asked later by the fire. Although Elspeth never got crossword clues, for twenty years he had persevered in asking.

'Hawthorn,' she said, proving that it is right never to stop trying.

'Why so?'

'"Ne'er cast a clout till may be out." People think it's the month but in fact it's the mayflower. Don't you remember? I've told you that millions of times!' But a mind that grasps crosswords will usually be too reasonable for rhymes or folklore.

Perhaps it was the extreme temperature, but by Saturday Ewan had contracted a cold. They ate hot cross buns by the fire and he went to bed early. Elspeth wished they had packed whisky and Ewan wished she wouldn't fuss. 'It's not fussing to want you to have a good time!'

'I'll be right as rain tomorrow,' Ewan said.

But he wasn't. Elspeth was aware that his night had been restless. Years of sleeping alongside her husband's tall frame had attuned her own to his. When he slept badly so did she – one of the penalties of a successful partnership. By morning he was coughing alarmingly and – even more alarmingly – agreed to stay in bed. There is only so much attention you can give a reluctant invalid. By afternoon Ewan shooed Elspeth out for a walk.

'But where shall I go? I don't want to do one of ours without you.' Ewan thought this daft but Elspeth, who could be stubborn, had her own rules. Well, she would strike out, find somewhere new. Then, when he was better, they could explore it together, add it to the others they had made their own over the years.

Although the walks Elspeth liked best started from the cottage, there was no chance she could discover new territory that way – it was all too well tried. So it would have to be a car trip, which would give her a chance to buy whisky – she felt that the least she could do for Ewan was provide that. Wells had a Wine Rack. She would go that way and then on towards Glastonbury. Never mind the old hippies.

With a bottle of Glenfiddich in the back of the car, Elspeth felt more entitled to her outing. But even then she wasn't about to abandon her husband altogether. She would keep him with her by doing what she and Ewan had done when they first met – drive where fancy took you, then take every left turn until you found the place you were looking for. It always worked in the end.

Elspeth drove by instinct, following roads she had never travelled, until all she knew was that she had come some way from Wells. But wasn't Somerset a strange county? Even such a short distance from where she had started the snow was quite deep, lining the hedges with precarious spines of powdery white. The white gave her a chill feeling. She half wished that she had packed a thermos flask.

There, she hoped she was not becoming one of those people who for ever wished they had done things differently! She had the whisky, after all.

Left, left again – it was funny, when you thought about it, that you so rarely came back on yourself – left here, and here and here: now stop.

She had fetched up a dead-end – not so much a dead-end, because there remained ahead a track which a lighter vehicle could traverse, but not the Volvo. Plenty of room for a person though.

Elspeth stepped out of the car, pulling on her fleece-lined anorak. Would she take the whisky just for the fun of a nip? No, it was for Ewan – unsealed it was not so much of a present. Luckily, she had brought her boots. The snow was melting into mud as Elspeth walked along the lane. On either side the hedges grew high, covered in wild clematis and the fine, light dusting particles of snow which gave the wrong seasonal feel: it was Easter not Christmas. Although still early afternoon, the light had begun to fail – or perhaps more snow was gathering, blocking out the weak sun. Now there was a wooden gate ahead, its mossy slats slightly out of true. And just beyond, Elspeth made out a small stone building with a cross aloft. A chapel.

In spite of her expectations, the door of the chapel yielded quite naturally and Elspeth stepped inside. A sweetish, musky smell greeted her – not altogether disagreeable, but not wholly pleasant either.

'You can put the lights on if you like.'

The voice, neither low nor loud, was pitched from somewhere in the shadowy back part of the chapel – which in a church is called the 'apse'.

'I'm sorry?' She wasn't alarmed yet.

'No need to be! The switch is on your left, just shoulder height.'

The chapel lit up to reveal a man seated on a bench at the wall furthest from the altar, on which was arranged thorny branches of green and flowering white. To the left stood a slight wooden statue.

'See there, the Hawthorn Madonna,' said the man. 'We are very proud of her here.' Since he was sitting down, it was hard to be sure but he appeared to be of medium height – quite ordinary, in fact.

'It looks old,' said Elspeth, trying to be polite.

But at this the man merely laughed – a brusque barking sound, like some large, unconcerned sea bird.

'You can touch her, if you like.'

'Surely not!' A touch of reproof. Elspeth was only mildly religious, but she knew what was to be respected.

'Why not? You won't hurt. 'Sides – she's meant to be touched at Easter times.'

Some local rite or ritual, Elspeth thought.

She walked forward, setting her boots down carefully on the flags. The figure was made of a knotty dark wood with a natural-looking twist in it which greatly added to the feeling of someone limber and flowing.

'Does she have a baby?' Elspeth did not know why she had asked this – nor even that she was going to ask it until the words flew, with a life of their own, from her lips. Once out, they seemed to hang in the air, with the breath that was making icy clouds before her face.

'Is it a baby you want, then?'

'Oh, yes!'

The words were out before she knew it, but she had no thoughts of taking them back. After all, it was what had lain behind all her other thoughts during the nights when she didn't sleep – and maybe even more so during the ones when she did.

'Touch her then and ask.'

It was odd how she didn't mind that he mentioned it – the subject she and Ewan had put away for good between them. But Ewan was at home sick and here she was in an unknown place – with a stranger . . .

Ewan said later that it was the whisky that had done it.

'She got me into bed, got me tight and raped me!' he used to say. And Elspeth would blush a little, perhaps because she didn't like the word 'rape' to be used of anything to do with Jack. On the other hand, she didn't want to take from Ewan his pride in their son – or her husband's part in creating him.

Jack was born, slightly premature, late on Christmas Day. But of course, Easter was early that year – and the mayflowers not out for a good few weeks after.